Praise for Titania Ladley's *Kabana Heat*

Rating: 90/100 & A Keeper "...plenty of unapologetic, unabashed, and very naughty scenes that have me wishing that someone would spray a fire extinguisher all over me... [a] most charming naughty romp."

~ *Mrs. Giggles*

Rating: 5 Stars "If you want heat, passion and molten hot sex then this is the absolute perfect book... Titania Ladley has created a story that is so passionate that the pages nearly steam... As a reader I cannot wait to read whatever Ms. Ladley has in store for us next."

~ *Ecataromance.com*

"Ms. Ladley has created a story that does a great job integrating the natural exotic romance, and culture of Hawaii with moving characters. The sex in Kabana Heat is hot enough to melt your screens."

~ *Just Erotic Romance Reviews*

Look for these titles by
Titania Ladley

Now Available:

Aurora's Triangle

Kabana Heat

Titania Ladley

A Samhain Publishing, Ltd. publication.

Samhain Publishing, Ltd.
577 Mulberry Street, Suite 1520
Macon, GA 31201
www.samhainpublishing.com

Kabana Heat

Print ISBN: 978-1-60504-305-0
Digital ISBN: 1-60504-128-9

Editing by Laurie Rauch
Cover by Scott Carpenter

First Samhain Publishing, Ltd. electronic publication: August 2008
First Samhain Publishing, Ltd. print publication: June 2009

Dedication

To all my readers and fans...what can I say? Without you, none of this would be possible. *Mahalo!* Thank you for always believing in my stories and loving them enough to keep supporting me. I'm humbled and grateful beyond words.

Dear Reader,

To enrich the story and add more of a Polynesian feel to *Kabana Heat*, you'll find various Hawaiian words and phrases throughout. For your enjoyment and convenience, I've provided a Hawaiian glossary at the end of the book including sources. I hope you enjoy *Kabana Heat*!

~ Titania Ladley

Chapter One

Kabana Island, Hawaii

"*Aloha.*"

At the sound of the sultry voice, Mitch Wulfrum jolted out of his lazy beach nap. His eyes flew open and he beheld what could only be described as the outline of an angel against the blazing ball of the afternoon sun. With the remnants of sleep, and now the sun's strong rays blinding him, her face registered as nothing more than a shadow. But everything else about her, damn it, transmitted straight to his otherwise latent libido.

"You didn't answer your door, so I took the liberty of coming down to the beach to look for you."

"What...who are you?" Stumbling to his feet, he drew himself up to tower a good five inches over her. At six-three, he generally looked down on most women. This one wasn't quite as small. With her long, fluid limbs and voluptuous curves, she stood much taller than he'd become accustomed to.

"I'm Kiona 'Alohi."

Kiona. The name had some sort of aphrodisiacal affect on him, washing through his bloodstream like that first alcoholic buzz after slamming a stiff cocktail. And it certainly had a ring of familiarity to it. But with his brain suddenly hijacked into a state of sexual inebriation, he couldn't quite place it.

She held out a slim hand, her bronzed, island-girl tan making the red-painted nails look as appetizing and ripe as berries. His gaze trekked up her bare arm to narrow, feminine shoulders glistening gold beneath the sun. She wore a snow-white halter dress with a plunging neckline, the narrow strips clinging to bulging breasts. Mitch let out a low whistle when the faint outline of her brown nipples perked under his scrutiny and pressed like rock-hard pebbles against the cotton fabric.

Even though his loins began a steady, painful ache, he tortured himself by continuing his blatant inspection. His stare traveled down over her flat abdomen and rounded hips, to long, brown, lean legs. An image flickered in his mind of toned thighs clamped on either side of his head. *Gulp.* He circled his watering tongue around in his mouth at the erotic image. For a moment, he could swear he tasted pussy, smelled its musky, sweet aroma. His hearing became muffled as if he'd become lost in the heaven between her legs.

"Okay...so you don't have to shake my hand if you don't want to."

He'd just spied the scarlet-painted toenails peeking from beneath the straps of leather sandals when her clipped, Hawaiian-accented tone jolted him from his gawking.

"Oh, sorry." It wasn't a full-on handshake, but he took what he could, closing his fingers around hers just before she withdrew. Heat warmed his clammy digits as he held tight to soft female ones, their slim length melding into his firm grip.

"Mitch Wulfrum," he provided as she removed her hand from his with a solid jerk.

"Yes, I know." When she spoke again, his stare finally popped up to the heart-shaped face. She wore dark sunglasses perched on a small, feminine nose. He studied the lenses, delving deep—what shade would her eyes be?—when a sudden need to penetrate the hidden orbs overtook him. But all he could see was his own reflection.

"You know me?" Shit, why couldn't he get out more than a two- or three-word intelligible sentence with this woman?

She let out a derisive chuckle. "Everyone knows who you are." With that melodious laugh, dimples emerged on her cheeks. Her seductive, warm scent wafted up on the arid breeze to tease his nostrils. The combination of the womanly aroma and the girlish dimples packed a powerful punch to his loins. He concentrated on the sound of swishing palms, the pounding of the surf—anything to keep the blood from rushing to his cock and embarrassing him with a schoolboy hard-on beneath the thin fabric of his swim trunks.

Mitch sighed, her blunt comment finally sinking in. He was still uncomfortable with the fact that, as the son of a farmer from rural Kansas, he'd made it so quickly to stardom. "I guess everyone here knows me?"

She drew off the sunglasses and smiled thinly. Velvet. Her eyes were golden, velvety orbs outlined by the black fan of long, seductive lashes. They left him speechless, nearly causing his knees to buckle beneath him. But then he caught the unmistakable glimmer of annoyance in the amber pools, and he regained his balance. The outer edges of her perfectly shaped dark eyebrows angled downward, further emphasizing the cold glare beneath them.

"Here? You're being coy, Mr. Wulfrum. Something I find odd and a bit disbelieving coming from a hotshot, box-office-hit movie star such as yourself—one who's a permanent fixture within the glitz and glamour of that pompous bubble you call Hollywood. You know as well as I do everyone in this whole entire world recognizes Mitch Wulfrum on sight. What game are you playing with me? Didn't Jager Manning tell you I'd be here to meet you today?"

At the mention of his publicist, everything fell into place. Through Jager, he'd vaguely known her name...uh, make that, he'd dismissed it like an arrogant bastard. But he wasn't *that* insensitive. Somehow, hearing it from her lips had made it sound like an entirely different name. Perhaps because of the accented way she'd pronounced it compared to the way he had read it on paper?

He groaned. "Ah, you're *that* woman. I, uh, wasn't expecting you until this evening."

"*That* woman?"

He flinched at her incredulous tone. "Well, yeah. The one Jager set me up with. Right?"

"Right. That one." Pursed lips bloomed like a blood-red, dew-dappled rose. The delicate jaw and high cheekbones made him long to cup that exotic face and inhale the bloom of her lips. "I already introduced myself to you. Didn't Jager provide you with a name?"

He furrowed his brow. Of course. Jager had briefed him on the minor details in written form. But it hadn't shown up within the documents in full color like the flesh and blood of her did. Mitch scanned her creamy bronze skin again, his fingers itching to touch the smoothness. Jesus alive, it wasn't just flesh, it was *tempting* flesh.

He'd known—as had she—this wasn't going to be a true marriage, so why expect him to obsess over the details? Now, had Jager attached a photo with the name, yes, *that* would have helped brand her into his brain for sure. Mitch frowned. Had he been so insensitive as to not want to at least see a picture of the woman he was to marry?

"Yes, I guess he did."

"Guess? Well, that sure is a relief," she mumbled with a

derisive snort. "Me and this cockamamie plan—we must be very memorable. Which means you're not as dense as I first thought."

"Well, gee, thanks." He ground his teeth together. He deserved to be cut deep by her sarcasm, because somewhere inside the celebrity he'd become, he knew his neglect of her made him appear to be an assuming jerk. It had been a long while since he'd faced that initial fast, hard ride to the top of fame, but he should always remember where he'd come from. As it should, the hot flare of self-irritation that shimmied up his spine doused his ego with a cruel dose of reality.

She wasn't the least bit taken by him and his star status.

The first primal attraction to this island goddess had been real all right—if his rising erection were any indication. But it appeared it was all one-sided...or possibly she was a woman who'd paid little mind to the media's heavy publicity with his last few hit movies or huge corporate endorsement ads. Despite the fact he deserved her disinterest, something about it gave him the sense of being an annoying gnat buzzing around a blooming hibiscus.

And Mitch refused to ever go back to that pathetic way of life.

"Forget it," she snarled. It seemed his sarcastic thanks proved to be her final straw. Kiona spun on her sandals in an effort to flounce away. But apparently the low, spiked heels weren't meant for beach strolling. She gasped and teetered sideways, her shoulder slamming into Mitch's chest when one heel sank into the grainy shore. Instinctively, he threw his arms around her curvy form, dragging her up to keep her from toppling into the surf.

She blinked, her mouth a fraction of an inch from his. "Whoa," she murmured, and he caught her warm exhale on his own lips. He sucked in a surprised breath, starving for more of her, for just one wet taste.

The annoyance of only moments ago faded, morphing back into total erotic sin. Mitch captured a new edge to her scent, that of unmistakable arousal. Her eyes softened behind a thin layer of determination, determination, he could see now, she'd erected to keep up her façade of indifference. Pleasure burst in his bloodstream, gratification of both the egotistical and the sexual sort. Her curves and cushions molded to his hard body like no other woman's ever had. He knew by the flare of her eyes and the intake of breath that she could feel his rigid cock against her hot "V". Though he knew it bordered on arrogance, he thought to use his fame like a weapon, wielding it to tamp down the woman's sauciness.

Yet...her exotic beauty and cool resolve to remain unfazed by him...ah, but it had an irresistible power of its own, strong enough to deflect his wretched conceit.

And that, you dumb bastard, is a first.

"Are you okay?" he whispered, acutely aware of her nestled against his throbbing shaft.

Her tongue snaked out to moisten her plump lips. He tortured himself further by imagining it lapping the pre-come from the tip of his granite-hard cock.

Stupid fucker. Don't torment yourself with thoughts like that...until you've got her head in your lap.

She winced. "I...I think I sprained my ankle."

Mitch sighed wistfully, using all the theatrics of an award-winning actor. "I think I sprained my heart."

Kiona's complexion paled by two shades. Her tawny gaze flitted back and forth between his eyes. "Is that a lame line from one of your movies or something?"

"Definitely or something. But I'd hoped you'd have watched all of my movies, and would know the answer to that already."

She stiffened. "I don't watch television, or go to the movies. I do, however, read a lot."

"Tabloids?" Mitch trailed his fingertips down her bare back, delighted when he elicited a shiver out of her. Her skin was smooth, silky, warm against his flesh. He imagined tasting the length of her spine, wondered if her skin would be salty or sweet on his tongue. He stopped his bold exploration when he reached the zipper at her waist, retraced his path back up and pressed her closer so that her thinly clad breasts smashed against his bare chest. His other arm hooked around her hips and held her up a fraction of an inch off the sand.

Kiona rolled her eyes, the expressive look making something flutter in his chest. "No, of course not."

He raised a skeptical brow.

"Well, I do flip through them when I'm waiting in line at the market. I don't buy or subscribe to them, though, that I assure you." She wiggled, attempting to get her feet back on shore. When he easily prevented her escape, she narrowed her eyes and a gleam of retaliation lit their sparkling depths. "But I couldn't help noticing the rumor plastered across the front of *Stars Gossip*. You know, the one about you possibly being...gay?"

Goddamn those fucking reporters. He shifted his stance, seriously considering dropping her in a heap at his feet. "Well, I assure you I'm not gay."

She grinned smugly, again revealing the charming indentations in her cheeks. Sunrays glinted off the rows of perfect white teeth while her rich tresses tossed wildly in the wind. Instead of shoving against him as he assumed she would, she settled her arms around his neck and winked as she dragged the edge of her sunglasses over the back of his shoulder. He shivered, watching as her shadowed dimples twinkled like two onyx gems on the bronzed planes of her cheeks.

"Yes, something tells me you're not gay...at least not completely."

"Baby, you can bet all of Kabana," he proclaimed, lowering his gaze to dip into her upthrust cleavage, "I'm one hundred percent straight. But how in the hell do you expect me to convince the billions of people on this planet after one tabloid decides to soil my good name? So what? I went to a party, got a bit wasted. When I sobered up, my head lay in some bisexual man's lap, and an orgy pumped in high gear all around me. Needless to say, I got the hell out of that place, but the damn paparazzi seemed to have shaped the story into their own version in order to boost sales."

"Your good name, you say?" She leaned back in the circle of his arms, seeming to ready herself for later flight. Her eyes glittered with dark mischief. "Well, it looks like you'll be convincing them all right, by having Jager hook you up with a woman like me—a woman dumb enough to hop into your black kettle."

"I would say you're definitely going to be getting something out of it, too." *And maybe while we're at it, we can turn up the heat and get that kettle to steaming?*

Her gaze wandered out to sea. "Yes, but something much different from you. I'm not gay, nor do I have to worry, as you do, what the world thinks of me. Just one person, one person is all I care to convince..."

Waves crashed at his feet, the surf roaring as the tide began to move in. The breeze whipped the salty ocean mist around them, and its heady scent became laced with her sinful, sultry essence. She twisted, her heels finally touching the moist beach. Her movement made her briefly grind against his erection. Mitch stifled a groan. God, how he longed to throw her to the sand and bury himself between those long, tanned legs.

"Mmm, how about convincing *me*, sweetheart?"

At her questioning stare, he clarified, "Kiss me. I dare you to be an actress for just this one moment in your life and kiss me. Try to trick me, make me think you're not only my fiancée, but madly in love with me."

Panic burst in her eyes. She shifted her gaze up and down the beach. "No, I don't think that would be—"

Before she could finish her retort, he bent his head on impulse and captured her mouth with his. He longed to know what she would taste like, how her lips would feel on his, if she would surrender or fight him. She sighed into the kiss, indulging him with one moment of capitulation in which her softness melted into him and her pineapple-flavored mouth opened to his hungry one. He gathered her close and dragged her softness up and down so her pussy abraded his cock. Fire ignited in his groin, fueled by her wanton, muffled cries of tortured ecstasy.

Mitch was just about to drop to his knees and cover her body with his when she tore her mouth free. She pressed her palms against him, the sunglasses digging into the meat of his chest. "No."

"Ah, Kiona, yes. You know the answer's yes. The moment I opened my eyes, the second your scent filled my lungs, I knew I had to have you."

"Now *that* definitely has to be a line from one of your movies." She shook her head vehemently. "I said no."

Disappointment stabbed at him, an ice pick spearing his ego. Not one woman had turned him down since the release of his first blockbuster movie.

Until now.

"I understand." He bit off a wounded response and slowly released her. She stumbled backward, and one breast all but popped from the halter strip. Her hands shook as she tugged down her dress and swiped her fingertips across her swollen lips.

"No, you don't understand." What was left of the passion in her eyes turned back into that gleam of determination and haughtiness he'd first detected. Her gaze darted around, up the beach again, down the other direction, as if to assure herself they hadn't been seen.

Wasn't he the one who should be worrying about being seen? Ah, but then again, if any reporters had gotten a picture of his lip-lock with her, it would surely help boost the non-gay image he hoped to project. Still, her rejection stung. So to assuage his wounded self-image, his pride returned full-force. Yes, who *wouldn't* want to be seen with Mitch Wulfrum?

"Mr. Wulfrum, I'm telling you right now up front, this can't happen ever again, even after we seal the agreement."

He hadn't been expecting that. Mitch blinked at the stinging shock of it. "What? Can you repeat—?"

She spun and marched toward the stairs leading up to the beachside home Mitch had rented from Jager for his stay during the wedding. Sand flew up in clouds behind her as she retreated in snappy strides. Unable to resist, he watched as the muscles in those long legs flexed, disappearing beneath the snug, short dress with each stride. The globes of her ass jiggled as she stalked away from him, and suddenly he found himself fighting off the erotic image of his shaft pummeling what he imagined would be a tight, slick anus.

"Damn it, where are you going?" He fell into step beside

her, mesmerized by the bouncing profile of her breasts. They tantalized him, the far one nearly bouncing out of its confinement again when she stopped abruptly and whipped around to face him.

"Where does it look like? I'm going up to Jager's house. We need to talk, to get some things straight before we take this bizarre plunge."

"Wait, I—"

Kiona jammed a fist onto her hip and twirled the sunglasses in the other hand. Her eyes glistened like twin Hawaiian sunsets behind black, storm clouds.

"Look, I'm here for one thing and one thing only." She wagged the shades in his face, emphasizing each word. "To get the contractual agreement out of the way. You need a wife to smother the supposedly false gay rumors in Hollywood, right? Fine," she went on, not allowing him time to so much as nod. "I can be that trophy wife who'll leave no one doubting your manhood anymore. As you should already know, I require a husband to satisfy my asshole *makuakane's*—my father's—wishes to see me married. Then and only then, he'll finally turn my trust fund over to me. And frankly, Wulfrum, I don't give a damn if you're a box-office-busting movie star or Hercules himself. I won't be sleeping with you. This will all be in name only, just as you yourself specified in one of the many contracts Jager drew up for us."

She whirled and started up the steps, taking them at a brusque pace. He followed on her tail. "But that was before I met you. It was just to protect myself. I had no way of knowing what—or who—I'd be getting."

Kiona threw him a scalding look over her bare shoulder as she climbed. "First off, if it weren't for the fact that I'm using you as much as you are me, I'd take that as an insult.

Secondly, Jager has known me for years. I'd think he'd have given you a photo, or at the very least, a clear description of what you were getting. Obviously for me, you're shoved down my throat every single day just by being you, so I knew what I was getting from the start. Well, to an extent, since you're even more arrogant in person than you come off to the public."

Ouch.

They reached the upper deck, a wide cedar expanse jutting out toward the sea. The Pacific winds whisked in again, thrashing her hair around her face, plastering her dress to the lush curves of her body and making him think of some Hawaiian goddess.

"Well, he briefly described you, but I trusted his judgment and never asked for a photo." He shrugged. "I know, dumb. Maybe I should have, but I'm a busy man, and I didn't really care since a real wife was the last thing I wanted."

A noise suspiciously resembling a cat's growl escaped her throat, but she said nothing.

"Look, it was never meant as an insult," he added a bit too eagerly. "Everything was all business, presented to you in black and white just as it was to me. I thought you were in agreement."

She bent and removed her shoes one at a time. Something about the fact she stripped them off now after leaving the beach, when it seemed more appropriate to have them on, made his gut clench. That and the sight of her bare, slender feet. His hungry gaze devoured the small tattoo on her right ankle, just above the gold anklet she wore. What was the design she'd chosen to adorn herself with? He strained, longing to get a clearer view. Almost deliberately, she twisted her foot to the side, denying him the pleasure of exploring it.

"Nothing's ever black and white, Mitch. Nothing."

He scratched his head, perplexed, reluctantly adoring the sound of his name on her accented tongue. For some reason she'd switched from the formal Mr. Wulfrum to his first name. And he liked the hell out of it.

"Okay, I'll go with that. So then, can you tell me what color we just painted together down there on the beach?"

"Yes." She pivoted, sashaying across the deck toward the house, weaving her way around patio furniture. Kiona stopped at the glass slider, wrapped her fingers around the handle, and turned back to him. Her gaze had transformed into something even colder than before, something pure cutthroat and businesslike. "Let's go inside, get the specifics out of the way. Then I'll tell you all about what just happened between us—and about the package deal you'll be getting with me. As if Jager didn't already tell you."

"Package deal? Jager didn't tell me—"

"All right, Hollywood, play dumb if you want. It doesn't make a bit of difference to me."

"I'm not—"

"You know, for an Oscar winner, you sure are lacking in your acting skills at times." She let go of the handle and flung out her hand. "But whatever. So anyway, yes, to answer your original question, it's a firm, non-negotiable package deal. You see, *People*'s Man of the Year, it's like this..."

Did she have to sound so condescending? "I thought you didn't read the tabloids."

"Saw it at the market. Couldn't miss it. It was plastered all over the cover," she shot back too quickly. "So, as I was saying, if you want to pretend you didn't know, and hear it straight from the source, here goes... I'm already in love."

He blinked.

“And like it or not, I won’t be giving him up to enter into this fake marriage with you.” Kiona slid the patio door open and disappeared inside his rented beach house.

Chapter Two

Kiona couldn't believe it. She actually sat on a leather sofa next to Mitch Wulfrum, famous movie star, American icon, unparalleled, world-famous playboy. Oh, it wasn't as if it should be a shock to her. She'd known all along that Jager, her *makuakane's* PR manager, had expanded his clientele and also served as publicist to Mitch and several other celebrities. But Heloki 'Alohi had secured Jager for his company, Kabana Pure Cane Sugar's promotional interests some ten years ago when Kiona was sixteen, well before Mitch's rise to fame.

Though Jager's promotional company was based on the mainland in California, he'd become a regular KPCS fixture over the years. He'd even attended a few family gatherings and become more visible on Kabana at certain crucial times when her *makuakane* demanded Jager's expertise in business matters. Eventually, Jager had bought a large slice of seaside land from Heloki and built a house on it. It was two miles up the coast from the cane fields and sugar mill, but close enough for conducting business while on the island. However, Jager was no fool. During his extended absences, he'd capitalized on tourism by booking the property as a very profitable timeshare.

As Kiona had grown to womanhood and had eventually become the CEO of her *makuakane's* company, she'd gotten very close to Jager in a brotherly sort of way. God help them, if

Heloki knew of the pact she and Jager had entered into, he would shit a coconut—and break Jager's handsome neck. Jager secretly knew of her undying love for Nakolo Huaka, her *makuakane's* former foreman in the cane fields. He also knew of Heloki's animosity and hatred for Nakolo—or Kol, as she fondly called him.

She'd cried on Jager's shoulder recently about Heloki's threat to disown her if she didn't sever her relationship with Kol and soon marry someone of a much higher social stature. Now, despite the obvious gay rumors swirling around Mitch, Heloki couldn't be happier with her decision to enter into a hasty marriage with the filthy rich and famous star. Heloki was no fool. To associate Kabana Pure Cane Sugar with such a renowned celebrity could only mean big things for his company, no matter Mitch's sexual preferences. But in the event Heloki had doubts, Jager had managed to convince him that Kiona had met and fallen in love with Mitch on her recent business trip to California, and that she'd given Kol up in the process.

It couldn't be further from the truth.

Other than seeing Mitch's face plastered on magazine covers, or on tabloid news shows, she'd not laid eyes on him until today. Her relationship with Kol couldn't be any stronger, but her *makuakane* didn't have to know that. In a savvy plan cooked up by Jager, Mitch would become ungay to the world, and she would finally gain control of her sizable trust fund...while keeping Kol on the sly under the pretext of being a woman happily married to Mitch Wulfrum. She and Mitch both required a public disguise of sorts. Therefore, though the agreement proved unconventional, it had seemed to be the perfect solution for all three involved.

That is, until she'd met Mitch. Until she'd had her body crushed against his granite-hard one, tasted his hypnotic flavor, and experienced his long arousal grinding against her wet pussy.

Kiona blew out a long breath and forced her wayward mind to ignore the memory of it, as well as the pounding between her legs.

"Jager, the bastard, I swear he didn't tell me this." Mitch raked a hand through the longish, straight strands of blond hair. Sitting only inches from her, he propped his elbows on his knees and clasped his hands together. The knuckles whitened and his eyes darted to hers making Kiona feel that fluttery sensation deep in her womb again. "So basically, I'm to marry a woman already taken."

She held onto that cold blue gaze long enough to see the blustery irritation brewing there. What the hell was Jager thinking not informing Mitch of such an important point in the deal? Her stomach twisted with worry. Hopefully, Mitch wouldn't seek to nullify the contracts they'd already entered into.

"Basically. But what does it matter?" She smiled, hoping like hell she sounded more optimistic than she felt. "This was supposed to be a farce for my *makuakane's* and the public's benefit anyway—right?"

He jolted to his feet and crossed to the bamboo side table. "Your father is the least of my worries. You don't know the paparazzi, how rabid and heartless they can be. You can bet they'll uncover your lover eventually. Yeah, I can just see the headlines now..." He turned back to her and drew a hand across the space above him as if to read the tagline on the news. *"'Kiona takes a lover! Is Mitch Wulfrum man enough to hold onto his stunning new wife...or was their marriage all a farce to cover up his true sexuality?'"*

Mitch spun back around and splashed a finger of brandy into a crystal tumbler. He tossed it down his throat with an audible swallow, then glanced over his shoulder and held up his empty glass with an arched brow. “Sorry, would you like a drink?”

Her gaze scanned the wide, tanned shoulders, the corded back muscles tapering into the blue and green floral trunks. She imagined her hands cupping those hard buns, wondered what his manhood would taste like in her—

Enough, Kiona! What in the blessed islands’ name is wrong with you? Kol, remember Kol and your deep, passionate love for him…

In spite of the self-scolding, Kiona’s eyes remained fastened on the perfection of his body, her perusal moving up and down each powerful leg. At the mental image of them flexing between her spread thighs in the throes of sexual thrusts, her heart fluttered and tripped in her chest, and something hot and wild tumbled into her belly.

She would not only like a drink, she desperately needed one. “Thank you, yes, I’ll take a gin and tonic on the rocks if you have it.” Attempting to steady her quivering voice, she went on. “But, Mr. Wulfrum, remember we were never to have a relationship, anyway. It was understood—from what Jager and I discussed—that we would both continue with our own private lives. Just as you specified originally, name only is how I always wanted it also. I wasn’t expecting…”

“It’s Mitch.”

She nodded. “Mitch.”

“And what you mean is you weren’t expecting this surprising mutual attraction.”

“No! I meant—”

“That strange, undeniable, instant pull between us. Well, neither was I,” he grumbled.

He mixed the drink and crossed back, towering over her. Kiona's gaze rose slowly, climbing up his tall body and locking onto those predator's orbs. She caught his scent, clean male sweat coated over the jarring aroma of animal arousal. Gods and Kane alive, if it didn't make her feel like swooning. Kiona dragged in a breath to steady the giddiness, clamped her legs together beneath her dress, and fought to hold in the sudden flood of moisture that soaked her bare labia.

"Here." Mitch sat on the coffee table facing her, and thrust the tumbler into her hand. It felt cold in her hot, sweaty palm, and she could swear she heard it sizzle, saw steam rise. Though her mouth watered, saturating her taste buds with the remnants of his earlier beach kiss, she tipped her head back and drank every drop of the cocktail. She had to wash him away, to resist this attraction that had taken her by surprise at first sight of those sleepy eyes coming to life. There was, she now knew without a doubt, much to be said for real-life, in-the-flesh meetings as opposed to tabloid or on-screen likenesses.

She swallowed, coughing and gasping against the blaze of the alcohol in her throat. The cold-hot fluid burned away his flavor, and she welcomed it, along with the heat that now warmed her belly, and the vague buzz that swam in her head.

Kiona swiped her damp lips. "You're wrong, you know..."

"Oh no, Kiona. No, I'm not." He sipped his drink, regarding her over the rim of the glass. Suddenly, he plunked the tumbler to the wood tabletop and scrubbed the tops of his thighs as if to give his fingers something to do. Then one hand moved slowly across the space between them, reaching out and curling around her wrist. Even as she stiffened and salvaged a shred of indignant resistance in the process, her hand went willingly within the bondage of his...straight up to his mouth, where he sucked her finger in between his teeth.

"Lover on the side or not, you want me as much as I want you," he murmured around her index finger. "I can see it in your eyes, feel it in the electricity between us. It crackles, goes right to my gut."

"Please, don't do... Oh, God." Kiona gulped back her refusal and soared on the erotic sensations. They were akin to wet molten lava smothering her fingertip. Ashes of desire caught and combusted into licking flames, roiling, sizzling liquid heat. The force of it ignited that irresistible sexual pull from her fingertip all the way up her arm, and into her breasts. Her nipples tingled, hardening against the thin fabric of her halter dress. The heat tumbled down and pooled in her groin like a waterfall in Hades. She groaned, fighting the lure of limpid eyelids and the involuntary escape of panting breaths from between her parted lips.

At her reluctant yet wanton response, he shifted over onto the couch without releasing her finger, snatched her glass from her hand, and slid it onto the sofa table behind them. The cushions squeaked beneath the shift of bodies, and along with his musky scent, she caught that of leather. In the distance, out beyond the open patio door, she could hear the caw of seagulls. The pounding of the surf on the beach below seemed to mirror the powerful rush in her loins. A fragrant breeze of brine and tropical flora wafted in, making the vertical blinds click and clack. It swirled around them, stirring up a mixture of her perfume and his warm essence.

All at once, he released her finger, turned toward her, and drew her body flush to his, closing his mouth over hers in one sweep. His arms wrapped tight around her shoulders and waist.

"Mmm," he rasped against her mouth. "You turn the flavor of gin into decadence. Too bad we don't have time for a few weeks of pre-wedding play." His lips grazed hers, his tongue snaking out to swipe and delve, to drink every drop from hers.

"No, please..." Kiona didn't know why she allowed her torso to be angled and pressed to his chest, or why her body refused to obey her commands to flee.

But when his warm, fiery tongue parted her lips and entered her mouth with a devastatingly gentle force, the answer became obvious.

She wanted him in her bed and between her thighs, despite her love for Nakolo.

For the first time in years, she truly desired a man other than Kol. The realization of it, along with the shame and guilt she felt, made her mind reel with sadness. Even with his velvety tongue twirling around hers, even though every cell within her had come alive once again, she somehow dredged up a shred of resistance.

"No." Kiona tore her mouth from Mitch's at the very second he shifted her so her hip ground against his thick erection. With discipline she didn't know she possessed, she pressed her palms against the smooth, hard wall of tight pecs, forcing him back. She resisted the urge to knead and explore his chest...to skim just one palm downward and close her grip around him.

"I can't do this," she said on a moan. "Nakolo's my life, the reason I entered into this crazy agreement with you. So I can finally be free to have him without Heloki's interference. I will not do this to him, to us, and I won't go through with this if you don't honor my wishes."

His striking eyes iced over with a glaze of ire. He leaned back, then forward, finally getting to his feet with a lengthy sigh. "Okay. I see."

"Do you? Do you really? Mitch, I...I *love* him."

He stared down at her for a long moment, his gaze raking her body with that overwhelming, sexual aura of his. His swim trunks were strung taut over his full erection. She fought the throbbing of her clitoris, but there was no hope for it, especially when he reached down and gently cupped her face, tipping it so she was forced to look into his eyes. Heat enveloped her cheek. Her eyelids fluttered helplessly.

"Yes, I understand. And I must say I envy him." His jaw clenched. He yanked his hand from her face so fast, her mouth dropped open, and cool air assaulted her hot flesh. "I'll go get the latest addendum Jager drew up for us. Wait here." A knot of disappointment and relief plunged into her belly like a concrete brick. She watched as he sauntered from the room, his back tense with rigid restraint.

I have to get out of here.

Kiona located her sandals and donned them, her hands trembling. She must leave before she did something stupid and irreversible. Now. Forget signing the papers. Even though Jager was still in California, she could have him fax or courier it to her—which she should have done in the first place.

But her damn curiosity had gotten the better of her.

Determined to put miles between her and this magnetic man, she rushed toward the front door. Before she'd gotten one step beneath the arched entry that led into the foyer, he returned, halting her steps. His hand fisted around a roll of documents.

"I know you already reviewed the prenuptial agreement and all those technical issues Jager is handling through our lawyers." He moved to the opposite side of the coffee table and lowered himself into an overstuffed leather chair. Mitch unrolled the pages, slapped the paper-clipped forms onto the table, and set a Montblanc pen on top. "But this one...this is our private agreement that even the attorneys won't be privy to right away. Just you, me, and Jager."

And Kol.

"Yes, I know. It's why I came here, remember?" She crossed back to the sofa, bent and reached for the thin stack of papers weighted down by the pen. Dragging it over to her side of the table, she plucked up the ballpoint and sat back down. The leather surface beneath her rear was still warm from where he'd been sitting. She forced the pleasant sensation from her mind and scanned the top page. "Jager explained it all to me. It's both of our personal and private requests merged into one legal document, right?"

"Yes."

Were all those keeping-our-lives-separate demands they'd both insisted on going to come back to haunt her? Would they keep her segregated from her own husband?

Kiona lifted the papers, fixed her gaze on item number one. It was one of her own stipulations that they not share a bed. She did a mental eye-roll. Of course it would keep her segregated from him. Separate lives, more than anything, definitely meant keeping man and wife in separate beds and homes. So why did that suddenly make her feel as if she'd been deprived of a much anticipated Christmas gift? She hadn't felt that way in the least on the drive over here, yet now it stuck in her craw like sludge. It was the way she wanted it—wasn't it?—the way it should be for both her and Kol. And Mitch, too, for that matter. All of his requests were there for a reason, to shield his career. Her requests were designed to protect her relationship with Kol, and to keep her *makuakane* satisfied long enough to hand her the trust fund. That was that, plain and simple.

Sign it, you fool.

She pressed her lips together. "Where do I sign?"

He arched a dark-blond brow. "Don't you want to read through it first?"

What I want is to get the hell out of here and return to Kol before I make a horrible, irreparable mistake.

"No need. I trust Jager with my life." Just to be certain, she flipped to the last page and noted Jager's signature line was currently blank. Since it was a three-party agreement, the stipulations wouldn't be valid or enacted until Jager reviewed, accepted, and signed it as their mediator. She turned back to page one. "He did inform you he would have rights to final approval of all the terms?"

"Yes, he did, and that very point is in the document itself. You're free to read it—in fact, I recommend that you do. But since you appear to be in such a hurry, no need to worry. I'll fax it to him first thing tomorrow." He chuckled. "You know Jager. He'll review every word before he dares to put his stamp of approval on it."

"You're right, I trust him like a brother. But if he didn't think to add it already, I'll see that Jager includes the agreement for approval of outside relationships with no interference from the other party. Then just to summarize the rest, it should basically state we'll be living under separate roofs—unless we're to put on a show for Heloki or Hollywood. In which case, we'll be setting up a sort of stage house here on Kabana, as well as one on the mainland in L.A. during those special red-carpet events you wish to present me as your wife. As you'd suggested in part, it should also address the right to separate social lives, and my suggestion, separate beds and homes. That is what it says, correct?"

He shrugged. "Among other things."

"What other things?" She clamped the pen between her teeth.

"Maybe you should just read it?"

Maybe you should just cooperate so I can get the hell out of here?

Kiona thought hard, attempting to recall the other issues that had cropped up. Edginess simmered between annoyance and full-blown temper. But it quickly dissipated when she realized what he referred to. She lowered the pen. "By other things, you mean...sex?"

He smiled thinly, and she watched as he eased himself back in the chair and crossed an ankle over the opposite knee. "Yes. Sex."

She tore her attention from the smug, openly horny expression, and stared down at the neatly prepared documents.

"*No* sex. It's simple. And if you think it's going to be any other way, you're—"

He frowned, drumming his thumbs on the arms of the chair. "Right. No sex."

You can trust Jager to look after you, so just sign it and get it over with, Kiona. Sign it now, leave, and immediately escape that look of raw sexuality...before you change your mind and do something you'll regret.

She bit her lip with indecision.

But wait. You know damn well it would be foolish not to read such an important document before signing it. Read it and get it over with, Kiona.

"Well, then, that means every issue has been covered." Still, she studied each page line-for-line while Mitch fidgeted. Finally, she thumbed to the last page, assured it addressed every issue, and found Mitch's signature line with its sweeping, illegible autograph already in place. Once Jager returned to the island for the wedding later in the week, he would be reviewing every P and Q before he signed and finalized the arrangement. In the off chance she missed something, he would protect her, just as he always had.

For now, she needed to get this meeting over with and get the hell out of there. She still had a conference to attend back at KPCS, as well. In addition, Kol could be waiting for her at her condo, and she would need time to deal with him. Already her heart skittered at the mere thought of feeling his strong arms around her after the stressful day she'd just had at the office.

And the temptation she'd just deflected.

Impatience rode her hard. With a resigned sigh, Kiona scrawled her name on the line provided. "There."

"There're three copies," he said calmly. "One for you, one for me, one for Jager."

"Oh." She turned more pages comparing to be sure they were the same as the copy she'd already read, located the identical signature area, and quickly scribbled her name. She did the same for the next copy. Rising, she plucked the top copy from the stack then reached across the table and slid the other two toward him. "Here you go."

"If you keep your copy, you'll have to have Jager sign it separately. Is that all right?"

"Yes. Yes."

"You don't want me to fax it with mine?"

"No, that'll be fine. I'll meet with him when he arrives on island this week."

Something odd flashed in his eyes. Was it pre-wedding jitters? "Sure. Okay."

Go! Get the hell out of here.

She felt like a racehorse chomping at the bit to leap out of the gates. "Well, I guess I'll be seeing you." Kiona took two steps toward the door, paused and turned back when he spoke again. The handsome picture he made sitting there with his hair in a rakish mess and no shirt on made her mouth go dry and her pussy dampen.

No, no, no.

"Thanks. Thanks a lot for your help in protecting my career." He got to his feet, snatched up the papers, and briefly flipped through each page. She tried to ignore the bulge that remained in his shorts. The scoundrel stood tall, making no effort to hide his erection. "When Jager returns from the mainland, have him review your copy and sign it. I'll forward these duplicates on to him for his signature, then we'll be set to marry this weekend."

"Believe me, I'll most definitely have him examine every letter." She sidestepped around the coffee table. "Now I really must be going."

"I understand. You need to get back to your boyfriend, to remain faithful to him...even though you'll be *my* wife."

That permanent word *wife* gave her pause, as did the tone he used with her. It bordered on irritation, almost jealousy. She looked at him intently, twisted the paper into a tight roll, and tapped it in her palm. "Whether or not I am true to Nakolo is—and never will be—any of your concern. Now, I have a final meeting at the KPCS offices. As if that's any of your business."

"No, you're right. It's not my business. Goodbye, Kiona. I'll see you at the wedding on Saturday."

She studied him for a long moment, struggling to ignore yet another threatening word. *Wedding.* Her insides turned to a quivering mass of gelatin. Soon, she would be married to this man, this movie star. Kiona fought against the memory of those famous lips on hers, knowing for her *makuakane*'s benefit, she would receive one last kiss from Mitch at the staged wedding. Despite her refusal to do so, her thoughts shifted onto a more wicked path. Her body went rigid at the vivid memory of that hard-on in his shorts pressed intimately against her.

"Goodbye, Mitch. I'm sure Jager will be in contact." Blowing out a lengthy breath, she turned her back on him and dashed from the room.

Kiona made her way into the foyer and dragged open the intricate wooden door. She followed the curve of stone steps down to the wide three-car driveway. Relief washed through her when the sun bathed her with its heat. She experienced an odd combination of freedom and disappointment she didn't care to dissect. Her shoes clipped against concrete as she rode an urgency to flee to the other side of the island...to the other side of the world.

But she halted in mid-step when her gaze fell upon Kol's old-model pick-up truck. Her heart knocked so violently against her breastbone, it felt as if it had burst into a million pieces in her chest.

Nakolo sat across from Mitch's driveway, his brown arm perched on the open window frame of the truck. The ocean breeze blew in and ruffled his shoulder-length dark hair. Erotic sensations bombarded her, the memory of the soft strands tangled around her fingers, the aroused scent of him, that one poignant moment when she'd let herself submit to his rough and intense lovemaking.

She ignored the dampness between her legs brought on by that surprising encounter with Mitch, and instead welcomed the rush of hot blood through her system as she perused Kol's island ruggedness. *God, I love that man.* Her breath caught as desperate need seized her soul. She would have him today, as soon as she concluded the conference with her department heads. The knowledge of it drove her faster to his side and planted a seed in her head. Maybe she should call the office and reschedule? After all, she was the boss, second only to Heloki.

No, no, it was an urgent budget conference. It couldn't wait another day. But perhaps it could be delayed by an hour or so...

Kol's narrowed gaze followed her every step as she continued her trek, detouring away from her sports car and toward her secret lover. But she couldn't forget what she'd just done. Guilt swirled in her belly even as her love for Kol overwhelmed her.

She approached the truck and started to set her hand on his brawny forearm. At the last second, she caught the raw glint of rage in his liquid eyes. Instinct had her hesitating. Did he know what she'd just done? Did he know Jager wasn't the man inside his own house?

Kol defied his normally reserved calmness by drumming his thumb atop the rim of the open window. His jaw ticked. "Ki...I've been waiting for you." The clipped island accent was more pronounced than her own, a result of his lack of education and his deeper roots on the island. Only now it held a hard edge to it that she had never heard before.

"Kol... What's wrong?" She started to reach for him again.

He tensed, the inky black pools boring into her. "Don't touch me."

"What?" Kiona slowly withdrew her hand. *He knew.*

"I saw you."

"Saw me?"

"Don't play dumb with me, Kiona. I saw you kissing him and throwing yourself at him on the beach. I might be—"

"I did *not* throw myself at him. I stumbled and fell. And he caught me," she added softly, knowing it sounded like a lame excuse, even though it was the truth.

"I might be an uneducated idiot," he said in a soft, growling tone, "but it'd be foolish of me to ask who he is. Everyone in the world knows who Mitch Wulfrum is. What is he doing here? Why are you having a sleezy rendezvous with a goddamn movie star? Just what the hell is going on here?"

A ragged gasp tore from her throat. "A sleezy rendezvous?" Her heart hammered out of control. She twisted the paper tighter, her hands shaking in an attempt to keep from whacking him over the head with the roll. He made it sound as if she'd been having an affair!

But how could he know what brilliant plan she'd implemented? How could he understand what she was doing here, and what she'd done for him—for them—until she confessed it all to him?

Kiona forced down a scathing remark and the urge to flee, and instead gave him a level stare. He could be such a hothead at times, which had led to him, in a sense, being unwittingly responsible for her rash decision. She knew if she hadn't taken matters into her own hands before consulting with him, he'd stop her plan before it even got started. But she'd also been impatient enough to secure both love and money—so impatient, in fact, that she'd sealed their future without his knowledge.

A wave of panic had her clutching her churning abdomen. She supposed it was finally time to inform Nakolo of her upcoming nuptials.

Chapter Three

Her warm, enticing scent engulfed him, and her beauty never failed to leave him breathless. How was a man to fight that?

"Please, *ku'u aloha*, give me a chance to—"

"Don't call me your love after such a betrayal!"

Her exotic eyes at first widened then narrowed with abrupt temper. It seemed a snap of anger rode his sweet Kiona. He had rarely seen that look in the years they had been lovers. Nakolo had witnessed the glaze of passion in those golden orbs far more than he had fury. She normally saved her charming glare of vehemence for Heloki, her *makuakane*, and in Nakolo's defense at that.

"Give me time to explain."

"Yes, that would be just great. An explanation. Though I hardly think it'll help." Visions of her in the movie star's arms filled his mind, her large breasts pressed against Wulfrum, her pussy nestling against the bulge in the man's swim trunks. It taunted Nakolo, making his ire burn hotter, and yet something about it revved his system. Even now as he chided her, his cock remained hard, the denim stretching over its bulk.

What the hell was going on? He couldn't possibly be turned on by...no, that was ridiculous, sick.

She clasped her hands tighter around a roll of papers and held it against her chest. The move forced her breasts up and together making her cleavage a deeper, darker cavern than usual. Ah, her *nohea*, her captivating loveliness always made him dizzy. His body tightened, recalling all too well the taste of her flesh, the bounce of those mounds as he pummeled his cock into her soaking wetness with delicious brutality. Even in his shocked wrath at witnessing her obvious infidelity, she still had the power to turn him on.

And that pissed him off to no end.

Nakolo shook his head and slowed down his breathing. He could swear he heard the rumble of lava deep in his soul, threatening to spew. He had never experienced such anger in his life—not even at her father's rebukes. He prayed he could hold onto the thin line of control without letting go.

"I'm waiting for your excuses, *ku'u aloha*," he replied with an edge of sarcasm.

She lifted one trembling hand and worked a red-tipped thumbnail between her teeth, her other hand continuing to grip the paper roll. "They are not excuses, Kol. You will see. I can explain. But I have a meeting in less than an hour, so there's no time to discuss it...unless you get in with me and we talk about it on the way to the office."

He smiled thinly, shifting the gear into reverse. He could almost picture his blood pressure rising, followed by a deadly gasket exploding in his brain. It almost felt as if he held on by his fingertips to the rim of a volcano. One half of his mind screamed *fight, climb!* while the other half longed to just let go and get it over with, tumbling into blessed hell.

"Of course. A quickie. You know how much I enjoy those fast, hard fucks with you. But I have a feeling this time there will be no pleasure in it." Her eyes widened at his unusually crude words. He'd said them both for shock value to lash back at her, and because the madness simmering inside him was so overwhelming, he just couldn't help himself.

But she abruptly turned on the charm. "Now, Kol... That's not what I meant and you know it. Just take a deep breath." She didn't need to use that seductive, pouty tone with him. His Kiona always got her way.

At least out of bed—but not in it.

"Fuck that. What about Heloki?" His voice sounded callous to his own ears. He took her advice and dragged in a lungful of balmy air, attempting to soften his tone. "He might see me drop you off at the office."

"He's not there. He's at the southeast fields briefing the new foreman, and will be for the rest of the day."

Nakolo tried not to clench his jaw. *Yeah, briefing someone else for* my *job.*

He nodded in understanding, even though his blood boiled with hatred for Heloki, and his heart bled in confusion at the images flashing yet again in his head. Images of his lover kissing the famous playboy.

"All right, we talk on the way to your office. But you and I both know there couldn't possibly be an excusable reason for that *malihini* to have his hands all over my woman. And you, by the way, eagerly giving it right back to him." He added that last comment on a bark. Goddamn it, jealousy rode him like a fucking green demon. He despised the raw pain of it, the stench of it, the bitter taste it left in his mouth as he said the hurtful words.

Then why, he wondered, did he have such a raging hard-on? Why had his cock stood to attention at first sight of the handsome movie star and Kiona groping one another on the beach?

He shook the vision from his mind, not caring to explore the sick ambiguities swirling around in his head…and his groin.

Nakolo shifted in his seat, readjusting the tight denim over his erection, and studied her reaction to his spiteful words.

Her eyes blinked in surprise. She knew he rarely spoke with such vehemence and rage. He watched with some sort of sick satisfaction as she backed a few steps away when he revved the engine. "There *is* an explanation. I swear it. A very good one."

On a snort, he replied, "Right."

She wedged a tight fist against the luscious swell of her hip. "Do you want to talk about it or not? I don't have all day."

"I don't either, so goddamn right I want to talk. Can't wait to hear what you'll come up with." He raced the engine again, and it backfired loud enough—hopefully—for the fucking celebrity to hear. He prayed to Kane the guy was peeking out the window right now. *Take that, you asshole.* "I'll park the truck at our spot. Meet me there."

Nakolo didn't wait for her reply. He backed into Jager's long, asphalted drive lined with well-manicured landscaping, and sped off, screeching his tires—one last dig for Wulfrum's benefit.

He shifted into fourth and eased into fifth as the old engine sputtered and rumbled. Maneuvering the winding coast road, he first passed Kiona's seaside house on his left…within walking distance of Jager's house.

Nakolo glimpsed the familiar cane fields off to his right in the island's interior. He edged along cliffs, climbing toward Mount Makakoa, and looked down at the coastal village where he'd grown up. Finally, just beyond that, was the overlook.

Though their tryst location was perched on a gorgeous side of the island with lush vegetation and soaring cliffs, it was north of the inactive Mount Makakoa and therefore beyond the stretch of KPCS's cane fields. His village was just south of that, so they'd often used it as a safe retreat, as well. Inhabited only by seaside huts and small fishermen flats, the rural community and its nearby overlook were places Heloki would rather die than be seen in.

The pompous bastard.

Nakolo's muscles tensed once again as his thoughts returned to her betrayal.

How long had she been seeing Mitch Wulfrum? Had she been fucking him during her last mainland business trip? And while here on the island, had she been sneaking along the half-mile stretch of beach between her place and Jager's, slipping into the posh home and fucking Mitch beneath Nakolo's very nose?

Nakolo rarely stayed at her house overnight anymore, not since Heloki had discovered their affair, fired Nakolo, and threatened to disown Kiona if she continued to see him. Since Nakolo had been forced to see less of her, Kiona could easily escape up the beach for a midnight rendezvous with Wulfrum without Nakolo ever knowing. She was far more determined, hardheaded, and deceitful than her father realized.

Now she has betrayed me.

His hands curled around the steering wheel until his knuckles whitened. "Damn her." He pounded the horn with his fist. "*Damn* her!"

And damn that son of bitch, Heloki. No doubt, this was all his fault. He had finally gotten to Kiona and succeeded in brainwashing her into dumping dirt-poor Nakolo for a rich man.

Nakolo breathed in, breathed out. His heart thundered with fury and loathing, but he managed to maneuver the wide curve and turn left onto the gravel overlook. It was a peaceful place—

the spot where he had first experienced her all-out passion. Lined by soaring palms and the purple jacaranda they had often made love under, it would always be special to them.

If only Heloki would let it be so.

God, how he hated her father! Heloki's prejudice against Nakolo's lack of education, and the fact he'd been screwing the boss's daughter, had lost Nakolo his good-paying foreman job in KPCS's cane fields. While still working for Heloki, Nakolo had gone and sacrificed his own financial stability in order to keep the spoiled rich girl in his life. But now it had all been for nothing. It was as clear as the crystal Pacific waters he gazed upon. While he waited for her—always he waited—he knew he had been played for a damn fool. Insatiable, she had taken her pleasures with his body just to amuse herself until something better had come along.

Like a fucking hot *nohea* celebrity from the mainland.

Hûpô! *How can you ever compete?*

"That's just it, you stupid bastard. You can't. You can get pissed all you want, and in the end, she'll choose Mitch Wulfrum. What woman in the world wouldn't? He's rich, he's famous, and he has that handsome *GQ* model face and hard body any woman would die to call her own."

He dropped his head against the back window and prayed to his Hawaiian god. "Kanaloa almighty, what will I do without her?"

Wallowing in misery, he rolled his head to the right and saw that her car pulled in next to his truck. She had the sunroof retracted, and golden rays slanted down through the open space, bathing her like some breathtaking Polynesian goddess. Her blue-black hair hung loose around her shoulders and down her bare back. Nakolo drew in a breath, recalling with clarity the scent of that glorious mane while burying his face in its thickness.

He bit his lip, welcoming the comforting pain of it. *Now Wulfrum will have her, smell her, taste her—shit,* fuck *her.*

She motioned him over, and despite the obvious bulge in his jeans, he eagerly stepped from the truck and strode around to the passenger's side of her car. He knew she saw the tubular shape in his pants, knew it would turn her on.

And that made it even more difficult to remain pissed at her. Goddamn it.

He yanked open the door and climbed in, settling on the smooth leather seat. The air conditioner blasted around him while the sun warmed his face through the sunroof. Her scent was all around him, her curvy beauty filling the space in the bucket seat to his left. He ignored the swell of one breast half spilling from her halter dress, and averted his gaze from the long length of silky legs stretched out toward the gas pedal.

She slid the gearshift into reverse. "Let's go before I'm late. We'll talk on the way."

"Wait." He set his hand over hers and shoved the gear back into park. Her fingers stretched out beneath his. She twined them into his, clinging until he could swear his heart melted. The warmth, the softness, the emotion when she squeezed his fingers nearly made him sob. Was this the end? Was she about to kick him to the curb?

Or would he get the nerve to sever their magnetic tie first?

He shifted his gaze from their joined hands to her stunning, heart-shaped face. No matter how many times he looked at her, it always felt like his pulse did some sort of strange flickering, as if everything came to a shocked halt in his system.

"Kol, I'm going to be..."

He leaned over the compartmented console—where he'd

just noticed she'd stashed that mysterious paper roll—and closed his mouth over her blood-red lips. Nectar. She always tasted like the sweetest nectar in all of Hawaii. He drank deeper, sliding his tongue past her teeth to search for her silky tongue. Kol suddenly paused in his assault, trying to place the flavor he detected. Was that gin lurking beneath the usual sweetness of her mouth? Had she indulged in a seductive drink or two with the man?

No!

His arms encircled her possessively, and he yanked her across the cramped space so that she lounged across his lap. He ground his throbbing cock into her hip, branding her as his, reminding her who wanted her, who loved her, who she belonged to. It wouldn't take long, he knew. It never did with her—hell, how could it? Kiona was the most tempting vixen he had ever had the pleasure of claiming as his.

His, that is, until he had seen her in the arms of another man.

At the resurfacing of his bitter anger, he fought the rigid reflex of his muscles. Instead, he relaxed and slipped a hand into her gaping neckline, palming one heavy mound. She sighed into his mouth, surrendering, wrapping her arms around his neck just as he knew she would. Her pillow-soft lips skated over his in a circular motion, and with a she-cat's muffled growl, she went in for the rabid kill. He opened wide, fully accepting her as he always did. And always would. Sucking her wet tongue into his mouth, he dueled with it, sword to sword, forcing her into obedience as he delved deeper into her heat.

Her nipple sprang hard and taut against his palm. He rolled it between his thumb and forefinger, pinching, pulling, until she broke free of the kiss and dropped her head back against the window.

"Ah, Kol, I want you..." She panted, her eyelids fluttering. "But I don't really have time."

He released her breast and skimmed his left hand up her smooth leg until he reached her bare hip. No panties. He stiffened, halting his movements. Had she left them behind after offering up her wetness to the movie star?

"Fuck the meeting. You're the boss. You can be late."

And the least you can do is give me this one last time with you.

He forced her leg toward the dashboard, opening her for his exploration. Delving higher up under her dress, he found her pearl, hard as a pebble, slick as sin.

His mouth watered at the mental image of her perfect sex; he swallowed hard, starting his assault with a feather-wisp, spherical motion of his finger. She twitched and groaned, and it wasn't long before her hips began that seductive, stripper-like dance, reaching for more, stroking herself with his digit.

Kol slowly slid two fingers into her. Ah, so warm, so tight. She screamed when he pulled out and spiraled back in to claim her G-spot. He closed his mouth over hers to muffle the cry that carried through the open sunroof and out across the Pacific. He murmured a silent prayer to Pele, the goddess of fire, to give him strength to suppress his own fires until he could taste Kiona's pussy.

Yes, he thirsted for her as always, but how to get his final fill of her in this cramped little sports car?

Nakolo, the sunroof... It was as if Pele whispered the solution in his ear.

He withdrew his fingers and watched as her eyelids rose, the dark lashes like fans of seduction encircling the glazed whites of her eyes. Disappointment edged her sweet voice, as did the small little panting breaths left behind by the sexual excitement.

"What...why did you stop?"

"Move back to your side."

"Why? What's wrong?"

"Just do it." He guided her back across the console. If he didn't taste her and get relief soon, he would erupt for Pele, just like the volcano Kilauea.

Kiona forced out a breath and gripped the steering wheel. She pressed her forehead against the back of one hand. "Okay, it's probably for the best. I really do have to be—"

Nakolo lifted the lever and pushed his seat back so it dropped flat upon the rear bench. He was just under six feet, so it was difficult to move within the cramped space to climb onto the back seat, but with a little stretching and grunting, he managed. While Kiona gawked at him, he leaned forward and across her, located her latch, and flattened her seat as well.

Without a word of explanation, he settled onto the center of the rear seat between the two reclined front seats.

"W-what are you doing?" She remained sitting upright, though the upper portion of her seat no longer supported her back.

"Stand up," he ordered.

"S-stand up?"

"You heard me. Stand up. Remove your shoes, plant a foot on each seat, and stand up so your top half is through the sunroof...and your juicy cunt is in my face."

Her mouth fell open and a sound that resembled a wheeze tore from her throat. He watched as she blinked, scanned the inside of the car, and looked up through the sunroof. Nakolo knew the precise moment understanding dawned on her.

She licked her lips and breathed faster. "You're going to...to eat my pussy while I'm…?" Kiona jammed a hand through her long locks. "Whew. I think I'm going to pass out just picturing it. As always, being with you is exciting and wicked."

"Honey, you don't have any idea how excited *I* am." He unzipped his pants and let his aching manhood spring free, loving the glaze of desire in her eyes at first sight of it.

"Somehow, I think I do." She grinned and reached for his cock, but he clamped his hand around her wrist just before she made contact.

"Uh-uh. I'm about to explode as it is. You want to come, you get your beautiful ass up and stand on the seats. Now."

Her smile faded. For a full thirty seconds, she stared deep into his eyes, her own tearing up. He knew at that moment she finally understood his desperation and intense desire to have her, to reclaim what was his after seeing her with another man.

Kiona twisted, assuring the car remained in park, and removed her shoes. She reached for the sunroof's edge, pulling herself to a standing position. She was a tall woman and it was a small car, so with her feet placed as wide as she could get them on each front seat, the roof came to waist level.

She set her elbows and forearms on the roof and leaned on them. "I'm ready," she whispered down to him.

He scooted forward and drew up her dress, stuffing the front hem beneath the garment's waistband. And there it was, her jewel—*his* jewel. Nakolo's mouth watered and his balls throbbed, engorging like a balloon ready to pop.

"*Hemolele!* Mmm, my love, you are so gorgeous, so—" he swiped his tongue up her slit, eliciting a scream from her, "—delicious."

The flavor of cream and faint salt burst in his mouth. Holy islands, she was wetter than the sea. He drew back and studied her toned thighs and the top of the "V" they held dear. Except for a small patch of dark curls above her clit, she always kept her pussy shaved for him so he could feel her silky lips upon his tongue or encircling his shaft. The labia were smooth and naturally tanned, her nub pink and swollen, emerging at the top of her cleft like the early bloom of a hibiscus. God, what perfection!

Nakolo couldn't delay any longer. He wrapped his arms around her hips and reached behind her. Sinking one finger into her dripping-wet *puka*, he closed his mouth over her swollen bud.

She screamed again, this time far louder. He heard her hands slap the roof, and rejoiced when her voluptuous body spasmed in his arms, against his face. He flicked his tongue over her clitoris while gazing upward through the sunroof. She was like a siren of the sea. He watched as the Pacific winds blew inland tossing her hair in a wild mass, her breasts perky mounds, her face contorted in ecstasy.

Her pelvis did a swiveling dance, abrading over his face. She growled, reaching for that pinnacle that always came so easily for her. Nakolo pumped his finger faster, adding another, then a third. She spread wider, accommodating him, coating his fingers with her stickiness. With his tongue, he thoroughly explored every fold, crease, and little bulge, knowing the time would come very soon when he would have to yank her down into the car and plunge himself into her cunt.

She was almost there, he could tell by the stiffening of her dance and the animal mewls escaping from deep in her throat. But somewhere in the sexual blur of his mind, Nakolo heard the hum of a car engine. He whipped his head around to see a sleek Mercedes pull up behind Kiona's car.

"Goddamn it," he swore when he saw none other than Mitch Wulfrum unfold himself from the driver's seat and stride toward Kiona's car.

Kiona's windows were darkly tinted, so most likely Mitch couldn't see Nakolo. If Mitch had spied Nakolo's truck back at Jager's house, he'd probably know Nakolo sat in her car. But if he hadn't peered out the window at Nakolo's boyish antics, Mitch wouldn't know whose truck it was and might assume Kiona was alone and the truck abandoned.

Not knowing one way or the other added an edge of excitement to the unexpected situation. Nakolo's loins simmered with reluctant fire. Did he want to be discovered or not?

As Mitch approached the driver's side, Nakolo studied the strikingly handsome face, the tall, lean body...and the bulge in the jeans he now wore. Nakolo swore under his breath. Why was it he found the sight of this man sauntering nearer so very arousing while he orally pleasured Kiona? Where had his anger gone? And why hadn't he demanded an explanation from Kiona before he had dived right into satisfying his sexual urges?

"Mitch, what are you—what are you doing here?" he heard her choke out.

The whole bizarre situation Nakolo suddenly found himself in did strange things to his libido. Hot liquid fire whooshed into his bloodstream, the flames of it licking at his cock like an incredible blowjob. He felt Kiona start to lower herself down, but something reckless drove him to hold her in place and force her to remain standing while he went back to work on her dripping cavern.

With his cock now as hard as stone, he slid his fingers back inside her and went wild on her clit. As if a demon rode him, he let his sidelong gaze fall upon the mass in Mitch's pants. Kol licked and sucked, his eyes locked on Mitch through the darkened glass.

Son of a bitch, what had gotten into him? Was he actually turned on by this man's interest in his woman...and by the man himself?

"You forgot these."

Nakolo heard the jingle of what sounded like keys, and the plunk of it on the roof. But he was so aroused he didn't care to explore why Mitch Wulfrum gave his Kiona a set of keys.

Kiona let out a strangled reply when Kol rammed his fingers in deeper and swirled his tongue faster. "T-thanks. I-I'll talk to you—oh, God! *'Û!*" She reached down and cupped one hand on the back of Nakolo's head, pressing him closer, grinding her stickiness all over his face.

Nakolo drank and slurped, drawing in her musky, heady scent. He did his best to pleasure her so that he could feel her body and her drenched pussy shudder while his rival watched.

There, take that. See if you can do any better, Mr. Goddamn Fucking Wulfrum.

He listened intently, waiting for her suppressed orgasm as she struggled to hide from Wulfrum what Nakolo did to her.

Nakolo had to admit he'd never experienced anything quite so wicked in his entire twenty-nine years. His gaze remained on Wulfrum, studying the swelling bulge, wondering what it might feel like to...

Hâmau! That's enough, hûpô!

But it was no use. Nakolo had already crossed the line of no return, the one that finally brought him to the other side, that side of bisexuality he had denied and hidden his entire life. He tried to recall his rage, and prayed for its acidic comfort to boil within his blood and bring him back to the reality of his sorry life. It didn't come. All he could do was lick her harder, finger-fuck her faster, deeper, and visually devour the man who stood only a few feet from him with nothing but tinted glass between them.

He'd never told Kiona about his depraved fantasies. Hell, even if he wanted to, he probably wouldn't get the opportunity now that Wulfrum had stolen her away. But he could dream, couldn't he? He had that much coming to him after her betrayal. He could imagine how it might feel to have Wulfrum behind him, pounding into his ass while he ate Kiona's sweet cunt just like he did now. The torture drove him to reach down and palm himself.

"Kiona, are you sure you're okay?" Mitch asked, his suspicious voice carrying down through the open sunroof. Deep, oh yeah, such a deep voice. Nakolo could well imagine it whispering in his ear during the throes of sex.

"Um-hmm, y-yes," she whimpered, and that was when he finally felt the spasms rack his fingers. She ground her pussy into Nakolo's face. Sticky juices trickled out, drenching his hand and chin. Her musky scent wafted up to fill the space of the car while her sweet folds covered his mouth. Her breath came out in ragged staccatos of suppressed ecstasy, and he heard her slap the rooftop just before she let out a final guttural, "Ahh..."

A long moment of silence ensued. Kiona struggled to get her heavy respirations under control.

"Uh, is there someone in there with you?" Wulfrum's voice suddenly took on an edge of thick, knowing desire. It made Nakolo's libido speed up, and he palmed himself harder.

"N-no, of course not," she laughed hollowly, shoving her dress back down with one hand. She shifted her feet and stood taller in the opening. Her puckered nipples pressed against the fabric of her dress, and Nakolo knew Wulfrum couldn't miss them.

Nakolo leaned back, lapping her juices from around his

mouth. He stroked himself, and continued to obsess over Wulfrum's fit torso and crotch through the dark glass.

"What are you doing standing up in your sunroof? And whose truck is that?"

"T-truck? I-I don't have any idea."

Nakolo caressed her leg and trekked higher until he found one soft mound of her ass. He squeezed, and loud enough to be heard, he said, "Tell him, *ku'u aloha*. Tell him it's your lover's truck...and that you're my woman."

Kiona gasped, and through the sunroof, she shot him a withering look.

Wulfrum mumbled, "Goddamn it, I knew you had someone in there." He bent down and cupped his hands around his snarling face, straining to see through the shaded glass. "Come on out, pal. It looks like we all have a few things to discuss."

"Mitch, no. *Kulikuli!* Just shut up, damn you, I'll do it in my own time and in my own way."

"You mean he doesn't know about the—?"

"No, not yet. Please leave and let me do this my way. Get the hell out of here. Now. *Pau! Aloha!*" Kiona dropped down through the window and shoved open the driver's door, forcing Wulfrum to step back. She sprang from the car and wagged her finger in his face. He didn't flinch. He stood there with his arms crossed over that T-shirt-clad, wide chest of his, and sent her a baleful look. "*Ahahana!* This is none of your freaking business," Kiona spat, her accent becoming heavier with her ire. "You hear me, Mitch? Now. I said *aloha* now!"

Nakolo knew at that moment his suspicions had been right. There *was* something between these two, but he couldn't quite put his finger on it. Well, he had ten fingers, and one was bound to hit the answer sooner or later. He stuffed his still-hard manhood into his jeans, zipped them up, and awkwardly climbed over the flattened driver's seat.

As he clambered from the low car and stood to his full height, only inches less than Wulfrum, he hooked his thumbs in his belt loops and drawled, "All right, *pal.* Here I am, Kiona's lover in the flesh. Go right ahead. Talk. I'm looking forward to hearing what you have to say, you prick."

"Kol, please don't make this—"

Nakolo shot up a hand to halt her words, but his eyes never left Mitch. How could they? Nakolo had to admit the guy was a total hunk, even more so in the flesh. "*Kulikuli,* Ki. Just shut up for one goddamn minute, would you?"

Kiona gasped. "Ooh, don't you talk to me that way."

Nakolo supposed he was a bit star-struck, standing there only five feet from the Oscar-award-winning actor with the stunning aqua eyes, but he got his bearings just the same. He had always been a sucker for a pretty face, but he'd never had to field two at once—one male and one female, at that.

"Quiet, Ki. I think I have a right to know what the fuck is going on here. Wulfrum, you have some explaining to do. Where do you get off butting into our lives...and interrupting our lovemaking? And furthermore, why did I see your hands all over *my* woman back at Jager's house?"

Kiona whirled, spewing all her wrath on the egotistical bastard star. He didn't so much as balk when she shrieked, "Don't you *dare* answer that, or say a word about—"

"Why haven't you told him yet?" Apparently, Wulfrum already knew the answer to his own question. He soaked Nakolo with an arrogant stare that reeked of an immature *Ha-ha, I know something you don't know* attitude.

"Told me what, you mother fucker?" Nakolo fisted his hands, preparing for the worst. Damn straight, he'd bust up that perfect face in a second if the man didn't come clean with an explanation.

"Mitch, if you open your mouth, I swear I'll—"

"You'll what?" Mitch asked, his gaze finally swinging back to Kiona. "You won't marry me?"

Marry? Nakolo's world tipped on its axis. That was the last word he'd expected to hear. Lovers, even best friends, but never marry. He shook the confusion from his head and dug a fingertip in his ear. "*What*?"

"You heard me, I said marry me." Wulfrum stepped back and draped an arm over the rim of Nakolo's truck bed. Something about it both irked and turned Nakolo on. But he quickly shoved the confusing thoughts from his mind and tried to focus on what the cocky jerk had just said.

"*What*?" Nakolo repeated. He strode toward Kiona and gripped her arms. Her face was pale, and he could feel her entire body trembling beneath his grip. Nausea stirred in his gut as he struggled to tamp down his rage. "You're going to *marry* this man?"

Her amber eyes filled with tears. She stared up at him, the wind tossing her wild mane and churning the waves of the Pacific Ocean in a breathtaking backdrop behind her. Nakolo's own body quaked. He couldn't stop his knees from buckling, and it was only by the fact that he held onto her that he didn't collapse to the gravel parking lot.

No. No. No.

But he saw it there in her eyes, the lies, the betrayal, even the truth. She was *marrying* movie star Mitch Wulfrum.

"Yes," she finally whispered. "T-this coming Saturday."

"*This* Saturday? But...but you don't even know him. How can you jump into it so fast? Or at all, for chrissake?"

Mitch cleared his throat. "I, um, have to leave next week to shoot my next movie. It'll take more than a month. Then I have a promotional circuit to fulfill. This weekend is the only time I have to—"

"Mitch, shut up," Kiona bit out.

"Shut up? That's all you can say to him? You're going along with this?" Nakolo swallowed a lump of bile when she simply blinked at him. He let go of her as if she'd burned him, and stumbled toward his truck. "Fuck. This is crazy—*pupule*. What...why?" He spun back around, determined to make sense of the madness.

No! *He* loved her. He could never live without her, much less see her marry another man.

A man he himself had just lusted after.

Was Nakolo just as depraved as Kiona where this man was concerned?

Nakolo forced aside the niggling guilt and gaped at Kiona for a long moment. He watched as she buried her face in her hands and sobbed uncontrollably. Still, regardless of her betrayal, in spite of this huge master plan that had obviously been devised behind his back, he had an urge to go to her and comfort her.

Wulfrum merely stood by, shuffling his feet, finally seeming to know it was time for him to keep his damn mouth shut.

Kabana's early evening heat beat down upon Nakolo, warming his skin. But that heat, that Kabana pride and fire that had always burned inside him, ultimately could not permeate the sudden chill that had just closed around his heart.

She was going to marry someone Heloki would be proud of and welcome with open arms.

And it wasn't going to be Nakolo Huaka.

No. Not with Heloki and Wulfrum standing as a united front intent on keeping their princess away from a lowlife like Nakolo.

Not with all that money and fame Wulfrum could offer her. How in the hell could Nakolo fight that, except to work his ass off and one day hope to be worthy of her?

But apparently, it was too late for that.

"Kol, please, let me explain. I—"

"Forget it, Kiona, forget it. I understand. Totally." An icy tremble rippled through him, but he couldn't tame his fury. He punched the side of his truck, denting the passenger door. Savoring the throbbing pain in his fist, he yanked open the door, scooted across the seat, and drove away with a squeal, the hot, syrupy taste of her pussy still lingering on his tongue.

Chapter Four

"Jesus Christ." Mitch scrutinized the billowing tailpipe smoke, wincing at the pop and roar of the retreating old truck. He turned back to Kiona. "You always put up with that shit from him?"

She gasped, watching as Kol squealed around a curve in the road, struggling to keep the tires off the shoulder...and away from the thirty-foot drop-off plunging straight to the sea. She reached out a quivering hand and planted it on the warm hood of her car. The sun dropped closer to the horizon, nearly blinding her. Muted orange rays slanted across the island from the west, blanketing lush land before reaching out over the choppy waters off the northeastern shore behind her. Its heat enveloped her, warming her flesh.

But her heart had frozen solid at Kol's dejected departure.

Kiona shivered at the remembrance of that gleam of betrayal and pained anger in his dark eyes. Pressing a palm to her belly, she breathed slowly in and out to calm her jittery nerves and ease the dizziness that had suddenly seized her.

"I...I've never seen him quite that upset before. I-I have to go after him." She stumbled to the car door and dragged it open.

Mitch seemed to come out of nowhere. He planted a firm hand over hers. "I'm going with you."

She shook her head vehemently, yanked her hand from beneath his, and sank into the bucket seat. “Oh no, you’re not. This is none of your affair.” Kiona slammed the door shut. They’d left the motor idling during their lovemaking, so there was no need to take time to restart it. She shoved the gearshift into reverse and prepared to lift her foot off the brake.

Mitch pulled the door back open before she could press on the gas. She didn’t know how he managed to stand there looking so handsome and irresistible, but there was no denying his magnetism. Kiona had just experienced the man she loved with all her being racing right out of her life, and yet she couldn’t seem to take her eyes from the one she was to marry.

Mitch’s turquoise gaze softened, and his tense body gradually relaxed. There was a light of seemingly genuine concern in his stunning eyes.

Seemingly. He’s a professional actor, Kiona, and don’t you forget it.

“Look, I’m sorry. The last thing I intended was something like this to happen.” He stepped closer and wedged himself between the open door and the driver’s seat. “But from what I’m gathering, this boyfriend of yours didn’t know about me any more than I knew about him.”

She caught a whiff of his musky cologne, and she wondered if he’d quickly groomed himself before chasing after her. The thought of it pleased her somehow, and it drew her scrutiny up his lean body to his sun-streaked hair and flawless masculine face. A shiver went up her spine when he fixed his eyes on hers and squatted on his haunches, mesmerizing her with a roguish look.

“Did he?”

Kiona jerked her stare away, breaking the electrifying spell. She studied the vast ocean bathed by the waning evening light.

How she wished she could just sprout wings and fly out there to some uninhabited island and wallow in her self-pity.

"It all happened so fast, I never found the right time to tell him. And as far as informing you about Kol, well, I did just now at Jager's place, didn't I? It seemed irrelevant before that. Our contractual obligations made it very plain this would be a name-only arrangement, so I figured, why bother?"

"Um, correct me if I'm wrong, but they were mostly *your* contractual suggestions as far as separate beds, name only, and all that crap. I swear Jager didn't tell me about him, or believe me, I would have given more attention to that part of the agreement."

She shot him a heated stare. There was no stopping her voice coming out in a hissing, growling tone. "You signed, didn't you? And name only was part of it. Isn't that what it should mean? We lead our own lives whether we've currently got a significant other or not?"

He lifted his wide, beefy shoulders. "I guess somewhere in the back of my mind, I figured that could easily be overcome if we ended up clicking. But I didn't count on there already being a *him* to deal with."

"Right, being who you are, you figured whoever you got would be totally available for the infamous Mitch Wulfrum. But when you get right down to it, even that didn't matter." She couldn't help it. Her voice rose with bitterness that seemed to bubble out of nowhere. "All you wanted was the trophy stage wife and you know it!"

He held up his hands, palms toward her in a truce gesture. "Don't get testy. Just trying to get clear on things."

"Yeah, it's all clear as fog." She flicked a narrowed, sidelong glance at him. "But I do wonder why Jager didn't tell you about Kol."

"You can bet I'm going to corner the bastard and find out."

"Get in line," she snorted.

He let out a concurrent grunt and went on. "Look, just to reiterate, I might be an actor, but I assure you I'm not putting on. This all came as a genuine surprise to me. Figured it would be just you and me, babe." He arched a dark-blond eyebrow. When he spoke again, that wide and delectable mouth of his twitched, as if he found something humorous in his next words. "I am kind of curious about something, though... We agree Jager might have been negligent, but why didn't *you* tell me about Kol when we first met on the beach today?"

Her mortification bubbled hot, making her cheeks flame. She knew very well what he implied. That she had avoided the truth because of their unexpected attraction. Okay, so it might be a teeny bit true, but she wasn't about to admit to it.

"That's absurd. And the point here is, you—being the one to first plant this cockamamie marriage seed, by the way—didn't bother to inquire with Jager if I was taken or not. Kind of odd if you ask me."

"Then we're one odd pair. Besides, you were already cooking up something with Jager. He just put the puzzle pieces together and figured we'd be a good match to solve each other's problems. And you accepted, didn't you?"

"No, he approached me about you after I cried on his shoulder about my father hating Kol. But still, we wouldn't be here in the middle of this debacle if *both* of us hadn't bought into this madness." She swore under her breath for added emphasis.

"Which naturally led me to believe you weren't taken. But remember, that was all before I had the breathtaking pleasure of meeting you in the flesh." When he winked at her, her belly fluttered. A flood of heat suffused through her loins. Ah, but that was nothing compared to the fire that ignited when he reached out and trailed a finger from her jaw, down her neck and into her cleavage.

Kiona didn't know why she thrust out her chest and allowed him to touch her, to let him shift his hand around and cup her breast through the fabric of her thin dress. With Kol long gone and the urgency to explain to him she'd done this for their future, it was difficult to understand why her mind suddenly flashed with images of the three of them in bed together. Her nipple tingled and sprang to life when Mitch tweaked it through her bodice. She imagined Kol on her right side doing the same to her other areola. Kiona struggled to catch her breath, to remember it wasn't supposed to be this way. She shouldn't be conjuring up Kol while messing around with another man.

She shouldn't be with another man. Period.

Name only, remember, you twit?

Lono help her, she loved Kol with all her heart, truly she did. So how was it there seemed to be room for this?

"Stop, please stop." God, she hated the tone in her voice. It came out pathetically weak and unconvincing. "I-I need to go after him, to explain, or none of us will get what we want in this farce."

His eyes went ice blue. He withdrew his hand and stood up, towering over her, leaving her cold and strangely alone. Propping an elbow on the top of the open door, he ducked his head and drawled, "Of course. Go after him." He stepped back from the door. "Tell him you're going to be my bride in less than a week's time. Tell him how you'll become the highly visible wife of Hollywood's most notorious rake, Mitch Wulfrum, in order to dupe your father, and as I'm now learning, to keep Kol as your lover on the side."

Her ire went up, spiking hot and fast in her bloodstream. "Yes. But you're forgetting one huge point. I'll also become that wife in order to smother those vicious gay rumors ruining the career of that particular *notorious rake.*"

She couldn't help it. She slammed the door shut, emphasizing her last word, and took off in a squeal of tires much the same way Kol had. When she looked in her rearview mirror, her husband-to-be was already climbing into his luxury rental car.

Husband-to-be.

It echoed in her head, making her stomach flutter, but she couldn't afford to think of Mitch or their crazy agreement anymore. She had to get to Kol.

He'd turned toward town, the opposite route from the small seaside village where he'd grown up. Since he hadn't come back this direction, he must have fled to either her house, or to drink himself into oblivion at the tavern where he'd been bartending since Heloki had fired him.

Kiona took the coast road's sweeping curves and steep hills like a pro, gunning the motor with reckless urgency. She had to get to him. She had to find Kol and explain to him that she'd done this for both of them—for him. It was the only answer, the only possible way they could ever be together without her father breathing down her neck and threatening to disown her.

As she turned onto the long private road leading up to her home, she scanned her paradise. The tropically landscaped, colorful path swung out along a cliff offering breathtaking intermittent views of the sea. The sight of her pale yellow stucco house, its red-tiled roof gleaming in the waning light of dusk, and the many arches and courtyards surrounding it, made her grip the steering wheel tighter.

"I will not give up all this freedom and beauty, nor will I let

Kol go," she whispered to herself. "We have to make this work for us all. We *have* to."

To give up her independence and this home would mean her emotional death. She had barely been able to afford it on her moderate salary. Despite being aware the mortgage would stretch her thin, she'd still taken the plunge in anticipation of her sizable trust fund maturing and eventually reverting solely to her. Since that glorious day she had finally walked away from the mansion she'd grown up in, Kiona felt whole, like a woman at last in charge of her own life. Perhaps she'd become too used to the allure of her new life out from under her father's iron fist? Yet the more she lived it, the more she couldn't stop reaching for the day her life would truly be her own once and for all.

She ground her teeth together and took a curve with a screech of tires. She should have known her *makuakane* wouldn't free her so easily. Butting into her personal life with Kol, Heloki had threatened to detonate that one last bomb if she didn't obey him. He would cut off her trust fund and disown her if she didn't dump Kol and marry someone more respectable.

Kiona sighed. "Well, there's always Plan B to fall back on."

She could give up the trust fund and leave KPCS.

To do so, she'd have to sell her house, rent a small apartment in town, and maybe get a job waitressing down at one of the wharf restaurants frequented by wealthy tourists. It wasn't beneath her in the least. She and Kol could eventually marry and live like ordinary man and wife with a cozy inland home, three kids, and a dog.

It all sounded so tempting, and yet there were two things holding her back.

Most importantly, she loved her job. It was in her blood. She'd practically grown up watching the business expand, learning to run it from the inside-out at a tender age. It had been home more so than the cold mausoleum she'd been born and raised in, so Kiona knew every aspect of the cane business. She thrived on sugar's development, from planting, tending, and harvesting, all the way through advertising, shipment, and distribution. To never let the rich soil sieve through her fingers again, or be a part of factory refinement or ad promotion, simply depressed her beyond emotional endurance.

Then there was the second, most puzzling thing keeping her from finally implementing Plan B. Mitch. Guilt thumped cold and unforgiving in her heart. Before today, there'd only been KPCS holding her back from severing her ties to Heloki. And surprisingly enough, Kol had understood her feelings, since he too had sweated for KPCS and her father, and had loved everything about the sugar business.

But now there was a new solution staring her in the face. It tempted nooks and crannies of her heart she didn't know existed.

It was really quite a brilliant plan, she mused, placing one hand on her belly to stave off the taunting nerves and nagging guilt. There was something in this arrangement for all three of them, and if it took her all week to convince Kol, so be it. He would thank her later, when they were able to wake up every morning in her home—their home—in each other's arms without her father's watchful eye tracking their every move. Heloki would assume she slept with Mitch, and would never even dream she resided with Kol rather than her husband—who of course would be off attending post-Oscar parties and jetting to his next international movie set. In true form, once Heloki genuinely trusted someone, he backed off.

Way off, to the point of neglect.

And that was what Kiona was counting on.

She rounded the last curve and scrolled to her assistant's

number in her cell phone. Kiona punched the send button and waited for Malia to answer.

"Oh, thank goodness, there you are. I've been trying to reach you for the last hour or so." Malia's sweet voice always had a way of calming Kiona. What would she do without her?

"Sorry, my *hoaloha,* something very important has come up. Can you let the rest of the staff know I won't make the meeting this evening?"

The pages of Malia's appointment book rustled. "Sure. Want to reschedule?"

The orange ball of the sun was just dropping behind the palm-lined horizon when she whipped her sports car into her driveway and hit the garage opener button. The door rose and relief flooded her jittery nerves. It was just as she hoped. Kol's truck was parked inside.

"Yes. Let's make it eight tomorrow morning. And please, give them my apologies, would you?"

"No problem, babe. I'm sure they'll understand. In fact, I think they'd prefer a morning budget meeting to a night one. Kind of hard to stay awake discussing boring numbers after a long day in the office, you know?"

"Yes, yes, you're right. Hey, did you pick up your dress?"

"Damn right I did." She popped her gum. "Yesterday. And it's fab. The tailor did a great job altering it. God, I still can't believe you're marrying Mitch Wulfrum."

Something fluttered behind her breastbone. *I'm marrying Mitch Wulfrum.* If *I can convince Kol. Oh God...*

"Kind of strange, huh?"

"*Kind of* strange? Try unbelievable. No, make that phenomenal. And I'm going to be your maid-of-honor, a part of movie star Mitch Wulfrum's wedding party. *Ho.*"

"Wow doesn't even come close. Try being his bride-to-be."

Malia's voice quivered. She swallowed audibly. "I'd love to."

Kiona pulled in next to Kol's truck and quickly pressed the remote, closing the door behind both of their vehicles...and away from Heloki's suspicious eyes.

It never failed. Those prying eyes were out there somewhere. Always.

"Look, I've got to go. Thanks for being my buffer, as usual. I'll see you in the morning."

"Bright and early. Oh, wait. Your father called. I need to tell you about something he's—"

"Uh, can you just call me back in about thirty minutes or so?" She noted the door leading from the garage to the laundry and kitchen stood ajar, and yet the interior lights all seemed to be out. "I need to check on something."

"Sure. No problem. Talk to you later."

When Malia hung up, Kiona scrolled through her missed calls. "Damn it." Not only had her father tried to reach her through Malia, but he'd also called Kiona's cell three times, apparently around the time of her tryst with Kol, or possibly during their heated conversation afterwards with Mitch.

She flipped the phone shut, groaning inwardly as she dropped her forehead to the steering wheel. *Just what I need, Heloki's overbearing intrusions while I'm trying to make Kol understand what I've done for him.*

Kiona raised her head and narrowed her eyes. "Screw it. He can wait for once. This is much more important at the moment."

A streak of rebellion twisted around the tight knot of anxiety in her belly. She ignored the underlying jitteriness and snatched her purse from the seat where not an hour before, her foot had been planted while Kol had devoured her pussy. Liquid sparks ignited deep in her groin at the memory of his wet mouth and talented tongue doing wicked things to her cunt while she stood in the open sunroof and tried to carry on a conversation with Mitch. Nothing—*nothing*—in her entire life had ever turned her on more.

And she was certain Kol had known Mitch was there.

Her pulse pounded, courting renewed sexual anticipation. It drowned out the apprehension of only seconds ago, and as she climbed from the car, a gush of warmth trickled between her thighs. She entered the spacious laundry room, and made her way into the vaulted kitchen. The house still had that new smell to it, yet she caught the unmistakable scent of Kol's aftershave mingling with it. The interior of the home was dim, so she flipped on the overhead recessed lights, bathing the large gourmet kitchen in a cheery white glow. A quick glance around told her Kol was nowhere in the adjoining great room or dining areas. Her mouth watered. Maybe he awaited her in bed...

Tossing her keys, cell phone, and purse on the black granite countertop, she called out, "Kol? Babe, where are you? We need to talk."

She heard the snap of the diving board seconds before catching sight of the open patio door to her right. His sleek, wet body arced across the evening sky. That naked, muscular frame became outlined by the waning light of dusk in a suspended snapshot-instant she would never forget. He had kept the underwater swimming pool and deck lights off for fear Heloki or any one of his spies might see him. In so doing, nature's poignant moment between sundown and nightfall left only the vague pinpoints of emerging stars surrounding him. His dark form became brilliantly poised before the gray and faintly pastel-streaked blanket scattered with the twinkling diamonds. Just before his beautifully tattooed body darted into the swimming pool with a faint splash, she caught a glimpse of his cock silhouetted against the fading pink still hovering over the horizon.

At the sight of the long, thick shaft that had brought her untold pleasures, her pulse quickened and her pussy dampened further, aching to be filled by him. Without a word, she stripped off her clothes where she stood and passed through the open French door. She inhaled the sharp fragrance of hibiscus and listened as the palm trees swayed, their fronds making a click-swish sound that melded pleasantly with the rush of the surf on the beach below. Kiona sighed when the night breeze fluttered her long hair and caressed her bare flesh sending shimmery goose bumps up and down her body. Kabana's arid air had cooled with the arrival of nightfall, but she didn't think there was anything chilly enough to abate the heat that simmered within her loins.

The two-story house had been built on a private tract of jutting beach at the north side of the island. Though she knew the nearest neighbors were a good half-mile away on either side, she still got a sexual charge imagining being watched dipping naked in the pool...and making voracious love with a man. Thank goodness for the growing darkness. It wasn't worth the risk of being seen by her father, or anyone he might have put up to spying.

With defiance fueled by the cloak of twilight and the fire of her ardor, she toed off her sandals and padded across the still-warm concrete. Her large breasts jiggled, making the nipples harden into tight knots of desire. When she approached the brick-tiled edge of the pool, Kol broke the surface, his long, blue-black hair sleeked back and away from the sharp yet handsome Polynesian features.

He jerked his head to the side, spraying water like a wolf emerging from a spring. His liquid gaze latched onto her. She could swear she felt the alluring pull of his eyes, magnet to steel, moon to Earth's ocean tides.

"What are you doing here?"

"What...?" Her jaw clamped shut. "I live here. Remember?"

"Mmm, how could I forget? *You* live here, not me. Yes, so *lôlô* of me. It's the stunning Hawaiian bride-to-be's new love nest with the movie star." His incensed stare raked her nakedness, making her knees go weak with want. He shifted, lounging on his backside upon the water's surface, the bulging muscles slick and defined by the emerging moonlight. His penis nestled in his crotch and water lapped over its bulk as he kicked. She could see it was already hardening, and all she could think of was leaping in and straddling him.

Yes, swallow up that massive cock, and ride him frantically from dusk to dawn.

But his words cut like sharp ice through her thoughts, bringing her back to the coldness of reality.

"Kol..." She crossed to the shallow end and descended the underwater stairs until the tepid water rose to her waist. Holding out a hand, she murmured, "Come here. We have to talk. Now."

He chuckled hollowly as if he could easily resist her, but he rolled onto his stomach and swam to her. Getting his footing, he backed her against the pool's shallow wall. The way he licked his lips when he caged her in reminded her of a wolf cornering his prey, preparing to pounce and move in for the kill. The heat of his flesh permeated her skin, warming her, while the sharp smell of chlorine and the all-male scent that could only be Kol's, filled the space between them.

"I think we need more than just talk." The last words came out on a growl. In the dusky light, those black-as-sin eyes glittered with a mixture of rage and simmering passion.

Though the look bordered on menacing, she didn't glance away. Instead, her breath caught hot and unsteady in her lungs. Despite their lovemaking normally being on the rough side, she had never feared Kol.

Until now.

A sick sort of reluctant excitement leapt into her throat nearly choking her, forcing her words out raspy and quivering. She planted her hands on his wet, hard chest. "I-I...now wait a minute. Let me explain."

He leaned closer, and his warm breath fanned her cheek when he spoke. The angry timbre of his voice seemed to grab her from her very toes and shake her entire body.

"*Ahahana*! I saw you," he snarled. "You threw yourself at him and kissed him on the beach before slipping into Jager's house to do no telling what with the fucking star. Ah, but he must have had you already turned on. Your juices still dribbled down your inner thighs by the time you got to me. And you definitely got off when I devoured your pussy in front of him."

"No, Kol, you don't understand what—"

"Then, of all the shocking things in the world, he announces you're to marry him. *Marry* him!" His eyes gleamed wolflike in the twilight, so incensed and tortured. He trailed a wet finger along her jaw, across her trembling lips. "How, my hot little vixen *hoa kâunu*, do you expect me to accept any explanation at all? *'Ea*?"

"I didn't throw myself at him. I—"

His mouth closed over hers in a brutal attempt to silence her. Still, it made her head spin with desire. He tasted of temper and beer, and it made her hungry for more, for all of him. Kiona wrapped her arms around his narrow waist and pulled him closer. His erection slammed against her abdomen, making her whimper and cling to him. Buoyant in the water, she easily climbed upward, wrapping her legs around his hips so that glorious cock of his nestled in her throbbing "V".

Damn it, she would make him see the wisdom of her decision, using her female wiles if she must.

Kol ripped his lips from hers and untangled her legs from his hips. He spun her around in the water and slapped her arms onto the deck. She could hear his ragged breathing, feel his steely manhood grinding against one ass cheek. God help her but it made her long to feel his shaft sliding into her tight rear. She fantasized about it, clenching her anal muscles, causing hot pussy juice to seep out into the water. Ah yes, as always, his cock would stimulate that secret place deep inside her, while his fingers did magical things to her cunt and her clitoris, bringing her to the gates of sexual euphoria.

"There's no explanation worth hearing," he roared in her ear, reaching around to fill his hands with her heavy, tingling breasts.

Kiona fought the ecstasy that seized her when he suddenly tore into her pussy from behind. She gasped, throwing her head back with a guttural moan. It wasn't anal like she'd just dreamed of, but it would certainly do. Her legs trembled beneath the water, her vaginal muscles spasmed in near-ogasmic protest.

"I-I swear, I swear. T-there's a very good reason. Please, please just let me explain."

He slid out, in, fast then slow. Water sloshed around their joined bodies, firm skin slapped soft flesh. Her eyelids clamped shut against her will, and every nerve in her body fired off in sudden bliss. They had never done it in the pool before, and with the exception of today in the car, never out in the open, either. It was all so deliciously hedonistic, she couldn't think straight, couldn't focus on the words she needed to say to ease his suffering.

"Ah, Kiona," he said huskily as he reached around and stroked her clitoris in a small circular motion. Before she could absorb the onslaught of unbearable pleasure, he added the brief shock of pain, clamping his teeth onto her shoulder. Throwing her into a vortex of mixed sensations, he changed things up yet again, this time gentling his ardor, kissing his way up her neck to her earlobe and making her shudder.

"You will surely be the death of me," he rasped, intermittently sucking the lobe between his teeth and licking it as he spoke. "I don't think there's anything you could say that would make me stop loving you, even knowing you have chosen to betray me by suddenly—" he pulled back, rammed in, "—marrying another man. Do you know how weak that makes me feel as a man, to love and obsess over a woman despite her unfaithfulness? Do you?"

She could swear her heart fell to her knees. He was consumed with anger, jealousy, and passion all at once, and yet he could still reveal his anguish and vulnerability. To him, his love was unrequited. To her, there was no other. She loved him so fiercely, it almost hurt.

Kiona stretched her arms up and behind her, hooking them around his neck. She rested her head on his shoulder even as he continued to fuck her from behind with his long, rigid cock. "My love, my love, please don't be such a *pa'akiki.* If you'd just let me explain, I marry him for you. For us."

He snorted and disentangled her arms, pressing her forward again so that her upper body fell prone across the deck and her nipples scraped the warm, rough surface. The move brought her feet off the floor of the pool and her ass up out of the water.

"The only head that's hard here is my cock, and I'm going

to fuck you with it like you've never been fucked before. Maybe that'll make you understand just what you're giving up in order to have the movie star."

She started to stand upright. "But, Kol, I—"

He held her down with a firm, hot palm. His free hand moved lower in a long caressing sweep to her buttocks. The unexpected smack on her ass made her blink. But given the level of the water just below the curve of her rear, the water's surface had slowed down the velocity of his hand, causing a splash to accompany the whack.

Nonetheless, his intent only added fuel to the flames smoldering in her loins. Spankings were one of her greatest weaknesses, never failing to turn her on. "Oh, God..." she panted, clamping her eyelids shut.

"You love it, don't you, babe? You get off on being bad, just like today in the car, just like on the beach with him. All so you can be punished."

"No, I..."

"Bad girl...like this." Kol slid a finger down over her tailbone until he located her puckered asshole. She jolted, letting out a mewling scream of ecstasy when he sank the digit slowly, maddeningly, into her wet anus.

Kiona's nipples tingled as they scraped the wet surface of the pool's edge. Her head arched back. She stared up at the emerging stars, feeling much like a blazing celestial body, glowing, burning, shooting haphazardly across space. "Yes, yes."

He pulled back just far enough to leave the very tip of his cock in her pussy. Kol knew she always craved simultaneous penetration, so it was with a sigh of anticipation that she felt him also withdraw his finger. He poised the tip of the digit and his shaft at the entry of each hole, then slid his other hand around the curve of her hip and found her pearl.

Fluttering around the tiny bulk with the tip of his finger, he whispered, “My beautiful Ki, you know I love you. I love you so much. How will I ever bear life without you?”

He didn’t give her time to answer or protest his mistaken question. Her cry of ecstasy carried on the night breeze when he sank the digit and his cock into her damp, aching orifices in one coupled motion. Her inner muscles clamped down on him while he played havoc with her clitoris, strumming her like he might an *ukelele*. She sang out in musical response, her moans and groans a blend of long notes and staccato-like ragged breaths.

“You know I love you too,” she panted, twitching when the first ripple of orgasm gathered deep in her womb. “You’re not going to be without—ooh, I’m going to…”

Kol increased the speed, fucking both holes with fervor and expertise. She welcomed him deep inside her core, meeting his thrusts with a frantic need, almost as if it had been weeks, perhaps months, since she’d had sex. He filled her up, the tip of his shaft abrading her soaked G-spot while his finger stimulated the sensitive nerves inside her ass. Her womb flooded with wet heat and the heaviness of full arousal, the sweet, sweet rise of climax.

“That’s it, baby, one last time, soak my cock with your hot honey.” He continued to penetrate her ass with the finger of one hand while he swirled the index finger of his other hand swiftly around her clit. She could swear she heard the coming climax roaring all around her as he sped up the stroking motions. The power of it surged in her system, rushing right down to her very toes. “Squeeze that hot ass of yours around my finger while I screw you mindless.”

“Aah!” The deep carnal cry seemed to come from afar, from

some wild animal lurking off in the tropical forest. But somewhere in the fragmented thoughts and fiery flames engulfing her entire body, she realized it was her own release.

The unbearable pleasure assaulted her senses in a relentless swell of ecstasy. She dragged in a breath, letting the waning waves wash through her as she held his aroused male essence inside her lungs. The warmth of his body blanketed her backside, the cooling water embraced her lower half, and the winds blew through her damp hair. Her nipples felt raw and tingly from their continued abrasion over the pool's edge. She rose up and turned her head, searching for his mouth, knowing by the fullness within her and Kol's frantic thrusts that he was very close to his own release.

He removed his finger from her rectum and gathered her close. With her mouth against his, she murmured, "Come, my love. Fill me up with your hot—"

"Well, well, well. Isn't this quite the pre-wedding tryst? Only the man you seem to be screwing isn't your fiancé."

Kol drew in a swift intake of air. It resembled a bear growling in challenge at an intruder interrupting his meal. "What the fuck? Who invited you?"

Kiona whipped her head around with a gasp and pushed herself out of Kol's arms so that he withdrew from her. She dipped beneath the water and covered her breasts with the pool's edge, and stared in amazement at the man standing at the border of her patio. Moonlight spilled down to spotlight his charming good looks. The evening breeze ruffled his longish blond hair lending him a roguish look that had her heart thumping in her chest. He wore the same jeans and snug T-shirt he'd had on earlier, which had suspicion settling in Kiona's gut like burning whiskey.

How long had Mitch been standing there? Had he been

watching them make love in the pool?

The thought of it ignited a heaviness in her breasts and a delicious yet forbidden quickening in her loins. From across the space, his gaze glowered in the dim night. It was as if she sat in a movie theater and gawked at him on the big screen in all his splendid, stunning, male glory, making young and mature women alike swoon and fantasize about being in his arms, feeling those lips on theirs. Her gaze dropped to his crotch where she could swear she could detect the outline of a hard-on.

Those women, no doubt, also fantasized about that impressive cock sinking deep between their thighs, just as I have dreamed of it...

Her eyelids went heavy at the thought. No, she could *not* think that way. The marriage would be in name only, she and Kol would finally be together, and Mitch would lead his own private life, including her only in those carefully planned paparazzi moments.

"Mitch..."

He swaggered forward—the cowboy in the movie confronting his nemesis—and stopped right above her. His intent, probing look seemed to caress her breasts through the water and ignite each tip into a flame. She drew in a lungful of air and caught his clean, rich smell. Behind her, Kol muttered something unintelligible and started to move away, but she caught his hand behind her.

"What are you doing here?" she demanded, not liking the breathy edge to her voice.

Mitch hooked his thumbs in the belt loops of his jeans and lifted a brow. "Well? Have you told him yet?"

"Yeah, remember? I already heard." Kol jerked his hand from hers and pushed through the water. He pulled himself onto the side of the pool right next to Mitch's feet...naked with his delicious erection poking his abdomen. "You think you're going to marry her."

Mitch folded his arms over his chest. "According to the contract, there ain't no *think* to it."

Rage and confusion erupted in Kiona's heart when she looked from Mitch's arrogant expression to Kol's pained one. "I'll handle this, Mitch. Alone. I don't need your help to explain to him—" The ring of her cell phone in the kitchen sounded through the open patio door. "Damn. I have to get that. It's probably Father. Or Malia. She's apparently got something more to tell me about Heloki."

"Figures. If it's not this—" Kol jerked a thumb at Mitch, "—arrogant asshole interrupting us, it's your nosy *makuakane*."

"Turn around, Mitch," she snarled, glaring up at him. "Hurry, before the call goes to voice-mail."

The phone stopped ringing, but instantly started up again. If Malia was anything at all, she was at least persistent.

Mitch rolled his eyes heavenward and turned. "Make it quick."

Kiona pulled herself from the pool and raced to where her clothes sat in a pile just inside the door. She bent and gathered them up, covering herself. Turning, she called out, "Don't you dare leave, Kol. I'll be right back, and then we *will* talk about this. Tonight."

Chapter Five

With Mitch's back to him, Nakolo got a full-on view of a firm, jean-clad ass. Images assaulted his brain...his hands exploring those hard mounds, his fingers probing between them...followed by his cock.

Cursing under his breath, Nakolo snapped, "I won't let her marry you."

Mitch whirled around, his hands fisted at his sides. Something about it took Nakolo by surprise and made his own hands flex with want. "I think she's already made her choice."

He dragged himself up, getting to his feet, dripping nakedness and all, and faced Mitch in a mirrored stance. "She's mine."

Mitch let out a snort. His gorgeous eyes twinkled with humor. "Tonight, maybe. But come this weekend, she'll be mine."

"You fucking egotistical prick."

Without so much as a flinch at the insult, Mitch shrugged. "What can I say? It goes with the job."

Nakolo had no way of knowing if Kiona had informed Mitch of his unemployed status, but he was sure that underneath those cocky words, Mitch had also meant to say, "At least I *have* a respectable job—a multi-million-dollar one, at that."

He might as well have punched Nakolo below the belt, right in his manhood. No one prided himself on hard work and keeping a job more than Nakolo did. Nakolo could argue he was at least bartending until something better came along. But to have this narcissistic man insult Nakolo's male honor snapped the very thin thread of control he'd been holding on to. Rage such as he'd never felt before, boiled deep in his soul and erupted with a drawn-out growl.

There was no stopping him. He attacked.

Using an old football move, he ducked and rammed his shoulder into Mitch's stomach, snarling as he pushed with all his strength. Taken unaware, Mitch's breath was knocked from his lungs and he stumbled backward, grappling and wrapping his arms around Nakolo's shoulders to keep from falling.

The two tumbled into the pool with a huge splash.

But Nakolo was one step ahead. He yanked Mitch up, spitting and sputtering, and spun him around so his back blanketed Nakolo's naked frontside. He locked his arms around Mitch's shoulders, slamming Mitch's lean, slightly taller form against Nakolo's muscled one.

He couldn't have missed Mitch's sharp yet subtle intake of breath if he'd tried. It was like sensual music to Nakolo's ears, as was the shallow breathing that ensued. Curiously, Mitch only struggled for a few seconds, and weakly at that.

Ah, so the tabloid gossip was true...

Nakolo inhaled, surprised to find himself intoxicated by the scent of chlorine rising up off hot male flesh. He tightened his hold, jerking Mitch back against his raging erection. Mitch had interrupted, showing up right as Nakolo had been climbing toward the peak of release. It wouldn't take much more to make Nakolo blow, especially with his cock rubbing against the roughened, jean-clad ass of Mitch Wulfrum.

"Hmm, I get the distinct feeling you like this." No doubt about it, *Nakolo* liked it, that was for damn sure. In fact, holding a man in his arms proved way more exciting than it had in his dreams. There was something ironic and even sensual about the feel of Mitch's soggy, clothed body pressed along Nakolo's bare flesh. Hardness beneath the wetness, strength beneath the stilted anger that screamed all man. It was enough to turn any straight man gay, to the point of never looking back.

Mitch struggled, his biceps flexing as he pulled against Nakolo's bear-hug hold. "Goddamn it," he growled, twisting so that water splashed and his ass rubbed harder against Nakolo's cock. "Let me fucking go."

Some sort of demon seemed to possess Nakolo. He'd been curious and had fantasized all his life about being with a man. Now here he was in the near-dark with a sweet tropical breeze whirling through the palm fronds and a famous hunk in his arms—and alone in a swimming pool, no less, with Mitch's firm ass grinding over Nakolo's aching rod. It was as if a blazing drum beat in his loins, the flame igniting higher, hotter, before he'd even been able to discern the tempo. If his cock throbbed any harder, and if Mitch fought him any longer, he'd embarrass himself and explode right here in the pool.

"The rumors are true then, aren't they?" Nakolo whispered in Mitch's ear.

Kiona's husky voice drifted out to Nakolo as she talked on her cell phone just inside the door. Mitch's guilty silence met Nakolo's ears. Feeling a twinge of recklessness, a fleeting, depraved thought flashed in his brain.

Can't wait for her to come out here and see him in my arms. How will she react? Will she tell him to fuck off and shove the marriage up his ass?

His heart raced with glee, thumping inside his chest. He

gave Mitch a jerking squeeze to get his attention. "Answer me."

Mitch spoke through clenched teeth, but Nakolo noted he relaxed, finally leaning into Nakolo's arousal. "I'm not gay, goddamn it. Now let me go."

"Let you go? Ha. I bet that's the last thing you want."

Nakolo couldn't stop himself if he tried. What did he have to lose? He clutched Mitch tighter with one arm, so much so that his cock finally became wedged between Mitch's ass cheeks like a hot dog inside a soggy, but very hot bun. Nakolo lowered his free hand, skimming it down across Mitch's hip beneath the water.

And he closed his hand over the rock-hard, denim-covered shaft.

"Hmm, seems you have a flaming hard-on. With a *man* holding you against his erection, I might add. I'd say that means something."

Mitch's shallow breathing was interrupted only by faint moans as Nakolo stroked him up and down through the jeans. "Stop. Just stop," he hissed. "I was watching you two get it on. What man wouldn't get hard with front row seats to an exotic Hawaiian porno movie in the making?"

Nakolo pressed his mouth against Mitch's ear. He sucked the salty earlobe in between his lips. With his teeth clamped to the tip, he murmured, "True, but still, you don't want me to stop, do you?"

When Mitch didn't answer, Nakolo shoved his hand down Mitch's pants and closed his palm around Mitch's stiff, bare penis. Wow, talk about reckless. Nakolo had reacted without thinking, and had finally copped his first feel of a cock in his hand—one that, for once, was not his own. And how empowering it was! So fucking exciting and sexy!

Mitch groaned an animal sound that said it all. His head

plopped backward onto Nakolo's shoulder, and Nakolo gazed upon the most handsome profile he'd ever seen. Oh, he'd seen it on the screen before, but nothing could compare to a front-row seat.

Mitch's eyelids finally fluttered shut in surrender. "Mmm..."

Nakolo's libido leaped into overdrive. He closed his hand tighter around the bulk, stroking up and down his length as best as he could within the confines of the jeans.

"You're bi then...like me. Aren't you?" he rasped, flicking his thumb over the mushroomed head.

Mitch's hand cupped Nakolo's outside the pants, urging him to keep caressing. His words contradicted his actions. "No, no..."

"Oh yes, you can't fool me anymore. But for now, it's our little secret. Kiona doesn't even know about me yet—or about you, does she?"

Mitch panted, shaking his head. He started grinding his hips in a circular motion, fucking Nakolo's hand. Mitch's silky shaft twitched within Nakolo's tight palm, and it was apparent—oh, God, was this really happening?—it wouldn't take much more to jack him off to orgasm.

"I knew it, you're just like me," Nakolo insisted in a low voice for Mitch's ears only, delighting in the shuddering response it elicited. "You're torn between cunt and cock. You fantasize about dicks all the time, but can't have them—won't let yourself. You crave both women and men. At the same time..."

He shook his head vehemently, but still didn't make a concerted effort to escape. "You're delusional."

"Uh-uh, it takes one to recognize one." Keeping one ear trained on Kiona's chattering inside the house, he dragged his lips up Mitch's neck, devouring the clean flesh as he went, a vampire searching for a throbbing artery. With his nose buried in the damp, shampoo-scented blond strands of hair, Nakolo growled, "I've seen it on the movie screen, sensed it studying your pictures in the tabloids. Hell, I feel it now, just as real as I feel your hot body trembling against my hard-on. I could come just like this. And so could you."

"No."

"Oh, yes. You can't fool me. Man, would I love to plunge into this nice, tight ass of yours while you're fucking her snug little pussy. Doesn't that sound hot?" To demonstrate his suggestion, he ground his cock deeper in between the soaked, cloth-covered ass cheeks. "Mmm-hmm, or maybe suck your huge cock while you suck mine. Or how about I eat her sweet, drenching cunt while you tongue-fuck my asshole and ready it for you to sink your cock into me?"

Nakolo couldn't believe his own boldness and the shocking words coming from his mouth. But goddamn, was it ever a turn-on to let loose, to finally speak what had always been in his heart, and to at last feel the hardness of a man in his arms.

Mitch made a noise from deep in his throat that suspiciously resembled euphoria. Encouraged, Nakolo went on, "Doesn't that sound hot? Doesn't it make you want to—?"

"Kol. What in the world are you doing?" Kiona had wrapped herself in a terrycloth, white robe. She stood on the edge of the pool staring down at them. Her dark eyes were wide and disbelieving, her gaze probing the water's murky surface in the area where his hand explored. She obviously attempted to peer through the dim night and discover just what the movements were beneath the water.

Caught. He'd been caught with his hand in the cookie jar…so to speak.

Slowly releasing his hold on Mitch's rock-hard rod, Nakolo

slipped his hand out of Mitch's pants and replied, "Proving your fiancé here *is* gay just like they say."

"Fuck you." Mitch tore out of Nakolo's clutch and pushed through the water. It left Nakolo to ponder the sudden disappointment and loneliness that beset him. Mitch dragged himself out of the pool dripping wet and sodden. "Your boyfriend here has lost his fucking mind. And I suggest you get rid of him or the deal's off."

"What? You can't do that!"

He shook his head, spraying water on her, then wrung his shirt out. His eyes were cold, two sharp icicles slicing right through her. "I can and I will. I could sue you for breach of agreement, goddamn it."

She raked Mitch from head to toe, her perusal briefly stopping on the bulge in his pants. Kiona flicked her narrowed eyes at Nakolo. "What have you done? Both of you? Fighting with each other like two immature teens."

Nakolo shrugged and swam to the stairs. He stood in the pool and took one step at a time, carefully, deliberately, without taking his gaze off Mitch. "What have *I* done? Hmm, let's see. Well, for starters, the woman I love more than my own life unexpectedly announces—right after I've just brought her to paradise in front of another man, mind you—that instead of marrying me one day, she's going to marry a movie star. So next, I get pissed and call him on it. If that makes me immature, then so fucking be it."

"Kiona, you either tell this..." Mitch's lip curled in disgust. "This animal to get lost, or I call Jager and we void the whole contract."

"Contract? Now we have a contract?" Nakolo climbed from the pool and plopped down in a nearby patio chair, uncaring of his naked state. The wind whispered around him, tossing his long hair, drying his heated skin. "Kiona, you either explain to me exactly what the fuck is going on here, or I'm leaving and never coming back."

Mitch snorted and fell into the chair next to Nakolo. "And this is a bad thing?"

"Shut up, Mitch," Kiona hissed. She pulled a seat out from the round glass table and collapsed into the soft vinyl cushion. Leaning back, she stared up at the starlit sky and sighed. "I've been trying to explain it to you for hours, Kol. I'm marrying him as a cover-up, to satisfy Heloki, and so you and I can be together without Father's interference."

Nakolo sat up ram-rod straight. "What?"

"Name only," Mitch supplied, propping his sopping wet loafers on the tabletop.

"Fuck you. She's a gorgeous woman. I don't believe name only for one second."

"Please, Kol, don't be so cavalier. Try to understand, I did this because I love you."

"Love. Great. Maybe I should go," Mitch mumbled, starting to rise.

Nakolo shot him a damning look that had Mitch halting his movements. "Like hell you will. I want to hear every detail—from both of you."

Mitch groaned and dropped back into his seat. "Yeah, right. All the gory details."

"I don't want to lose you," Kiona cried to Nakolo, her large dark eyes glittering, pleading with him to understand. "And yet Father's hell-bent on cutting you out of my life. Don't you see? This is the perfect solution for all three of us."

Nakolo studied each of them in turn, trying to imagine the three of them cohabiting together on an irregular basis. Mitch gone most of the time, off doing blockbuster movies, while Nakolo and Kiona happily play husband and wife. Then suddenly, *bam.* Mitch comes back invading their home, and then what? Kiona hops over to Mitch's bed while Nakolo sits around waiting for him to leave for the next damn movie shoot so Nakolo can have his woman back?

Like fucking hell.

He tried desperately to hold onto his anger, but the more his mind fantasized about their beds merging into one big king-sized community bed, the harder his cock got. And the more he found himself warming to what he heard.

"Think about it. Mitch can live his life as he sees fit while keeping his career intact. Whether it's true or not, I don't know, but at least to the public, he'll appear as a heterosexual movie star with a loving wife. For me, yes, I'll admit this will help me to get my trust fund, but that's money I need for my future—our future," she added, leveling a pleading look at Nakolo. "You already know it's money Heloki's been holding over my head since I was a child. And most importantly," she added, leaning over to frame Nakolo's face in her hands and brush a light kiss across his lips, "we get to stay together, and Dad will never have to know. He'll back off as he always does when he thinks he's won, and assume I'm living with Mitch in wedded bliss. Only it will really be *you* living with me—well, except for those rare occasions when Mitch retreats here. Of course, it'll be necessary for me and Mitch to keep up appearances whenever we're in public, like in Hollywood for special PR functions and so on. You know, to *look* married."

"Wow." Nakolo's wary gaze swung from Kiona to Mitch and back again. Some sort of odd light of hope flickered deep in his pounding heart. "I don't know whether to be pissed that you planned this all behind my back, or ecstatic that you fucked Heloki over."

She slid her hands down and gripped his upper arms. Giving him a little shake, she murmured, “Please understand, I did this for you, for us. I knew you’d say no and stop the whole thing if I talked with you about it first. But this way, with the contract signed and sealed, you can’t back out on me. I’m sorry I chose to do it that way, but it’s our answer, babe, it *is.*”

“Look, pal,” Mitch said in a gravelly voice that made Nakolo shiver. “I understand your position, but the papers are already signed. It’s a valid contract.” He got to his feet and rounded the table so he stood beside them, forcing Kiona and Nakolo to look up at him.

Those famous blue-green pools held Nakolo’s gaze, and he could swear something feral lurked there, something for both Nakolo and Kiona. Nakolo shoved down the bubbly euphoria of it and instead focused on the bizarre plan they’d come up with behind his back.

“So the two of you, along with that damn Jager, cooked up this scheme? You marry in name only, Kiona finally gets her money, and Mitch Wulfrum, wealthy fucker that he is, gets to thumb his nose at the paparazzi and say, ‘See? I told you I’m not gay. Who *could* be, with such a smokin’ babe on their arm?’ That right?”

“Yeah, mostly. I want to suppress the gay rumors, and what better way than to marry, and be seen in Hollywood with a gorgeous woman such as Kiona?”

“Why thank you.” She grinned, her straight white teeth gleaming in the moonlight.

Her sudden glee made Nakolo’s heart reluctantly swell with his own joy. He wanted nothing more than her happiness. As he sat there looking at her, feeling the heat of her body so near his, he longed to run his fingers through her thick tresses and kiss that plump little mouth. Yet he wondered what it might feel like to be doing that very thing while Mitch watched...or better yet, while Mitch gave them both some hot attention. The image it conjured up in his mind had his cock rising back to attention and his anus clenching. After that scorching but incomplete round with Kiona in the pool, followed by his first highly arousing touch of a man, Nakolo imagined his balls were not only blue, but fucking navy.

With a grumble of annoyance, Nakolo rose and located his jeans. He jammed them on and said in a clipped tone, "Yeah, but what about the fact that you *are* gay—or bisexual?"

"Kol!"

Mitch stalked across the patio and shoved his face into Nakolo's so they were nose-to-nose. His chest was puffed out, his eyes narrowed as they locked on Nakolo's wary gaze, never wavering as he spoke. "It's okay, Kiona, really. I'm used to shallow-minded, cruel people attacking me with slanderous accusations. It goes with the territory."

"Right. Slanderous." Nakolo leaned slightly back and crossed his arms, acutely aware his forearms and his dick were both mere inches from Mitch. He longed to step closer and become engulfed by that seductive, manly heat again. But first, he wanted the man to face what had just happened between them. "Go ahead, deny it. Deny that you didn't enjoy me touching you just now in the pool."

Kiona gasped, but wisely didn't say a word in response.

Nakolo inhaled to calm his rapid heartbeat, fully prepared and determined to get the facts on the table. After all, this was a man with a plan to marry—to steal—the woman Nakolo loved. But Nakolo was through with letting the other men in Kiona's life slice him right out of the fucking picture. In this case, he'd sensed something that might be the key to some leverage. No way was he keeping it to himself, even if it meant shocking

Kiona with the truth about his own secret desires. It was a risky trump card, but it seemed she was determined to marry another man anyway, which didn't bode well for Nakolo's future with her.

Unless the look he'd seen in her eyes when she'd spied Nakolo's hand down Mitch's pants, turned out to be what he suspected...

"What...what are you talking about?" Kiona gripped the edge of the table and pulled herself to an erect sitting position. Her shocked gaze swung from man to man.

But was that also lust she attempted to conceal in her expression? Gods of Hawaii, please let it be true.

There was only one way to find out. His usual frankness. "I think you already know. You saw me fondling him in the water. And whether he's prepared to admit it or not, we *both* enjoyed it. Do you understand what I'm saying, Ki?"

"Jesus." Mitch's face went pale. He groaned and dropped his head back, staring up at the night sky. "Jesus fucking Christ."

"Y-you're telling me you're..." She let out a long, slow breath, her sparkling eyes latched onto Nakolo's. "You're gay?"

"Bi-curious might be the best way to put it, at least for now. Until it can be...explored more." Nakolo shrugged mentally. What difference did the truth make now? She was marrying another man. But God, it felt good to finally admit it out loud!

She pressed a trembling hand to her heart. He heard her swallow. "Are you serious?"

"As shit."

"Speaking of shit, I think I've had enough for one night." Mitch spun on his heel to leave.

Kiona scrambled up, her seat scraping on concrete, and raced toward him. She clasped both hands around his arm and tugged, managing to halt his flight. “Please. Please don’t go. W-we have things yet to discuss. Apparently, a lot more than I ever dreamed of.”

“Dreamed? Are you telling me you’re okay with what your boyfriend just accused me of?”

There was a long pause. A wave rolled in, slamming against the rocky shore below. Nakolo held his breath, waiting for what seemed like eons as the song of the sea played in the background.

“Yes.” Finally, that one word came out soft, almost tender. It spoke to Nakolo more than anything she’d ever said to him. “I’m wondering if he’s right.”

Mitch yanked his arm free. His jaw set. He spoke through his teeth. “So we’re back to that, are we? Believing the tabloids?”

Kiona planted her hands on her hips. Her robe gaped open, the edges of the terrycloth barely covering her nipples. She ignored Mitch’s distracted, penetrating stare that seemed to drop to her cleavage like a lead ball.

“It has nothing to do with tabloids and everything to do with what I just saw with my own eyes. I’ll admit, it seemed like the fantasy came out of nowhere, but yes, it surprisingly turned me on to see the two of you so close. Kol naked, with his hand down your pants. The look of reluctant lust on your faces. Both of you climbing out of the water with indisputable erections.” She inhaled, and then exhaled. “Oh yeah, a lot of women would find that very arousing.”

Just hearing her words and watching their interplay made Nakolo go hard again. The two of them were beautiful, the perfect female and male specimens. He’d touched them both, and he knew intimately the night-and-day differences between them.

His balls drew up and blood drained into his cock, making him ache to be sandwiched between the two. But he held to his spot, forcing himself to watch this heated, red-blooded exchange.

Across the patio, Mitch sought out Nakolo's gaze. The touch of it was like a firm yet reluctant caress. He looked back at Kiona and dragged a hand down the sleeve of her robe. "You're telling me you want this?"

She didn't answer at first, only stood there and shuddered at his touch while her attention shifted to Nakolo. "Babe?"

"Hmm?"

"Please tell me I didn't read this wrong."

He couldn't help chuckling. Nakolo crossed the space, stopping right in front of them. His gaze moved in a slow trek from Mitch's strikingly handsome face, to the deep cavern of Ki's cleavage. Diamonds of water glistened there, making Nakolo long to rip the robe off and slurp up every drop while Mitch watched. Instead, he hooked his thumbs in the waistband of his jeans and considered her words. He wondered how it was he could have felt such intense betrayal and anger for these two stunning creatures only moments ago, and yet now crave them both without thinking of his own self-respect.

He lifted one hand, cupping her jaw and tipping it up, forcing her to look deep into his eyes. "No. You don't have it wrong. I figure I could already be on the losing end of this deal by letting you marry him, anyway. So why not? Why not finally admit my secret?"

"To be with a man?" she asked breathily, her chest rising and falling.

"Yes. To be with a man I know has the same urges I do." He

glanced over at Mitch and finally saw the surrender he'd been seeking, the softening of the expression, the light of passion at last igniting in the eyes. Nakolo knew exactly how that felt. It was so damn freeing, and so fucking exciting, he felt giddy as hell.

Nakolo shifted his perusal back to Kiona. "While we're making love with you at the same time. The three of us, together. Crazy as it sounds, it's a dream come true for me...as long as I'm not being pushed out of the picture. As long as this marriage includes me too."

Just then, a cloud passed across the moon. It cast Mitch in shadows that emphasized his masculine features. Through the muted light, he looked directly at Kiona, holding her eyes to his. "Is this what you want? Really? A threesome?"

"Remember today?" she asked, her mouth curving into a sly grin.

The tension lines across Mitch's forehead gradually softened. "In the car?"

"Yes," she replied on a whisper. "I knew you knew. I could tell you got a charge out of it. It...it really excited me like never before. And Kol?" She flicked her stare to latch onto his. "You knew Mitch was there, and you enjoyed him watching us. It turned you on too. Didn't it?"

"Damn fucking right."

She nodded, her lips spreading into a beaming smile. "I could tell by your sudden...enthusiasm."

"I could tell by the way you came all over my face while trying to talk in a normal tone to him."

"Whew." Mitch raked a hand through his damp hair leaving it roguishly disheveled. "I can't believe what a sudden jagged turn this conversation just took."

"You like it jagged," Nakolo accused. "Just like you liked watching the ecstasy cross her face today when you knew someone else was getting her off."

Mitch shrugged. "What red-blooded man wouldn't?"

She let out a tinkling laugh. "Listen to you two. Can't you see this is the answer to our dilemma? Think about it." Standing between them, Kiona planted a warm palm against each of their chests. Her eyes danced with euphoria, the light of dusk making their golden pools twinkle. Nakolo's nipple tingled at the feminine touch while vividly remembering the masculine one, the man standing only two feet from him.

With Kiona connecting them.

Her sweet scent engulfed Nakolo, thrumming through his system until it took hold of his loins and squeezed. Bathed in silver moonlight, her blue-black, damp hair framing her face, Nakolo wondered how he could do anything but let her have her way.

"Oh, I'm thinking all right," Mitch replied, stepping away. "Thinking I need time to give all this craziness some serious thought, and probably consult with Jager on a few legal issues. Look, I'm going to get out of here, go get some dry clothes on. And go choke the life out of that fucking asshole Jager as soon as he arrives on the island," he mumbled good-naturedly, stalking toward the sidewalk that led around the side of the house.

Nakolo studied the slicked-back blond hair brushing the collar of the wet shirt, the wide shoulders tapering down into a fit torso and narrow hips. He gulped. And that tight ass that had fit perfectly against Nakolo's cock. He didn't want to see Mitch leave under such bizarre circumstances. Had Nakolo read Mitch wrong? Maybe Mitch had just been taken off guard in the pool? Maybe his erection had been all for Kiona, and had had nothing at all to do with Nakolo and the male-to-male, electrifying connection Nakolo himself had experienced?

His gut twisted with dread. If that was the case, it *would* mean he'd eventually be cut out of their marriage. He was just about to call out and plead with Mitch to come back and let them finish hashing this out, when Mitch crashed right into a bulky man.

"Sorry. Excuse me." Mitch tried to sidestep Heloki's rotund frame.

"*Kupaianaha*!" Heloki's thick-lipped mouth fell open in the full moon of his tanned face. "You're...you're Mitch Wulfrum."

"Yes, yes I am."

He thrust out a beefy hand and grinned. "I'm Heloki 'Alohi, Kiona's father. Jager has told me so much about you—as has Kiona."

Yet she didn't tell me a damn thing about Mitch. He'd almost forgotten how much that still smarted. Nakolo ground his teeth together. With his fists newly clenched at his sides, he shot her what he hoped was a heated look. But she'd become so staggered by her father's sudden appearance, she didn't notice.

Mitch hesitantly took Heloki's large hand and pumped it. "All good stuff, I hope?"

"*Auê*! Yes, yes!" Heloki chuckled and slid his hands into the pockets of his khaki trousers. His trademark floral Hawaiian shirt stretched over the ample abdomen and glowed red, orange, and white in the moonlight. "I was pleased to hear the story of your whirlwind courtship when she flew to L.A. on company business recently. Ah, and though a bit hasty, word of your engagement thrilled me. I'm so honored to meet you. You're one of my favorite stars. And I tell you—"

He cut himself off when his gaze fell upon Nakolo standing off to the side, shirtless, wearing nothing but jeans. Black beady eyes glowered across the space at Nakolo. Ire rushed along Nakolo's nerve endings. No one boiled Nakolo's blood like his ex-boss. Still, he kept his interest trained on his foe and wondered how he could hate the father so fucking much while obsessively loving the daughter.

Heloki's attention shifted to Kiona, his mouth twisted in disapproval. "What is he doing here?"

Kiona sighed. "I don't think that's any of your business."

"My business? This is highly inappropriate, young lady. Mr. Wulfrum is your fiancé. Show him some respect and see that this...this *scum* leaves the premises."

"Whoa, wait a minute." Mitch held up his hands palms forward. "With all due respect, sir, I hardly think that's necessary."

It seemed the tide picked up on the beach below. Nakolo could hear it roaring right along with the fury thrumming through his system. It was only Mitch's sudden, unexpected interjection that kept him from exploding.

He couldn't be actually standing up for Nakolo—could he?

Heloki raked Mitch from head to toe and back again. "You're defending your bride-to-be's former lover?"

He'd said it to deliver news he assumed Mitch didn't know, but Mitch didn't skip a beat. "I'm defending a seemingly decent man who hasn't uttered one word of disrespect to you. Or me, for that matter." He shifted his stance even as Kiona stepped forward to block Heloki's view of Nakolo. Mitch hooked a possessive arm around Kiona's shoulders and pulled her close. "Look, I love your daughter, and she loves me. I think that's all that matters, don't you?"

Kiona jerked her head up and gaped at Mitch. Wisely, she clamped her jaw shut and composed herself before Heloki noticed.

Heloki peered around Mitch to snare Nakolo with a vengeful look of glee. “I suppose you’re right, but it really is tactless. You don’t want to get tongues wagging, now do you?” Heloki nodded. “He should leave. And never return.”

“That, Mr. ’Alohi, I believe would be up to Kiona.”

“Yes, that’s right.” She slowly slid her arm around Mitch’s waist. Nakolo was almost certain the move was meant not only for Heloki’s sake, but for Nakolo, as well. He liked to believe it was intended to turn him on in their new game of voyeurism. Well, it worked, damn her. A hot glow spread through his belly and settled in his groin.

“But, Father, marriage to another or not, the fact is, Kol will always be a good friend of mine.”

“That’s ridiculous. You can’t remain friends with an old lover when you’re about to marry this decent man here.”

“No, it’s true. We’ve been friends for years, and will remain so. I won’t let go of that, and Mitch knows and approves.” She peered up at Mitch and sent him a cool smile. “He encourages whatever will make me happy, don’t you, sweetheart?”

Mitch mimicked her fake smile. “Of course I do, darling.”

“So there you have it, Father.” Her smile faded. “And please remember, it will be our business from now on. Not yours.”

It irked Nakolo that they spoke of him as if he didn’t exist. He sidestepped toward the edge of the patio gaining a better position to witness their exchange, while at the same time, making himself more conspicuous.

Heloki’s dark eyebrows arched into a single bush at the center of his forehead. “And you, my *kamali’i*, should remember your trust fund is my business.”

Damn the bastard, why did he continue to hold that over her head?

Kiona pressed her lips together. "What have you come here for, Father?"

"I've been trying to reach you all evening. Then I come here and knock at the front door, but you didn't answer. I assumed you were swimming, so naturally, I walked around back."

"I'd like to ask that from now on, you honor my privacy. If I don't answer my door, please don't intrude further."

Nakolo watched as Heloki's blubber started to tremble. "You didn't answer your phone, either," Heloki barked, leaning forward in that manner of his that always foreshadowed a meltdown. "Jager called from L.A. earlier to tell me Mitch had arrived, and I simply wanted to meet the man who is going to be my new son-in-law. Is that so bad?"

"No, of course not. But did you ever stop to think perhaps I didn't have a signal at the time, or maybe I was busy and couldn't get to the phone?"

Nakolo could see the silvery sheen of sweat breaking out across Heloki's wide forehead. "Busy with your lover, Nakolo?"

Mitch sighed. "Mr. 'Alohi, I hardly think that's any of your—"

"Look, I'm sorry," Kiona interjected, cutting in on Mitch's scolding comment. "Malia did tell me you were trying to reach me through her. And I did see you'd called my cell a few times, but it's past business hours. I figured it could wait until tomorrow."

"Did it ever occur to you it might be personal?"

"Look, I said I was sorry. It's been a long day, and I'm very tired. I'd hoped to deal with whatever it was you'd wanted tomorrow. For now, as you can see, I'm home safe and sound with my fiancé, planning this weekend's wedding. So what could be so important you'd see fit to stop by unannounced?"

Heloki's big body trembled with renewed rage. "*Unannounced*? I am your father, you ungrateful little—little bitch!" Kiona gasped, but Heloki barreled on. "I am the man who raised you and loved you even when your selfish mother chose to abandon you. *I* am the one who has sacrificed and sweated to build and shape the company, to bring you up and give you all these fine things—this house," Heloki spewed in a booming voice, flinging out a fat hand toward the home he'd helped her build. He then wagged his finger at her, leaning closer so his nose nearly slammed into Kiona's. "Don't you ever forget it. And do not *ever* talk to me with such disrespect again!"

When Kiona flinched, cowering closer to Mitch, Nakolo couldn't keep his trap shut any longer. "Goddamn it, get away from her." Nakolo's nostrils flared and his pulse pounded in his temples. Unable to hold himself back any longer, he charged at Heloki. "What the hell is wrong with you, you son of a—"

"Kol, no!" Kiona started toward him, but threw up her arms and halted her steps when her father retaliated.

Heloki drew back a stout fist. He swung at Nakolo, but he missed his mark, doing nothing but stirring the air and tumbling forward off the sidewalk into the flowerbed.

Just in time, Nakolo was spared. All in one smooth move, Mitch tugged Kiona behind him while yanking Nakolo toward him so his back crashed into Mitch's hard chest.

With his arm tight around Nakolo's shoulders, Mitch growled low in Nakolo's ear. "What, are you crazy? The man's wealthy, no doubt with lots of local influence. He could have your ass tossed in jail with one snap of his fingers."

"Not before I choke the life from that prick," Nakolo sneered, jerking against the strong hold while fully aware of Mitch's soft cock pressed against his ass.

Kiona berated her father, looking down on him while

chattering and slipping into her Hawaiian dialect.

Mitch and Nakolo continued their quiet exchange.

Mitch chuckled. He replied in a soft, gravelly voice meant for Nakolo's ears only, "I don't know why, but I like that in you, the macho temper when it comes to protecting your woman. But you end up in prison, there're a lot of other men who'll *like* you too—and I guarantee it won't be nearly as pleasurable as our encounter in the pool."

He'd murmured that last part so tenderly, Nakolo wondered if he'd imagined it. Nakolo replied in the same tone. "Ha. Not quite the time to discuss our mutual attraction to each other." Nakolo elbowed Mitch and broke free.

Kiona bent and tried to assist Heloki to his feet. "Please, please just go. We'll talk tomorrow at the office."

Heloki swatted her hand away. "I can get up by myself." With the help of a nearby patio chair, Heloki dragged his bulk up and brushed the soil off his knees.

"Father..."

"I'm going, damn you, I'm going." He waddled a few steps up the walk, then turned back to face her. His eyes narrowed, glittering in the lunar light. "But I warn you, the minute I hear or see any evidence you and that lowlife are more than just friends, the trust fund goes to charity."

Chapter Six

Upon Heloki's abrupt departure, Kiona had raced to her room and plopped down on the bed, Kol on her heels. All she wanted was to moan and mourn the day she'd been born to a woman with no maternal instincts, and a father who insisted on running every aspect of her life, right down to what toilet paper she bought.

Now she jerked herself up off the mattress and crossed to Kol, where he stood with one ear pressed against the closed door.

"You can listen all you want, but Mitch is an actor, remember? What he says, and how he says it, isn't necessarily always the truth." She whispered it to him as they stood there like two kids, their ears perked, as if trying to eavesdrop on the grownups after being sent to bed too early.

Following the Heloki debacle, Mitch had asked to stay and use her phone and computer. He currently occupied the office area of her living room returning calls and sending emails. And chewing out Jager for various faux pas related to the current situation the three found themselves entangled in.

Mainly, he demanded Jager tell him why Kol had been factored into the situation without Mitch's prior knowledge.

Would Mitch back out of the deal? God help her, she hoped not!

"Yeah, how could I forget?" Kol winked. "His handsome face is plastered all over every tabloid and TV station in the country."

"True, he is handsome."

Kol's mouth thinned, though she didn't know if it was from jealousy, or the cold hard facts of this entire awkward matter. "Very," he mumbled.

How that one word of admittance coming so easily from Kol could give her such a charge, she didn't know. But it did. Her pussy throbbed as images of their two hard-muscled, glistening bodies flashed in her head. One slightly taller, blond, and athletic, the other dark-haired, deeply tanned, and cut like a diamond. She could vividly picture Kol's bulging arms wrapped around Mitch from behind...his hard-on pressed into Mitch's ass.

Whew.

"But he lied to you—to us. Believe me, he *is* bisexual, whether he'll admit it or not. I sensed it, even felt his arousal in my hand."

"Oh, God," Kiona moaned.

His warm hand came up to cup her jaw, and his eyes bore into hers. "That turns you on, doesn't it, babe?"

She glanced away, unsure if his tone was accusatory or heavily laced with desire.

"It's okay. You can be honest with me. I won't be mad."

Kiona knew it was true. She was also certain of Kol's love for her...as well as his shocking but oh-so-hot yearning for another man. That gave her a strange sense of security in admitting her true feelings.

"Yes," she finally whispered. "It turns me on like crazy. I-I want it so badly. I want to get to know that half of you I never knew existed, and see it finally getting satisfied. I want to be between the two of you, beside you, watching, touching, experiencing it all. I can't explain it, but today? Today when you were eating my pussy and he was right there next to the car? *'Û*, did that ever excite me!"

His eyes twinkled with the light of hope and passion. He bent his head, his lips grazing hers. "I know. You drowned me in your juices, remember?" His wide mouth curved up in a soft smile. "I love you, Ki. So much. I never thought I could ever admit my secret to you, and now here we are. I can't think of anything more fucking thrilling than you being cool with it—hell, all this enthusiasm is way more than I could ever ask for. Thank you."

"Don't thank me too soon," she warned. "We still don't have Mitch's agreement."

"He signed the contract, right?"

"Yes, but with you now included in the bargain, he could easily cry breach, as he said before."

He sighed, dropping his hand. "But maybe this is what Jager'd planned all along? We both know he's got a sly way about him. Hell, Jager's probably making excuses to Mitch while talking him into going along with it." He shook his head. "No, I don't think he'll keep crying breach after Jager's done with him."

Hope fluttered in her chest. "Do you want Jager to persuade him?"

Kol thrust a hand through his long hair. "Do you want me to want it?"

"Yes."

He smiled, and something mischievous and joyful glowed in his eyes. "Would you still love me if I said I want Jager to convince him something fierce—almost as much as I want you?"

"I will always love you." She held her hand to his jaw loving the feel of the soft whiskers that always shadowed his jaw every evening. "That's what I've been trying to tell you all day. It's why I did this."

"Yes, I get it now." He turned his head and rooted at her hand, planting a butterfly-soft kiss in the palm. "You wanna know what else I think?"

"Always."

"I think Mitch'll still marry you, even knowing you and I will remain lovers."

"You think?"

He nodded emphatically. "Oh, yeah. He has too much at stake not to. Besides, I see the way he looks at you with obvious lust—no acting there for sure. Huh, and the attraction between him and me? The coward denies his sexuality, but holy hell, I could've sliced the heat with a butterknife. He wants both of us, whether he'll admit it or not. He might be coming off as odd and wishy-washy—probably worrying about tarnishing his near-stellar image if he makes a bad career move by letting me stay on—but he'll go through with marrying you, at least. I guarantee it."

"And...and you're okay with me...with us all...sleeping together if it comes to that?"

Kol blinked. Beyond the door, she could hear the deep sound of Mitch talking on the phone.

"Only if I'm included." His eyebrows suddenly furrowed, dipping into a black angry slash. A stormy gleam lit his eyes. "You don't plan on sleeping with him alone when I'm not there, do you?"

"No, no, of course not."

His gaze latched onto hers, challenging. “You promise?”

“I promise.”

He let out a pent-up breath. “You know this is fucking hard on me.”

“Of course it is,” she assured him, rising on tip-toe to brush her lips against his. “But it’s the only way for us all to win.”

He drew her into his arms nestling his half-erect cock against her abdomen. “We’ll take it one day at a time, how’s that?”

“Sounds like a great plan. We’ll see what comes of it.”

“Comes? I think he’ll come all right. Like I said, he’s got the hots for you, babe.”

She grinned, winding her arms around his neck. “And for you. Which makes me very horny,” she purred, kissing his neck.

He leaned back against the door, dragging her pussy up and over his rigid manhood, and groaned, “You’re a naughty, gorgeous diva he won’t be able to resist.”

“After all those compelling gay rumors,” she said with a giggle, “the last thing I was expecting was for him to be attracted to me. Yet he does seem to be pondering the possibility of a two-man, one-woman threesome.” Kiona considered that, once again assailed by a powerful wave of desire. She clenched her pussy, rubbing harder against him so that her clitoris throbbed in delicious response.

“Mmm,” was all Kol could say. He clamped his big hands on her ass and levered her up higher.

“But that doesn’t necessarily mean a man is lusting after that other man. From what I understand in a few articles and erotica books I’ve read,” she went on, kissing him randomly across the mouth, cheeks, and nose, “a lot of men prefer the kind of ménage where there's no physical contact between the two males."

Kol pulled back, shrugging with reluctant agreement. The look of disappointment that crossed his face didn't go unnoticed. He wanted there to be male-male contact, and the concept of that only made the excitement in her loins pulse harder.

"Actually, I take that back. I'm as certain of this as I am of your love for me, Kol. Like you, I believe deep inside, Mitch Wulfrum *is* bisexual. He revealed an obvious attraction to you, as you insist he also did to me. When you were in the pool with him, I saw the magnetism with my own eyes. Hell, I *felt* the electricity in the air."

He brushed a lock of her hair off her forehead. His eyes, they were so volatile and ever-changing with his moods. They now twinkled with desire and some sort of new gleam of exhilaration she'd never seen before. Had he really been suppressing that side of himself all his life? What torture that must have been.

"Are you saying for sure you want it that way?" Kol asked, a hopeful tone lacing his voice.

Kiona shimmied down his body and found her footing. She crossed the plush-carpeted master suite and fell onto the king-sized bed. Fixing her gaze on the ceiling, she sighed lustily, "I...I'm not sure what I'm saying. But it sure is an exciting idea in theory."

A rap sounded at the door. Kiona rolled her head to the side and watched as Kol gripped the knob and yanked the door open. "What?"

Mitch stepped into the room, his glance first cutting to Kol, then, with a slight flush to his face, he looked directly at Kiona. "I was just thinking when I was talking to Jager... Why can't you just do without the trust fund?"

The sudden question made her blink and stammer. "I-I... Well, it's—"

"Hmm, interesting thought." Kol shut the door and followed Mitch as he trekked to the bed. "But a stupid one. She's been waiting for her money for over a decade."

Mitch ignored Kol and sat on the edge of the mattress, his hip so close to hers, she could feel the warmth of his flesh burning through his still-damp jeans. His dazzling eyes lit on her, caressed the length of her body in one warm, long sweep. She could smell the faint scent of chlorine mingled with the aroma of soap. Behind him, she could see Kol's face taking on that feral animal's expression as he stood back and watched Mitch and Kiona converse on her bed.

"You have a job, right?"

Kiona shivered, trying to concentrate on the words coming from his mouth rather than the sexy ones blazing in his eyes. She threw an arm across her eyes. "Yes, but he pays me a pretty measly wage. Well, not really measly, but it's barely enough to cover my bills, living expenses, and a small pension payment."

"What?"

"Yep," Kol offered, rounding the bed and lounging on the opposite side. He stretched out at Kiona's right side, propping his head on a fist. "He talked her into building this house. Dangled free land in front of her, paid the down payment, tempted her with freedom and her independence. But really, his motivation was to get her strapped to a hefty mortgage, keep her here on Kabana, totally dependent on him for life. Putting her on the payroll, earning a just-enough salary while holding back her trust fund guarantees she'll work hard for him at KPCS, while the house keeps her chained to the island. He's a clever man."

Mitch arched an eyebrow. "He pays you a just-enough salary, and you're the CEO of the company?"

She nodded, embarrassment warming her cheeks at his incredulous tone.

Mitch scooted closer and closed his hand around her wrist. He drew her arm away from her eyes. "That's bullshit. You shouldn't put up with that."

"Same thing I've been trying to tell her for years," Kol mumbled.

The hot vice on her arm sent a tremor of liquid desire spilling into her womb. As each second passed, lying there on a bed with her lover on one side of her, and a heartthrob star on the other, Kiona had a difficult time thinking about anything but that male-on-male embrace in the pool—and seeing Kol's hand down the front of Mitch's pants.

Oh, God.

"I love KPCS. I practically grew up either in the office or in the fields. I'd work there for free if I could." She let out a lusty sigh. "But that's not possible with a mortgage, car payment, credit card bills, living expenses, and the like."

"So without realizing it, he's forced you to do something as rash as contracting to marry a stranger so you can get access to your trust fund. Money that's rightfully yours in the first place." He shook his head in disgust and let go of her arm. She clenched her hands into fists to keep from brushing aside the lock of pale hair that fell across his brow. "Sounds like one of my movie plots."

Kiona sat up. "Well, do you see now? I need you to marry me. I need that trust fund." Her heart rapped against her ribs with worry. "You didn't order Jager to file for breach of contract, did you?"

Mitch frowned. He reached over and plucked a lock of hair from her breast. She still wore the robe, but even with the cloth covering her chest, the nipple puckered on cue, making a trail of heavy desire snake through her system.

Rubbing the strands between his fingers, Mitch murmured, "Regardless of what I discussed with Jager, you shouldn't have to do something so drastic just to pay your bills."

Kol snorted. "That's Heloki for you. Trusses people up like a damn puppet, makes you owe him, then you have to resort to doing *lôlô* things to pay your debts or stay in his good graces. Good at pulling strings, obsessed with keeping her on a chain—hell, everyone, even me." His eyes narrowed. "Until he fired me for sleeping with her."

"Really?" Mitch glanced at Kol. She watched as his gaze freely roamed Kol's body from head, to toes, to crotch. "So all because of Heloki, she's working her ass off for pennies, while you're drawing unemployment."

Kol shrugged, but Kiona knew him well. "Doing some bartending while I look for something better. Can't sit around and do nothing."

He may look it, but Kiona knew Kol was far from feeling nonchalant. Her libido stirred hotter when she noted the vaguest bit of cock peeping over the waistband of his jeans. The unmistakable thickening of a rising hard-on strained against his zipper.

"Mmm," Mitch agreed, and Kiona could swear she saw admiration and respect flicker in his eyes.

"Shouldn't you get out of those wet clothes?" Kol suddenly asked.

Kiona's lips parted on a wistful in-drawn breath when Kol reached down and palmed himself through his pants, adding, "Wouldn't want you to catch your death before the wedding, now would we?"

Mitch locked his blue-green gaze onto Kol's dark one. "Are you offering me...?" His perusal moved lower to study Kol's crotch. "Offering me sex with my bride-to-be?"

Whoa. Kiona swallowed a lump. "Uh, I don't think—"

Kol scooted closer to Kiona and drew her robe partially open, exposing her breasts. Cool night air rushed through the open French doors, fluttering the curtains and sending a ripple of goose bumps up and down her body. Kol's warm hand lifted one globe, palming, massaging, so that Mitch had no choice but to lower his gaze and watch.

"No, I'm offering you sex with your bride-to-be and her man—her permanent man who stays right here by her side no matter who she marries. So what do you say, Wulfrum?" Defiantly, Kol leaned down and circled his tongue around her areola. She sucked in a breath at the wet-hot sensations bombarding her nipple while another man watched. Sticky cream oozed out of her aching pussy. *Is this really happening?*

"You ready to explore that bi side of yourself?" Kol challenged when Mitch simply sat there motionless, speechless.

Who was this man, Kiona wondered, this wicked devil suddenly emerging in Kol's place? It made her head spin, had her panting with a sexual fever. Yet she really didn't have to ask herself who he was. It was as if she'd known the panther lurked within all along, but hadn't known there was a cage, or how to unlock it.

Oh, but gods of her islands, she had the key now—in the form of Mitch Wulfrum.

To torture and tempt further, Kol kept his stare on Mitch as he drew her areola in between his teeth, and bit down. Kiona arched into Kol's mouth even as she heard Mitch mutter a curse under his breath. Every now and then, she got whiffs of her own arousal mixed with the scent of chlorine in Kol's hair as it dragged soft and tickly over her upper chest. She watched Mitch's eyes as they devoured her naked breasts, sliding over to take in the powerful sight of Kol's flexing biceps and sculpted, bare upper body. Mitch's jaw clenched, his propriety apparently fighting with the male demons ruling his libido.

But what really struck her was the way he seemed to become periodically fixated on Kol, not in the male-watching-another-pleasure-a-woman way, but in the way she'd read about men openly lusting after other men, or seen in those porno flicks she and Kol had watched together. Yet it also seemed Mitch warred with himself over the need for both man and woman.

It was true. The movie star was bisexual.

"Come here, Mitch," she finally whispered, raising her hand to him. Bubbly exhilaration rippled up her spine. *Ah, yes, a woman's deepest, darkest fantasies are made of exciting moments like this.* "You don't have to choose. You can have both of us."

Oh God, did she really just say that? And was she truly about to have sex with the man she loved, and the celebrity she'd had a secret crush on for years? She was like the lead female role in one of his movies, center stage, all eyes on her. Only this far surpassed all of his box-office hits. None of them featured a threesome, and none of them were ever this naughty.

"Jesus Christ." Mitch didn't ponder her offer long. He stood up and ripped off his wet clothes, exposing an erection to rival Kol's. She knew Kol's eyes were also on Mitch, but it was Mitch's moan of approval that had Kol picking up the pace, sucking harder, skimming his callused hand up her leg, over her undulating hips, along her swollen slit.

At Kol's eager caresses, her robe fell fully open, exposing

every inch of her tingling flesh. She cried out, nearly coming undone when Kol sank a finger into her damp channel at the very moment Mitch eased a knee onto the bed and stared down at them while he stroked his long cock.

"If it's okay with you, I'd like to hold off, save you—us—until the wedding night," Mitch rasped, pumping himself off.

Kiona simply blinked, stunned into speechlessness. His words were sweet yet full of erotic promise. He was on the bed with them, palming himself frantically, yet he wanted to save their consummation for their wedding night? Touched by a deep sentiment she couldn't quite name, she looked down at his erection, back up his beautiful body to that gorgeous face of his. Breathless. She felt totally breathless and dizzy with excitement.

"What?" Kol croaked, his head popping up.

Mitch lifted a shoulder even as he continued to stroke himself. "Don't ask me why. I mean, I'm definitely going to take advantage of this moment—but not fully." His hungry gaze raked her body, finally falling on her exposed pussy. It felt as if a flame had seared her wherever his eyes touched her. "For some reason, I want to save it for our wedding night. I want that initial moment of sliding into her to be when she's my wife."

Wow. At his surprising declaration, Kiona's pulse thumped out of control.

Kol chuckled hollowly. She knew it to be in reference to Mitch's *our wedding night* comment. She detected a hint of jealousy in Kol's tone, but still he pushed the confirmation of a three-way encounter. "What about me? You're forgetting me, goddamn it."

"No. No, I'm definitely not forgetting anything. I meant you too. This may not be the American way, but fuck that. When I marry her, it looks like I'll be marrying you, as well. We'll have

Jager do something to fix it, hell, I don't know. But I do know I need to wait to have both of you on *our* wedding night."

Our. He didn't clarify, but she knew it meant he'd included Kol, and the sound of it made Kiona's heart soar with joy. Heat flooded her loins as random images of their wedding night flashed through her brain.

But how would they go about this without actually doing it?

Kol's expression softened and she saw the exact second understanding and relief took hold of him. "Then how do you suggest we do this?"

Mitch jutted his jaw toward Kol by way of pointing. "You take her from behind while I watch. While I lie there and let her suck me off."

Her mouth watered at the image his suggestion conjured up in her mind. Kiona's very talented lover would make love to her while she gave movie star Mitch Wulfrum a blowjob.

Holy shit.

She wasn't sure if Mitch was copping out over the male-on-male contact, or if he truly wanted to hold their consummation sacred until after the ceremony. But it didn't matter to her either way, because she was so fucking turned on she could barely think or breathe.

Oh yeah, Kabana was heating up like the blazing depths of Mount Makakoa. She didn't need to study Kabana's famous volcano to understand its inner workings anymore. Kiona let the lava build and boil, and knew once she erupted it wasn't going to be a geological event, but rather a celestial one that would rock her whole universe.

Mitch glanced around at the luxurious bedroom with the

Polynesian décor and the huge four-poster, wrought-iron bed angled in the corner. Kiona shrugged out of her robe and now lay totally nude upon the white comforter, her blue-black hair trailing across the fluffy pillow she rested her head on.

His perusal slid to Kol, his dark head bent as he busied himself tasting those luscious-looking, full breasts. Island-tanned, tattooed skin bunched and rippled over muscles made so, Mitch was sure, by hard labor and hands that refused to remain idle. Like now. Kol shoved her long, silky legs apart with one large hand, and she bit her lips, her exotic eyes going limp with desire when Kol finger-fucked her while voraciously sucking one dark-brown, erect nipple.

Mother fucker, was this some kind of erotic dream he'd tumbled into, or had he truly lucked out? Mitch stroked himself, knowing he could blow just like this, kneeling next to her lush, writhing body, watching as Kol, so dark and so fucking male, brought her to climax.

But Mitch wasn't going to deprive himself anymore. He'd already tortured himself watching them in the pool. He needed release, although call him a traditionalist, but he wanted more than anything to delay his consummation with them until the wedding night. A blowjob, he decided as his pulse beat like a jungle drum in his chest, would see him through just fine until then.

"Get the pants off," he said huskily to Kol.

Kol didn't even pause. He seemed to instinctively understand, and without taking his mouth from her breast, he fiddled with the button and zipper of his jeans and kicked the garment off.

Christ Almighty. The man had a body like a bronzed god. Long and lean and muscle-packed, with ass cheeks as tight and smooth as rocks. Mitch groaned, rubbing his cock as he imagined sinking himself in between those hard buns, gloved by the snug inner muscles.

His gaze shifted to Kiona. Her tanned, slender legs were spread, her hips doing some sort of hula swivel as she met Kol's caresses with hearty thrusts. Except for a small square patch of dark-brown curls above her cleft, her pussy was shaved, and the silky, cream-coated lips glistened with her elixir. Mitch watched as Kol swirled his finger around the swollen clitoris then slid one long finger into her cunt. He loved the sound of the feminine, feral cries erupting from deep in her throat, and the way it appeared to fuel Kol's attentiveness and determination to please her.

Mitch let the lust ride him hard. He stepped one knee over her legs and straddled her, moving Kol aside in the process. Looking down, he raked his hungry stare from the stunning eyes, down over the pursed, reddened lips, to the full tits and narrow ribcage. Her abs were flat and slightly rippled as if she worked out, her hips gently flared, her legs feminine yet vaguely corded with smooth muscles. He could well imagine them ringed around his hips, her ankles locked behind him as he slid his cock into that soaking-wet pussy.

"What now, fiancé?" she purred, cupping and squeezing her own breasts.

"Turn over," he said gruffly, even as he reached down and flipped her onto her stomach.

She yelped in surprised delight. Dark locks of hair spilled down her long back. He brushed the glossy strands aside with a groan and studied the subtle notches of her spine leading a seductive path down to the slope of the most beautiful female ass he'd ever had the pleasure of examining. The bare cheeks were round and firm, just right for gripping during a bout of hot, sweaty sex. The creases where ass merged with thighs were very appetizing at the moment, so much so that he licked his lips, imagining how her flesh, her asshole, her pussy would taste.

"Aah," she sighed when Mitch rubbed his palms up the backs of her thighs and filled his hands with her buttocks. As he continued to massage her and listen to the sweet song of her approval, he shifted his gaze to scrutinize Kol. He lounged on his side, touching himself, seeming satisfied to watch their interplay.

"You okay with this?" Mitch asked.

Kol's liquid-dark eyes lit with lust. He nodded slowly. "Yeah, I think so."

Satisfied with his reply, Mitch let his perusal drift to Kol's erection. Jesus, if it wasn't the most delicious cock he'd ever seen. Okay, so the tabloids were right—Mitch had a penchant for men. But he wasn't about to ruin his career and admit it publicly. He'd had a few discreet interplays in the distant past with men who were sworn to secrecy and could be trusted...or with men who were being paid off regularly through Jager to keep their mouths shut.

But this whole arrangement seemed to have turned into some sort of dream-come-true fantasy that had fallen into his lap in a matter of hours. Every aspect of it—except for her meddling father—seemed to fit all three of them very well. She drooled over the idea of a threesome, and seemed to have no problem with—in fact, was turned on by—two men interacting within that trio.

Then there was the perk that both Kol and Kiona were gorgeous, and Mitch had no qualms about admitting that he himself wasn't bad looking either. Together, the three of them made a stunning bedroom trio, while in public, he and Kiona would present as a happily married, eye-catching husband and wife.

Perfect.

He hooked one arm under her hips and yanked them up. It opened up her butt cheeks and gave him a full-on view of the tight ring of her anus and the drenching pussy hole. The sudden sight of it from this angle sent a lightning zap of carnal need through his groin and made his cock tingle. He inhaled and caught the musky essence of those juices. Licking his lips, he bent and allowed himself just one lick.

"Mmm," she mewled, her hands fisting in the thick blanket. "I'm so ready for this, you both have no idea."

Kol's eyelids went limp over glittering dark orbs. He was still lying on his side, propped up on an elbow. He palmed himself, watching intently as Mitch sampled his woman. Kol looked so goddamn hot Mitch could no longer deny his need for a permanent man in his life. The realization both stunned and empowered him.

God, how he hoped like hell this was the answer to his prayers.

Mitch rolled the milky-sweet flavor of her juices around on his tongue. "Damn, you taste so good."

"Be my guest," she panted, rocking backward so her ass rose higher. "Have another taste."

Mitch chuckled but shook his head. "Uh-uh. Not 'til the wedding night." He shot a look at Kol. "Get over here and get behind her."

Without a word, Kol obeyed. Shifting up onto his hands and knees, he crawled around behind Mitch. Glancing over his shoulder, Mitch watched with sweet torture as Kol licked his lips and raked his gaze up and down Mitch's backside. Mitch involuntarily clenched his glutes, and his asshole tightened at the sudden heat that enveloped him. It was as if a torch had been brushed up and down his flesh, searing deep into his groin.

"You don't move very, very soon, Wulfrum," Kol warned with a sex-crazed timbre as he rubbed a hand across his faintly whiskered chin, "I'm going to be forced to fuck that nice ass of yours...and blow your little after-the-wedding rule all to hell."

Mitch could do nothing but swallow a lump of excitement.

"Kol, do as Mitch says and get behind me." Apparently eager to get the action going, Kiona searched over her shoulder and reached out until Mitch took her hand. She led him around so that he knelt in front of her. "Oh, my God, I can't believe this is happening."

"That makes two of us," Mitch murmured.

"Three," Kol amended.

Mitch lay on his back crossways in front of Kiona. She had a wild-eyed look about her as her scrutiny took in the length of him, finally settling on his erection. He watched her lips compress, heard her swallow, then her plump mouth parted in speechless awe.

Hell, if she wasn't the most beautiful, exotic creature he'd ever had the pleasure of being intimate with, he didn't know who was. His gaze shifted to Kol. Make that one of the two most beautiful, he concluded as he watched Kol take the spot Mitch had just vacated. Kol reached down and cupped her cunt, palming it, giving the swollen clitoris a few circular flicks before dipping his finger into her pussy.

Kiona whimpered, never once taking her eyes off Mitch's shaft.

"Mmm," Kol murmured, sucking his cream-coated finger into his mouth. "Wulfrum's right. You're so delicious and sweet." Then he poised his long, veiny cock just below Kiona's pussy. There was a tiny, glistening, pearl-drop of pre-come just now oozing from his slit. Mitch could see the whole exquisite thing surrounded by the inverted "V" of Kiona's toned thighs, as if he looked at it through the framed hands of a photographer. His mouth watered. He could well imagine what a mix of their come would taste like on his tongue, bitter-salty and creamy-sweet all at once.

Mitch settled back and propped one arm behind his head while jacking himself off with his free hand. He was hard, so fucking hard he feared he'd blow before she even got her plump lips around him. He swiped his mouth, hungering for pussy, cock, whatever he could get his hands and tongue on.

How had he gotten this lucky? he wondered as he watched Kol grip the base of his penis and start swirling the tip around her damp folds. She moaned in response, throwing her head back. Her long hair spilled down her back, enveloping her shoulders, waist, and torso in a cloud of sexy darkness. Unable to resist, Mitch reached up and skimmed his palm up her arm, combed his fingers through the silky tresses. It stirred up the essence of her shampoo, clean, fragrant, exotic. Totally Kiona.

Kol's gaze locked on Mitch's at the very moment Kol pushed into her pussy and lightly slapped one of her ass cheeks. Mitch blinked, momentarily stunned by the sudden strike.

"Suck him, babe," Kol ordered, never taking his penetrating stare off Mitch. "Suck that nice cock while I fuck your tight little pussy."

Kiona let out a sharp gasp at the whack, her mouth spreading into a dreamy-soft smile.

Ah, so she likes it a little rough. Mitch suppressed a need to squirm, erotic heat whooshing into his loins and making his penis throb. He rubbed harder, faster on his shaft, the desire for her mouth on him becoming a desperate need he could no longer delay.

He threaded his hand in the hair at the nape of her neck. “If you’re not ready, I’d be just fine watching, but...”

“Uh-uh. There’s no going back now.” She bit her lip and moaned when Kol started picking up the pace, thrusting into her with deeper, quicker strokes, every now and then whacking her rump. She leaned down and Mitch got a whiff of pussy mixed with her perfume. “I-I want it. I hunger for it, all of this.”

Her impassioned words made Mitch’s heart surge up and rap against his breastbone. His blood ran hot, snaking through his veins and engorging his cock. He couldn’t wait any longer. He guided her head, pushing it down so that her open mouth perched just above the head. Her warm breath fanned his fiery flesh, her wet tongue flicking out to take one maddening lick, just like he’d done to her only moments ago. Her gentle grip encircled the base of his cock just above his tight sac, angling his granite-hard rod up and away from his abdomen. And he let out a feral roar when the wet heat of her lips finally closed around him. His head dropped back onto the bed in surrender when her tongue did a dance around the head, then she opened her mouth wider and took him whole into the hot cavern of her throat.

Mitch could hear the slap and wet slurp as Kol fucked her from behind, and the continued pace of the movements made her struggle to keep her own tempo as she devoured Mitch, giving him the most divine blowjob he’d ever received. Kol let out a long grunt of satisfaction. Mitch hissed and panted, his body arching when her hand slid down and cupped his balls, massaging in rhythm with her up-and-down motions.

She sucked him like a pro, her hair spilling down to tickle his thighs and abdomen. Every now and then, she teased him with the faint scrape of teeth or the sliding of her hand higher when she stimulated his corona with the wet-hot blade of her tongue.

The edge of the orgasm was just out of reach, threatening to blow at any second. Mitch didn't think he could take anymore, but he was wrong. With his body angled perpendicular to Kiona's, it didn't seem possible, but Kol was somehow able to maneuver to Kiona's left side so he could plant both of his hands next to Mitch's right shoulder while still buried inside her. Mitch caught the subtle aroma of Kiona's pussy juices again, just beneath the scent of manly sweat. His senses were on overload, the lingering taste of her come in his mouth, the faint smell of her perfume mixed with that of Kol's essence. There was the sight of naked flesh—God help him, both male and female—all around him, and the erotic, maddening feeling of her warm mouth on him. Holy shit, but the bombardments were enough to make him blow any minute, any second...

Kol's strong body tensed, the muscles defined and glistening with sweat. "I have to taste you." It was a raspy whisper that made Mitch shiver. It felt as if Kol's gaze drilled into Mitch's eyes, spearing him in place. There was a strange glimmer in the dark-chocolate pools that begged for understanding. But no one grasped their meaning more than Mitch did—the curiosity and the desire to be with both a man and a woman.

So with Kol's cock still buried inside Kiona while she continued to suck Mitch off, Kol leaned down and captured Mitch's lips with his own. It was one of the most erotic sensations he could ever recall experiencing. The wet, hungry mouth of a man devouring him on one end, while the soft dampness of a woman's mouth pleasured his cock. Mitch tasted the faint flavor of beer, and he thought how the kiss, this whole experience, was more intoxicating than any bottle of alcohol could ever be.

Their tongues sparred, sucked, tasted. Kiona swirled and

slurped with her talented mouth, giving Mitch the urge to bite down on Kol's tongue. There was a glorious tightening deep in his groin, an ache so harsh, it almost hurt. With the slaking of his lust nearly upon him, Mitch needed to fill his hands with both femininity and masculinity. In the madness and flurry of limbs and gyrating bodies, he skimmed his right palm down Kiona's flat belly and located her clit. It was as hard as a pebble, soaking wet, and continually being stretched and pulled by Kol's slow and deliberate thrusts as he struggled to maintain their connected triangle.

Mitch stimulated the sticky little pearl, and Kiona moaned her appreciation, her tongue vibrating against his rod. "Mmm, *Mikeke...*" she murmured his Hawaiian name around his cock.

Mitch crossed his left hand over and kneaded Kol's breast, pinching and pulling on the puckered areola. Kol's response was to growl into Mitch's mouth and push his tongue deeper still. Mitch accepted it hungrily, opening wider to devour the hard male mouth while his hands played with the flesh of man and woman.

So fucking hot. How had he gone all his life without this? The question echoed in Mitch's head even as Kol's warm mouth suddenly went still on Mitch's, followed by his muffled grunt of release. Kol twitched and sucked air into his nose, keeping his mouth sealed to Mitch's lips. Kol moaned louder, dipping his tongue deeper, sucking and dragging it along Mitch's back teeth.

Kiona's climax came next, her high-pitched moan of ecstasy stifled by her rabid devouring of Mitch's cock and pre-come. She whimpered, squeezing the base of his shaft with her hand, holding onto him for leverage as she slammed backward time and time again onto Kol's rod. Mitch could well imagine her cunt muscles contracting around Kol's manhood, drawing out the last of his ejaculate.

Then it happened. A second wave of mind-boggling bliss so intense, Mitch had to tear himself from Kol's kiss and let out a long growl of pleasure. His balls drew up just before that unbelievable sensation of hot come shooting into her mouth. Mitch's eyes crossed then clamped shut. He lifted his head up, stabbed his hands into her hair, and held her skull so that there was no way she could escape him. He watched her lips stretch wider, her beautiful face buried in his crotch as she did her best to swallow what she could. The rest of his come spilled down around the base of his shaft and into the crisp brown nest of pubic hair. He sucked in breath after breath, riding each peak and wave until the final plummet.

"Oh, wow, did that really just happen?" Kol murmured, panting. He withdrew from Kiona's passage and plopped backward onto the bed, his stiff cock coated with her white elixir.

Kiona gave Mitch's penis one final lick and kiss. She swiped her sticky mouth with a trembling hand and collapsed next to Kol. "I-I think it did," she said breathily.

Mitch angled around and rolled toward them, flinging his arm across both bodies. Hooking a hand on Kol's far hip, he yanked, forcing them all closer so that Kiona was tucked against Mitch's chest facing him, and Kol was positioned spoon-fashion behind her.

"Damn right it did." Mitch sighed. "Son of a bitch, the possibilities are endless. And now I can't wait for the wedding so we can do it again. But the wedding night's going to be different..."

"Uh-uh." Kol had his arm flung over his brow. His tanned, sculpted chest rose and fell with his heavy breathing.

"What do you mean, uh-uh?" Kiona asked.

"I mean," Kol replied with a snarl in his tone, "there's not going to be a wedding. Unless...”

Chapter Seven

"Unless? Unless what?" Kiona sat upright and twisted around to gawk at Kol.

He shot off the bed, his jaw clenched. Now that the heat of the moment was over, panic seized him, making his throat tighten and his chest ache. Kiona and Mitch had contracts holding them together. Kol had nothing. But he wanted it all—he wanted *both* of them, without the worry of being cast aside once the glow of their wedding had worn off. "Unless you let me be a groom too."

"Now wait one goddamn minute." Mitch rolled over and got to his feet. The naked, masculine sight of him took Kol's breath away. The man was Kol's new lover. For now. But what guarantee did Kol have that Mitch wouldn't dump him and simply become Kol's rival for Kiona's affections once all this excitement wore off? But damn the mother fucker, Mitch didn't seem to be the least bit concerned. Instead, he planted his hands on his hips and glared at Kol. The wide expanse of the bed, with Kiona set right in the center, was one of only two things separating Kol from the man he wanted with such a fierceness it frightened him to fucking death.

The other thing was his fear at being rejected by them both.

"We already had this all worked out," Mitch snapped. "What the fuck's your problem?"

At Mitch's scathing tone, Kol snatched his jeans up off the floor. Screw this. He'd be damned if he'd let anyone discard him so soon after all that mindboggling sex. It hadn't been two seconds after coming down from his orgasmic high of making love to Ki and kissing Mitch while she sucked Mitch off, that a terrifying thought had occurred to Kol. What if he could never experience that heaven again with them? Kiona was so goddamn beautiful, and Mitch was such a stud, what if they eventually decided they didn't need him anymore? What if the public adored them as a couple so much, they decided they didn't need Kol anymore? He knew he was being irrational, yet the thought of how right it had felt to be with them both, compared to suddenly having to be without them just because he didn't have a damn signature on a piece of paper, well, it was making him fucking *pupule.*

But he couldn't help it. He'd just indulged both sides of himself for the very first time in his entire life, and nothing was going to stop him from keeping it that way. He had rights here, too, and he wasn't going to let up until they could reassure him he wasn't just a goddamn third wheel.

So to hell with Mitch's public image. Kol being a second groom in their wedding would fix the problem, wouldn't it?

Well, it would have to, or he'd die before he'd let her marry Mitch without him.

Kol took one brief second to shoot a withering look over his shoulder as he jammed his legs into the garment. "No, you and Ki had it all worked out nice and tidy with your fucking contracts and all. Without even consulting me first."

He left his jeans unzipped. Confidence flared briefly when both pairs of eyes riveted down to study his whorls of dark belly hair leading from his navel and arrowing down toward the barely discernible tip of his softening erection. He knew his long hair was touseled from their bout of amazing sex, and he hoped like hell his inky eyes glowed with desire neither of them would ever be able to resist.

"Kol, what is it?" Kiona sat up. "What's wrong all of a sudden? I thought you were fine with this."

"I...I was." He combed both hands through his hair and laced his fingers together on top of his head. He sighed and whirled around toward the door. "Or maybe I became seduced just enough by the two of you, that I forgot how much I'm getting screwed in this deal."

"You're not getting screwed." Mitch started toward toward Kol, but when Kol spun back around, Mitch stopped in mid-step.

"Huh, easy for you to say," Kol mumbled.

"How do you figure you're getting screwed?" Mitch asked. "We just had some incredible sex, and you were definitely a part of it."

"Yeah, that was some incredible sex we just had." He winced at the quiver in his voice. "But from where I stand, it was just that. Sex. Now what about me? What about *my* guarantee? I want more than sex. I want what we just did to last for the rest of my life. But ya see, I'm the only one here without insurance. You can stroke me all you want, swear to goddamn hell that I have nothing to worry about, and that you'll work it out with Jager like you said earlier, but the fact is, I'm still the third guy out here. I need more. I need it in black and fucking white. I need to stand up there and say I do, right along with you. You both have the law on your sides. I don't. There're no legal papers to keep me from being booted out of this little trio we just initiated. Can't you understand where I'm coming from, man?"

"After what the three of us just shared together, no, I

can't," Mitch growled. He dragged his T-shirt over his head, his half-hard cock angled from his body. His shorter blond locks stood on end and his bright eyes gleamed with ire. It made Kol think of a roaring lion. He could just picture himself as one too, in a fight to the death with Mitch, a pair of alpha lions going head-to-head over their chosen lioness. Just as they were now.

Who would win the fight? Or would they, instead, join together to take down their kill?

Society.

Mitch's paparazzi.

Her goddamn father.

No, it appeared Kol was losing this fight.

He gripped the doorknob. Son of a bitch, was that the sting of tears in his eyes? "If you don't get it, then fuck it. I'm out of here."

"Kol, no," Kiona whimpered. "Please don't go."

"Wait." Mitch was already across the room, his warm hand curled firmly around Kol's upper arm. "Look, pal, you're being ridiculous and totally paranoid. I promise you, you have nothing to worry about."

"Paranoid, maybe," Kol grudgingly agreed, trying his damndest to ignore the whoosh of fire that shot from Mitch's hand wrapped around his arm to his aching groin. He added a few swear words under his breath and jerked his arm free. "But how about you try standing in my shoes? If you think I'm just going to hand her over to you and agree to this little arrangement without making sure I've got some sort of protection, too, *you're* fucking ridiculous. It ain't happening. I'll walk away right now before I ever let myself get in too deep, only to be dumped."

Kiona finally scooted off the bed and donned her robe. "Kol, wait a minute. Please don't go."

Kol yanked open the door.

"Where the hell are you going?" Mitch groaned.

"To get myself a contract too."

"What?" Mitch stepped closer, his wide shoulders filling the doorway and blocking Kol's view of Kiona. Was that the way it would always be? Mitch coming between Kol and Kiona? "You can't just go find a random lawyer and draw up some convoluted contract. This is going to be a marriage—between a man and a woman. You can't add another man to the picture, at least not legally."

"Why the hell not? No law against a person making up a contract about anything they damn well please, convoluted or not."

"We can't do a three-way marriage." Mitch blew out a breath and leaned against the doorjamb. The handsome, masculine picture he made was straight out of one of his movies, and goddamn it, it made Kol's loins leap into overdrive. "There's not a court in the world that would uphold it. And there's no way the tabloids would let that one slide. My career would be over before the ink even dried on the first issue."

Kiona belted her robe and pushed her way between Kol and Mitch. Kol caught the scent of Mitch's clean sweat mingled with Kiona's sex, two distinct aromas that made his mouth water and his mind go all mushy. But given the stakes, he quickly refocused.

"Fuck your career." Kol gritted his teeth and fought the urge to punch the wall. "This is all about you, always has been. Well, screw that. I love her and I'm not taking the chance of you pushing me out of the picture and stealing her away from me. Or maybe I should just get the fuck out of Dodge and let you have her."

Kiona gasped. When Kol spun around to stalk off, she gripped his arm with both hands. "Kol, wait. Please don't do this. Please, I'm begging you."

He turned back around, slowly, deliberately. His gaze dropped to her small hand, scaled back up to snare her glittering eyes. He longed like hell to take her in his arms and never let her go. But if he got right down to the truth of the matter, she'd teamed up with Mitch behind his back and had basically betrayed him. If she couldn't see what a risky position she'd put him in, then amazing threesome sex or not, maybe he *should* just go. Emotions swirled so violently in his head and chest, he wasn't sure if he was bluffing or not, but knowing his own temper and his damnable pride, he was certain he could easily walk out that door and never come back.

And that thought scared the piss out of him.

"Sorry, darling," he said with a sneer, "but I've been waiting long enough for you. I want you, and I'm not afraid to admit I want him too. But I'm also not stupid enough to stand back and hope I never get kicked out on my ass just because my signature's not on some damn piece of fucking paper."

She stared at him with her mouth hanging open. At that moment, it was just the two of them. Mitch faded into the background of Kol's peripheral vision. "You've been waiting long enough for me? What's that supposed to mean?"

Kol fisted his hands to keep from reaching out to her. He didn't want to hurt her by walking away, but shit, wasn't he the one really getting injured here? "You were supposed to be *my* wife. We only waited because of Heloki, to give him time to turn over your money and eventually accept me." He snorted, but the harshness of the response became softened by the burning lump in his throat. "Fat chance of that happening."

"I asked what you meant when you said you'd been waiting

long enough for me." Her voice was whisper-soft, strained with the pain of a possible break-up. "You didn't give me a straight answer."

Damn you to hell, Heloki. This is all your fault.

Out of the corner of his eye, Kol noticed Mitch shifting his stance when Kol reached up and trailed a fingertip around Ki's mouth. "I've told myself countless times I'll wait until the end of time to have you be mine forever." Kol's gaze narrowed on Mitch, silently warning him away. A lone tear escaped the corner of Kol's eye and trailed down his cheek. It was humiliating, and yet he defied Mitch to call him on it. "But that was before he came along. How can I compete with that?"

"Goddamn it," Mitch muttered. "I didn't know about you until today, until well after all the agreements were reached and contracts signed. You're not going to fucking blame me for this. It's—"

Kol had Mitch backed into the corridor wall before he could stop himself. His pulse thundered in his ears. He stared into Mitch's eyes, lost in their stunning color and thrilling gleam, fighting the urge to cover Mitch's mouth with his own. An image filled his head of fucking him against the wall while Kiona watched in excitement. But this wasn't the time to indulge in his sick little bisexual fantasies.

"I blame Heloki, goddamn it. Not you," Kol finally barked.

"Kol, don't—"

Kol held up a hand to silence Kiona and keep her at bay. "I mean, look at Kiona. Any man would be a fool not to take her up on her offer."

Still, she took two shuffling steps toward them. "Kol, please don't—"

"No, babe, you don't," Kol growled, never taking his attention from Mitch. "Now listen to me, both of you."

Kiona remained silent, suddenly at a loss for words. Kol stood toe-to-toe with Mitch, one hand pressed menacingly into Mitch's chest, the other planted on the wall to the left of Mitch's head. Oh, but he could just as easily wrap his arms around the bastard.

"I just got an earth-shattering nibble of a fantasy I've always carried deep inside me, that I've never even revealed to you, Ki. I want it damn bad. And I don't think I'm the only one." Kol looked from one to the other and got no objections. "But do you two really think I'm going to allow you to marry each other without getting some sort of security or contract or whatever the hell it'll take to make sure either one of you can't fuck me over later?"

"I would never do that," Kiona insisted with a lift of her chin.

"I think we can discuss this without you crushing the fucking life out of my lungs." Mitch's deep voice was raspy as he attempted to escape. He pushed against Kol, but it wasn't hard enough to dislodge him. He finally gripped Kol's wrist, hurled his hand aside, and shoved against Kol's chest.

Kol stumbled backward and blinked. Ah, so the man did have some balls after all. And that turned Kol on like crazy.

Mitch rubbed his chest, his eyes narrowed to mere slits. "Don't you *ever* do that again, you hear me, you son of a bitch? It was earth-shattering for me, too, but goddamn it, what the fuck's wrong with you? You don't always need to resort to bullying to get your point across."

"Shit." Kol closed his eyes, sighed. "I... I'm sorry." He spun around, sauntered into the living room, and plopped onto the sofa.

Kiona and Mitch followed.

"Kol, please..." Kiona dropped to her knees and laid her

head in Kol's lap. He caught the faint scent of her pussy juices. It made his libido rev, but he forced it aside. "I'm sorry that I did this without discussing it with you first, but I already explained my reasons to you."

She lifted her head and gazed at him with tortured eyes, imploring him to understand. It tore his heart out to see the raw pain there, made his chest ache so badly, he thought it must be what a heart attack felt like. "*Aloha wau iâ 'oe*, Kol. I love you, you know that. I want to be with you until the day I die. I would never, *ever* kick you to the curb, whether I was married to another or not."

"Married to another or not," Kol repeated with a snort. "This is some fucking crazy shit."

With a sigh, Mitch collapsed onto the couch next to Kol. Kiona let her gaze drift to him, watching him intently as he laced his hands behind his head and stared up at the ceiling. Kol indulged as well, spellbound by Mitch's handsome profile, just as he had always lusted after him on the movie screen. Kol waited with his breath clogging his windpipe, hoping to God Mitch would say something that would soothe him and clear up this whole mess.

"You know," Mitch said in a tone that almost came off bored, "there's a very easy solution...if I might interrupt your lovers' conversation to get a word in?"

"Huh." Kol chuckled hollowly. "I think it's gotten a bit more complicated than just two lovers."

"Well, do you want it to be more or not?" Mitch demanded to know with a snarl, never taking his gaze off the ceiling. When Kol didn't respond, Mitch went on, his tone almost cold. "The fact is, Kiona and I have entered into a legal arrangement. And no matter what you say or do, you can't stop it. I'm sorry, but it's just the reality of the situation."

"Mitch, please don't—" Kiona started to protest the coldness of Mitch's statement, but her words were interrupted by Kol's flinching response to Mitch's cold words. Maybe Mitch was right. Maybe it was all over, and there was nothing Kol could do but walk away.

"Will you both just listen to me? Damn." Mitch blew out a disgusted breath and propped his feet up on the coffee table. "Kol, you want an agreement, fine. I already suggested we talk to Jager and get things set up. I don't think that'll be an issue. He'll come up with something I bet you'll feel comfortable with. Of course, by law, we can't make it a three-way marriage, but I have an idea. I think there's a way to solve this whole problem while allowing us all to live together without Kol feeling threatened..."

"It's going to be fine," Kiona crooned, grazing her palm up Kol's arm as they strolled hand-in-hand toward their secret spot on the beach. The scent of coming rain hung heavy in the air, and the winds were picking up, whipping the tall palms back and forth, making that eerie swishing noise. A night storm brewed far out to sea. Although there was still time to safely bask in the charged air ahead of it, Kiona loved taking the risk.

"I know Mitch didn't give us details before he left," she went on, "but I trust him. I really think he's come up with a solution we can all live with—even you. He and Jager'll work it out so all of us will be happy with the arrangement."

"Easy for you to say," he grumbled, slicing a look down at her. "You have the protection of a contract no matter what he comes up with. Me, if Mitch decides to have you all to himself, I'm SOL. Losing my gal, my ego, and the continued fulfillment of my darkest secret all in one day."

The breeze tossed her long tresses and the silk robe she'd donned before they'd climbed down the rocky incline to the shore. She gazed up at him, mesmerized, visually devouring the rugged picture he made. An involuntary, delicious shiver rushed up her spine. He reminded her of the tortured hero in a novel she'd once read, just before he'd shifted into a dangerous, snarling werewolf. As if to underscore that thought, beyond Kol's silhouette, a dark cloud slid across the sky and blocked the moon. The sudden dimming of lunar light further lent him a menacing air, obscuring his face and making his coal-dark eyes appear fathomless...like a vampire.

Kol was a lot like that, she decided. The tormented, seemingly immortal soul caught in the clutches of man's evil and carelessness.

Her own father's evil spite.

They arrived at the molten rock area and rounded the first large boulder. Between it and the next one sat their private rendezvous spot, a twenty-foot wide patch of beach hidden on either side by the tall rocks, and inland by a cliff topped with thick forest. They'd met here many times in the past years. It was their own patch of the world where they could indulge in their native Hawaii while letting all of their primitive instincts loose.

Kol spread one blanket on the sand, and set the other within reach in case they got chilled.

She stepped onto their makeshift bed with him and scrutinized his anguished eyes. A powerful surge of love and wanting erupted inside her, rising with the tide, making her heart pound like the surf. Waves crashed against the seaward side of the rocks showering them in a fine, cool mist. His jaw and upper lip were shadowed with rugged stubble, and when she reached up to frame his face, she thought how she longed to have it abrading the soft flesh of her inner thighs as he pleasured her there with his mouth.

"You will *not* lose me. I did this *for* you, not against you."

He pulled her close, molding her body to his hard length. "I get that now, and I love you for it. But do you think this might be a mistake? That we jumped into the sack with him too quickly?"

"No." She shook her head vehemently even as her gut churned like the waters behind her, dark and foreboding. *Had* they—she—made a mistake? No, she couldn't believe that, not after devising the perfect plan, nor after that amazing three-way connection they'd all had a few hours ago. It had to work out, that was all there was to it. It was the ideal solution for each of them.

He pressed a soft kiss to her forehead. "And you don't worry this might turn into a huge disaster for all of us, each in our own way?"

"Kol. No." She reached up and tipped his face down so that she could look directly into his eyes. "Now that I've learned more of your secret fantasies and seen you in action with Mitch, nothing will convince me it was a mistake, or that it will become a problem. This will all work out, I promise you. And *if* on the off chance something does happen where we can't or won't continue to maintain a relationship with him, then we go on as originally planned. Me and you together forever, and me and Mitch nothing more than a public relations image. For me, you come first. Always."

His eyes tracked his hand's movement as he combed his fingers through her long hair in an adoring fashion that made her heart melt. She quivered at his warm, sensual touch.

"That is so good to know," he whispered. "I hope to hell it stays that way."

"It will."

"Can I ask you something?" He looked away, out to sea where the inky black waves thrashed with their white, foam-tipped spikes.

"Yes, yes. Of course." She squeezed his torso and pressed her cheek to his sculpted chest. The sparse hairs tickled the side of her nose. She turned her face into him, burying herself in his warm scent, that earthy fragrance that could only be Kol's.

"Did you think there was something there, something *kupaianaha*? I mean, it was amazing, too amazing too fast. Don't you think?"

At his cautious tone, she lifted her face and met his gaze. The passion in his eyes, combined with his tender assessment of their lovemaking with Mitch, made her realize the magnitude of his true sexuality. She felt lucky to have been included in his secret, and there was a constant giddiness edging her mood when she thought of their future together.

For the first time since Jager had suggested her alliance with Mitch, she was certain she had done the right thing.

"Yes, it was incredible, perfect."

She started to add more, but something about his pensive manner made her remain silent. Latching pleased eyes onto hers, he eased her slightly away and slid the silky fabric off her shoulders. He tossed the garment aside, leaving her completely nude for his pleasure. She barely noticed the gusty breeze as it cooled her hot flesh.

Lightning briefly lit up his heated stare. He raked her from head to bare feet, and she could swear she felt the singe of it scorching her nipples, her belly, her damp pussy, as if she'd been struck by that far-off lightning. Finally, he muttered, "Damn, but you're the hottest woman on the whole fucking planet."

"Thank you." She perused his erection with an open stare. It strained against the denim of his jeans. "You're not too bad yourself."

She suddenly needed to feel his arms around her again, so she stepped closer and set her palms on his warm chest. The cool, wet sand sifted between her toes, and the dull edge of a seashell scraped along the side of one foot. The tall palms thrashed, singing that whooshing tune as the air ahead of the storm moved further in across the volatile sea. She tipped her face back up, devouring his glazed yet oddly brooding expression, her own emotions resembling the excitement of that reckless ocean, wild, vast, determined to have its way. Kiona never thought it possible to love Kol more than she did now, more than she had before Mitch came along, but she did. What they'd shared with Mitch only sealed her love for Kol more so, and it seemed to have opened emotional doors she never even knew were there.

"I've got to say it again. Our lovemaking with Mitch was incredible to say the least," she murmured. He set his hands over hers, lifted one and kissed the tips of her fingers while she continued to reassure him. "It was off the charts. So off the charts, there's no way it'll not happen again. Not if I can help it."

"Really? Ya think so?"

"Mm-hm." She held his head between her hands, threading her fingers into the thickness of his hair, and gazed into the raging storm of his eyes. "Not only that, but do you realize how much you agreeing to this arrangement has deepened my faith in us, and how much it's strengthened our relationship? Even with Mitch in the picture, maybe even *because* he's in the picture. Just think, you can be you now, and I can be me.

Together. We have a whole new exciting life ahead of us that not even all of my father's money or power can destroy. I love you, Kol. I love you more now than ever before. Thank you for not walking away."

Suddenly, he yanked her against his chest and clutched her to his hard body, running his hands haphazardly over her back, her arms, her ass. He groaned low in his throat as if those were the very words he'd hoped to hear her murmur. "No matter how much my pride wanted me to, I could never leave you."

She giggled. "Yes, I was a bit worried your enormous pride would stand in our way."

He smiled, but the grin faded just as quickly as it had emerged. "Are you sure? Are you sure that me being..."

His words trailed off, but she knew exactly what he alluded to.

"Kol, my God." She reached up and cupped his jaw, forcing him to meet her gaze. "There is nothing—*nothing*—at all wrong with it. You have this new side to you that's extremely sexy and attractive to me, and I'm so glad you finally revealed your desires to me. Besides, you might think it's selfish, but nothing is going to keep me from enjoying that again. It's a huge turn-on."

"Really?"

"You bet, my *hiwahiwa.* I had a fantasy too, one that I had never revealed to you." She rose up on tiptoe and grazed her lips back and forth over his. They were dry but soft, slightly parted as if her words had stunned him. "And that was to see you making love with another man."

"I guess that means as far as keeping secrets, we're even now," he growled harshly, surprising her. He massaged and pinched her buttocks so hard, it was just short of excruciating.

But instead of making her shrink from him in fear or pain, it drew her closer as it always did, making blood rush to her cunt so she became hornier, more in need of him.

"Touché."

He fisted his hands in her hair and buried his face in the crook of her neck. "Ah, Ki, you make me so crazy," he rasped in her ear.

Fiery pleasure unfurled in her belly when he sighed and dragged her down onto the blanket with him, her body sprawled across his. The sudden move made her breasts jiggle. Her nipples puckered tighter, and goose bumps rose in a sudden shimmer up her spine, making her scalp bristle. His gaze didn't miss her body's reaction, dipping down in a hot, visual journey that made her breasts go heavy and moisture gather between her thighs.

"Wasn't expecting that. I was afraid you'd be disgusted instead." Kol shifted her so she lay beside him, shoved his jeans off releasing his straining hard-on, and then pulled her back into place on top of him. He wiggled beneath her so that she straddled his hips. The intentional move made the head of his erection settle at the damp opening of her vagina. "Looks like we should have been a bit more honest with each other, *'ea*? But I was so afraid of losing you," he whispered, skating his hands down her back, cupping her ass cheeks, holding her pussy captive against the tip of his shaft.

"Never." She could barely get the word out. The strong pressure on her rear forced her pebble-hard clitoris to grind into his taut abdomen and his penis to slide an inch inside her. Hot, aching desire coiled in her loins making her breath catch in her lungs and her fingers dig into his strong shoulders.

"Are you sure?" His eyes glittered with a potent mixture of arousal and uncertainty. He reached up and trailed a thumb over her bottom lip.

At first, she clamped the salty digit in between her teeth, but quickly started to suck and swirl her tongue around its length. She loved the oral sensation of sucking and running her tongue over something stiff in her mouth, enjoyed the power of hearing him moan in response as he now was. But he seemed to get a grip on his initial response. His doubtful pause and penetrating stare had her gripping his wrist. She pulled his finger from her mouth and placed his hand upon her left breast. His wet thumb grazed the fleshy skin, but she curled her fingers over the back of his to make him hold her more firmly.

"Do you feel that? Do you feel my heart knocking against my ribs, beating strong and fast like a *koa congo* drum?"

He nodded slowly, molding the mound so that her nipple spiked against his palm and fire back-lashed into her womb.

"It beats for you, excitedly, always out of control. You must know you are at the top of my heart's totem pole. Always."

Kol pulled her down for a kiss so forceful, so intense and sweet, it made her toes curl. "Have I said I love you yet today?" he panted against her mouth.

"Yes," she whispered, tracing her tongue around his full lips. "But once is never enough for me."

"And apparently, one man isn't enough for you," he growled against her mouth. As if to prove the meaning of his accusatory words, he bucked upward, sinking every inch of his cock into her canal.

She drew back at the tone of his voice, even as her cunt clamped around his shaft and her clit jolted when it rubbed abruptly over his pubic bone. His mood could be so unpredictable, passionate and sweet one minute, seething with ire the next. How could she concentrate on the wonderful sensation of being filled by him when his words so easily doused her fire?

"What...I don't know what you—"

"Tell me about it."

She stared down at him, filled to the tip of her womb, not knowing what to do, what to say. Should she just kiss him into silence and reach for the orgasm that had already started to ripple inside her? Or should she climb off of him and gather her robe, and then run to her house? She wasn't sure, so she remained still, his girth deliciously stretching her tender hole, his narrow hips wedged between her quivering thighs.

Cautiously, she studied him, waiting, holding the sultry air captive in her lungs. His chest rose and fell with his rapid breaths, and sweat glistened on his brow as he continued to glare up at her. She watched intently as the unruly wind thrashed around them, blowing her hair over her shoulders and curtaining them in a world of their own. The scent of her own come wafted up to stir around them, and by his long, indrawn breath and the blissful fluttering of his eyelids, she knew he smelled it too, the beast scenting his mate.

The gusty breeze ruffled the blanket he lay on—the god of the ocean and winds, Kanaloa's doing, no doubt—making it bunch up along one brawny arm. Those arms had held her with such tenderness in the past, yet they could easily snap her in half.

Kiona shivered, but not from the cooling night or the fine mist that now and then splattered her bare back. And it wasn't even from that fleeting, dangerous thought she'd had of his powerful arms, for no matter how rough their sex got, no matter how angry Kol got with her, she knew he would never hurt her. Instead, it was those eyes that made her quake. Fathomless, black-as-coal devil's eyes that could hold her spellbound one second, yet shoot fire at her the next.

The man is so damn intense. Which is one of the many reasons why I love him so much.

His chivalry didn't surprise her when he reached for the extra blanket and slung it around her shoulders. Pulling her down so that her mouth hovered mere centimeters from his, he murmured in a voice thick with passion, "Tell me about how it turned you on. *All* about it. I want so badly to get off inside you while you whisper in my ear how his cock felt in your mouth when you gave him one of your talented blowjobs. I *need* to hear—" he clutched her face between his big, warm hands and gently shook her to emphasize each word, "—how it turned you on to watch me kissing him. Touching a man. I want to hear about everything, every taste, every smell, every quickening of horniness in your sweet little cunt. I want to imagine it all when I fuck this tight pussy you've got closed around me."

Even as thunder clapped out to sea and lightning flickered overhead, Kiona heaved a sigh of relief. The storm neared, tumultuous and powerful. Just like Kol. Only he wasn't angry as she'd thought. He was incensed by a flaming desire for something that was new to him, that he needed to hear and know and experience. He was demanding to live—for the time being—vicariously through her intimacy with Mitch, and begging for assurance. He needed to know how much the concept of he and Mitch truly turned her on at the very moment she showed Kol her undying, committed love.

She couldn't have taken any aphrodisiac more potent than that raspy, verbal command. Kiona rose up and began to move on him, bouncing slowly up and down in that age-old rhythm so that her slick tightness stroked him.

"Oh, yes, it turned me on *very* much," she said huskily. "Do you have any idea how hot that was?" She planted her hands on the blanket on either side of his head and kissed his mouth, his ear, his neck. Her insides ached hot and wet. This new sex-play between them made her so horny, her climax loomed only a few more strokes away. "To see you kissing and touching him? God, it made me so wet. Just thinking about it makes me feel all hot and aroused deep inside my pussy, like I'm going to melt all over you."

"You sure?" The inflection in his hoarse voice was honeyed by eroticism and relief all at once.

"Never more sure of anything in my life." Kiona pushed herself back up, propping her hands on his chest, and reveled in the cool, misty winds caressing her skin. Her hands skimmed over his hard chest, and she pinched his pebbled nipples, delighted when he groaned in response. "And I want it that way forever. I want us all to be able to share our dreams and deepest, darkest desires with each other. Can we do that from now on, Kol? Can we put aside the animosity and just enjoy this amazing gift that practically fell in our laps?"

Thunder rumbled offshore—or was that Lono, the god of thunder himself, calling to her? At this glorious moment, she didn't care who or what it was, she just wanted to enjoy one of their last moments together as an unmarried couple in love.

She looked down at Kol, waiting for his response, his hard Polynesian features fully visible to her each time lightning flashed in the sky above. With the storm brewing, and the excitement of making love on the edge of danger in the middle of the night, it made her pulse leap out of control and her muscles go taut and hot.

Kiona lifted her ass up far enough so that her pussy settled at the very end of his cock. She felt him twitch in protest against her drenching hole.

"Well?" she panted. "I'm waiting."

He hissed in a breath between clenched teeth. "That's a cruel technique to try to get your way," he murmured, lifting his head and capturing her mouth in an explosive, wet kiss. The move made her gasp against his mouth when his penis slipped another inch inside her. "How can I say no to that when you're gonna make me blow before I even get all the way back inside you?"

A wicked giggle escaped from deep inside Kiona's throat. "Call me a wily vixen, but I'll do whatever it takes." To prove her point, she pulled away, releasing him from inside her. She rocked her hips wildly, undulating so that her slick slit rode up and down the front of his penis, coating him with her cream.

"Mmm," was all he could say as he dropped his head back against the blanket, folded his arms behind his neck, and stared up at the flashing sky with a glazed expression.

What a gorgeous man you are.

Looking down at him, she studied his flexing biceps and his well-muscled chest defined by the intermittent light. It made her suddenly ravenous to get his cock back inside her.

His faraway look gradually tracked from the flickering sky to latch onto her eyes. At that very moment, she rose up, aligned herself, and took him in. She clamped her eyes shut, bit her lip, and groaned at the sudden fullness that seemed to touch her very core and send her pulse racing out of control.

Thickly, softly, he whispered his love for her. "*Aloha wau iâ 'oe*, my *milimili.*"

She slowly opened her eyes and stared down at him, struggling to stave off the orgasm. His face shone fierce and strained with passion. The muscles in his burly arms twitched, as if it took all his strength not to reach up and overpower her, not to let his raw emotions go, to just fuck her hard and fast.

At his words and the unfettered expression on his handsome face, there was a flutter behind her breastbone, a quivering of the heart that made her blood run hot and pound in her ears. The surf thrashed behind her. Black clouds rolled in overhead. Thunder clapped and rumbled, tumbling closer to shore, and lightning flashed faster, more volatile as each moment passed.

"And I love you, too, with all my being," she choked out, shuddering when he reared up and sank even deeper inside her, the tip of his rod grazing her G-spot. She clenched her pussy muscles and sighed when come trickled out and dribbled over his balls and groin.

"Tell me," he finally roared, rolling her over while keeping himself anchored inside her. She hooked her ankles behind his waist, knowing the beast she loved so very much had finally broken loose. He drew back, ramming his shaft so deep, her gasp was cut short and she instead screamed out in ecstasy. "Tell me how his cock tasted, how he felt in your hands. Now, before I come."

She clung to him as the first ripple of the climax reached for her. "Hard," she panted, alternating kissing him with biting his neck. "Hard and long and faintly salty."

"Oh, God..." Kol muttered, almost choking on his words. "Oh, fuck."

"Delicious. He was so delicious." She bucked up, accepting his frantic thrusts. His sweat dribbled onto her breasts, slicking their bodies and reducing the friction between their nipples and abdomens. She could smell his arousal mixed with sweat and the musty scent of rain. The storm and its impending danger drew nearer, she knew. But nothing short of a tsunami could tear them apart.

"It was like satin over steel on my tongue, so long and thick that I—"

"You're going to make me come." He pulled out and pushed back in, shoving her across the blanket and onto the wet sand with each forceful plunge. The grains scraped over her back, but she didn't care. All she wanted was to reach that pinnacle as the storm broke free around them. "I'm going to..."

"I tasted a bitter drop of his come...on my tongue...even before he came." She bucked up, meeting him thrust for thrust. Her lungs burned, her muscles strained as she grasped at him, clutching, slapping his sweat-soaked, water-sprayed back. "I could smell his expensive, masculine cologne...and a mixture of clean soap and arousal."

"Kiona, my love, I swear if you don't stop, I'm going to—"

"And then I glanced up along his flat stomach and—oh God, it was *so* hot—you were kissing him...tonguing each other." It was like she was reliving their lovemaking again. She could imagine it so easily, every taste, smell, touch, like it was right in front of her, a porn movie playing on the screen of her mind. Cream gushed warm and sticky from her canal, soaking him, soaking her. She fought for air as she picked up the pace, pistoning her hips faster so that her tight slickness jacked him off in quick strokes.

"He was touching me, reaching down and rubbing on my hard clit, pinching your nipple at the same time. To have that connection...his cock in my mouth...yours inside me...you two kissing, all three of us touching. You have no idea how excited and wet that made me."

"Kiona..." He stiffened, halting his movements.

She added, "Ah, and you were fucking my pussy at the same time he was fucking my mouth. You were so hard, so big inside me, and his cock was so tasty, I couldn't suck it fast enough. Both of you made me so horny and—"

He grunted, reaching down to curl a hand behind her neck. He yanked her up, slamming her mouth into his, clamping onto her with frantic hunger. She thought she tasted the salt of tears, but there wasn't time to investigate as storms seemed to erupt everywhere, around, above, beneath, and inside her. The rain finally moved in, splattering down on them, cooling their heated flesh. She heard the rumble of thunder directly overhead, and simultaneously rode the violent quaking of their bodies as one. A potent combination of ecstasy and love flooded her loins and spilled into her bloodstream. Her eyes were closed, but she could see the flash of lightning behind her lids, and she could smell raw sex and electricity in the air.

She whimpered into his mouth, the climax rising, the pleasure of it spreading out from her twitching clitoris and contracting vagina, to her very toes.

Kol tore his lips from hers, letting out a final howl as they both reached the ultimate crest together. His hot seed spilled inside her, warming her womb and making her sigh. Then he jerked himself from inside her, scooped her up off the sand, and ran for the safety of the house.

"Yeah, I think everything's going to be fine," he whispered in her ear as he raced up the beach. "Just fine."

Chapter Eight

Days later, Heloki sat behind his massive cherry-wood desk, his fingers steepled against his mouth as he eyed the chattering young *malihini* woman sitting opposite him. Nothing would ever again be fine for Nakolo Huaka if Heloki had any say in it. And he most certainly did—or would once he had his brilliant plan set into action.

Anjelee Montrose was a freelance reporter who had only a few notable credits under her belt, but she seemed hungry to sink her claws into the notorious *Superstars* magazine again, to get a more impressive byline the next time around. For some reason, Jager hadn't informed Heloki of her connection to the tabloid—perhaps in all the haste to hire her, he'd missed it?—but in doing some probing of his own, she had just revealed it to Heloki.

Jackpot.

According to what Jager had uncovered, it was rumored she had a reputation for hardcore fact-collecting methods that sometimes netted her a story well worth its gossip in gold. Although she wasn't at the top yet, but rather on the lower few rungs of her career-recognition ladder. Bottom line, she was hungry for assignments her current colleagues in the journalism field seemed to be landing before she could get her greedy hands on them.

Just the kind of motivation Heloki needed to get his sometimes cunning daughter back on track, and that lowlife Nakolo off the island and away from Kiona. What's more, Heloki had to have some sort of leverage to hold over celebrity Mitch Wulfrum's head if he didn't conduct his life with Kiona in the manner Heloki expected of him.

After all, the man was going to be Kiona's husband. And what kind of groom allowed his bride-to-be to continue to be friends with her ex-lover? Heloki's only child and heir was beautiful, extremely so. She would be the perfect tool to boost KPCS's sales in conjunction with the star.

An image of his daughter at three flashed before his eyes, her long midnight hair trailing down her back, and her little body clad in a worn, *lei*-printed dress. It was in the days prior to the business's sudden financial success and his building of the current manor he lived in. Tears had sparkled in Kiona's big golden eyes and trailed down her plump little bronzed cheeks. She stood on the front porch of their small cottage, her thin little arms wrapped around Heloki's leg, watching as her mother, Wanaka, climbed into a cab without a backward glance.

Wanaka had deplored the backbreaking, dirty work they'd been forced to do in the fields in the beginning when Heloki had struggled to get the cane business up and running. She'd longed for the big-city, mainland life of L.A., insisting her native Kabana—and the hundreds of acres that had eventually grown into KPCS—was nothing more than a primitive, useless place. She had never let him forget it, constantly complaining in her heavy Hawaiian dialect, claiming he would fail and that she would laugh when he did.

Heloki took in Kabana's gorgeous western-shore view out his window, glanced around his richly furnished, spacious office. *Yeah, well look who's laughing now, you bitch.*

He didn't know what he'd ever seen in the selfish, cold witch. It had gotten worse with each passing day, and Kiona's birth had seemed to be the final nail driven into the coffin of their marriage. Wanaka never had a drop of maternal blood in her, and it was with great relief for Kiona's sake that he'd finally watched Wanaka go.

But he had vowed that day that he would not see Kiona leave. So once KPCS had started turning a profit, he'd initiated the trust fund for her, allowing it to grow handsomely over the years.

That money had been his only assurance of keeping her nearby. Kiona had grown into a brilliant, very valuable KPCS employee, and though she might be absent at times jetting around the world with the movie star in the near future, she and her famous husband-to-be would become wonderful KPCS public representatives.

More profit. He could hear the cash registers dinging now.

Yes, Kiona marrying the star would work in the company's favor. And it wasn't as if Heloki would be the only one netting any gain here. She would finally get her much coveted trust fund, and she would be the perfect wife for Wulfrum to flaunt before his hordes of fans and the public, a plus for Wulfrum, as well.

So why was it, Heloki wondered as Ms. Montrose continued to chatter across from him, that if Kiona was so stunning, and it was such a win-win situation for them all, that Wulfrum had allowed such depravity? Why had he seemed to take Nakolo's side and allow the man in their pre-wedding presence? Was Wulfrum really that stupid, or was there some sort of deceit going on that Heloki—and Wulfrum himself, perhaps—hadn't been made privy to?

But Heloki would find out, perhaps with the help of this

annoying tabloid-connected woman.

Heloki wasn't exactly into the tabloids, be they magazines or TV shows. Oh no, he had much more prestigious, demanding things to do with his time at KPCS than wasting it on arrogant celebrities or public figures.

This was why he had picked Jager's brain. The day after he had met Wulfrum at Kiona's, Heloki had requested that Jager find a photographer as a wedding gift to Kiona and Mitch. It was planned as a hush-hush, intimate ceremony with a limited list of friends and family invited. The media, as far as Heloki and Jager knew, had not been tipped off.

Until now.

He slid the low-five-figures check across the desk. "You'll get the balance when the job is done."

Anjelee's green cat-eyes widened as she chomped on a pink wad of gum. She snatched up the check, purple nails clicking on the desktop, and whistled. "Wow. Now that, I must say, is the biggest freaking check I've ever had the pleasure of accepting."

"That's only half, Ms. Montrose."

"Half. Right." She blinked, dragged her gaze up from the check and focused on Heloki. "Well. Fine by me." She tucked it into the knapsack he imagined held all her camera equipment and miscellaneous spy gadgets.

Heloki hauled his bulk up out of the chair, his silent signal he was done with her and her incessant babbling. "Be sure to do all the shots one would expect of a wedding photographer. Then I want anything and everything else you can get—any way you can get it, you understand? Of all three of them."

"Oh, yeah. I get it." Grinning, she got to her feet and slung the strap of the bag over her shoulder. Dimples emerged on her cheeks as she chomped, her bubble gum popping, grating on

Heloki's nerves. He averted his eyes from the silver barbell disgustingly adorning her eyebrow, and the winking little diamond pierced into the side of one nostril. What the hell was wrong with young people today? No telling where else she'd pierced herself.

The sick little bitch.

With the flick of a hand, she shoved her long, blonde hair behind her tank-top-clad, thin shoulder. As if that didn't do the trick, she tucked her hair behind one ear. The move revealed a row of earrings lining the cartilaged rim of the seashell-shaped ear. He sighed, forcing his gaze to instead take in the random streaks in her hair. They were a shade of bright neon pink that reminded him of the color of sticky, wet cotton candy. To add to the peculiar eyesore, she wore camouflage, knee-length pants that hugged her subtle curves, yet the garment was loaded with masculine cargo pockets.

'Û! What a freak. If it hadn't been for Jager's recommendation, Heloki would have thrown the leanly built eccentric out of his office long ago. No, he would never have allowed her in in the first place.

What had this society come to? Didn't females want to be feminine anymore? he mused in disgust.

"The ceremony begins at six tomorrow evening. I expect you to arrive an hour before to get familiar with the place in the event you should need to take a few...discreet shots. The florist will have Jager's rear deck decorated and set up with a large canopy to keep out any prying media who might get lucky enough to hear of the nuptials and try a fly-over or spy by boat. For now, I expect you to do what you can to prevent any leaks, and to shield the bride and groom if it should still become a media circus. If you demonstrate your worth, any photos I approve after the wedding will be yours to disclose to the press as you see fit. I've already informed Jager and Kiona of my...photography gift, so everyone should be amenable to you circulating around the house. Are there any questions?"

She nodded as she crossed to the door. "The gay rumors? If I should see anything along those lines, should I...?"

Heloki waddled around and propped a generous hip onto the corner of his desk. "Gay rumors?"

"Yes." She'd been about to pull the door open, but instead crossed back to the center of the room. "You know, the speculation that Mitch Wulfrum is gay?" She chewed and popped. "Don't tell me you've never heard it before?"

If he hadn't been sitting down, he might have fainted. His pulse thrummed somewhere deep inside his ample chest. Heloki squelched the urge to dig a finger in his ear. Instead, he croaked, "No, I must say I haven't heard that one."

"Don't see how you could've missed it," she remarked with incredulity. "It's widely known hype that's been all over the tabloids and entertainment shows for weeks, maybe months now." She snorted and shrugged, her small breasts bouncing beneath her tight white tank shirt. "But I guess it's likely the buzz is a crock of shit if he's marrying your beautiful daughter—right?"

Gay? Kiona's marrying a gay movie star? How the hell did I miss that shocking news? And more importantly, why would she do such a foolish thing?

Was Kiona more like her mother than he'd thought, obsessed with L.A. and getting out of Kabana? Had he missed that too?

Heloki reached across his desk and plucked up the package of antacids. With trembling hands, he managed to dig one out of the tight roll and toss it into his mouth. Sweat dribbled down his temples and spine. Suddenly, he couldn't breathe. It seemed the life was being choked right out of him.

"If you're asking me if I know whether the man's gay or not, no, I don't know. While I might watch movies, I don't exactly follow all that absurd Hollywood gossip, much less care about everyone's promiscuous sex lives. But if you witness any such behavior, I expect you to earn your pay and get it discreetly on film. Every bit of it."

That one pierced eyebrow arched. "Every bit of it?"

Heloki sucked on the tablet, deploring the chalky taste, but gods of Hawaii help him, he felt as if he might hurl his lunch. So this wedding was a farce? Was she marrying him just to get her hands on her trust fund—or was she using Wulfrum as a flight out of here?

No. Kiona cannot leave her native land, or KPCS. Heloki needed her. KPCS needed her. Therefore, he would instruct Anjelee to get photos of anything at all that might help Heloki keep his daughter in Kabana, assisting him to run his company.

He got to his feet and slid his hands into his trouser pockets, trying his best not to imagine the famous Mitch Wulfrum in a nauseating lip-lock with another man.

And then returning home to share a bed with his daughter.

He suppressed a gag. *I'll kill the bastard if he marries her, and then I find out the sick rumor is true.*

"I just paid you half of a very large sum for your services, Ms. Montrose. I expect you to earn it. So yes, that means everything—any way you can get it. Do you understand what I'm saying?"

Her heart-shaped, pink mouth curved up in a wicked grin full of blinding white teeth. "Totally. But if I get anything...extra, does that mean a bonus?"

The conniving little twit. “We'll see.” Even from across the room he could smell the scent of her bubble gum. He ground his teeth together as he reached for another antacid tablet. “It depends on just how extra it is. Now, if you don't mind, I have a company to run.”

“Sure, but one other thing before I go.”

He groaned and popped the tablet onto his tongue. “Make it fast. I'm losing my patience second by second.”

“Considering you mentioned earlier that they're spending the night at Mr. Manning's house before leaving on their honeymoon Sunday morning, um, well, getting that extra stuff might require a key.” She held out her hand, palm up, and wiggled her fingers in a gimme gesture. “You wouldn't happen to have one I might...borrow, would you?”

Several hours later, Jager Manning knocked on the door of Anjelee Montrose's Kabana hotel suite, compliments of Heloki 'Alohi. Jager's flight from California had just arrived not an hour earlier, and with the wedding fast approaching, he needed to get this mess straightened out, one he'd inadvertently caused.

Shit, he prayed to fucking God Mitch didn't find out.

Or Heloki.

He heard the jingle of the chain-lock, then the click of the deadbolt disengaging. The door swung open, and the musky scent of her perfume wafted into the hallway to tease his nostrils. He'd smelled its kind plenty of times before.

It was the wicked type strippers often wore, the sort that brought to mind leather and lace, soft skin and gyrating curves.

Jesus Christ.

"Yes? Can I help you?"

He blinked. *Can you ever.* His pulse seemed to cease beating. It did a double-take in his chest, followed by a suspicious galloping rhythm, but it was apparent why.

Damn, but he hadn't been expecting this. She'd had a sexy voice over the phone, all right. But at the sight of her hot little body, it didn't quite do her justice. It proved somewhat tongue-tying. "Uh, are you Anjelee Montrose?"

"In the flesh."

No kidding.

He took in the lean frame, the tight white tank-top emphasizing the just-enough small breasts—mother of all gods, was she braless beneath that thin fabric?—and the flare of hips shaping the green camouflage-print capri pants. His perusal skimmed downward, quickly registering bare feet and purple-painted toenails. He jerked his eyes back up to her interesting face. It was heart-shaped with a small nose sporting a faintly discernible knot on the bridge, one nostril pierced with a teensy white diamond. Dimples emerged in her slightly plump cheeks when her wide, fleshy mouth curved into a pink-tinted grin. One perfectly plucked dark-blonde eyebrow was adorned with a silver barbell, making him wonder what other...body parts she'd decorated with stainless steel. He watched as she flicked her long, streaked blonde hair over trim shoulders.

Wow. Make that *pink*-streaked blonde hair.

On second thought, the woman wasn't his type in the least. She was the epitome of the word eccentric. A vision suddenly filled his head, one of a tight, pretty little pussy, the hood pierced right at the top of her shaven, moist little lips and clit.

Jesus, help us all.

"Hey, I know you." She wagged a finger at him. "You're Jager Manning. I recognize you from the KPCS website. Nice pic, looking all fancy-schmancy, like a real executive-type kind of guy." Her almond-shaped, emerald eyes openly raked him from head to loafers as she chomped a big wad of gum. The orbs reminded him of cat's eyes, cunning and glowing with feline pride. "Who, it looks like, has just gone from the office to the golf course. Headed out to play a few holes?"

He tried to keep his mind focused on the topic of his attire rather than the few holes comment she'd quickly switched to. His stupid, taken-off-guard brain started blinking pictures in his head of two tight little orifices just waiting for him to—

"No." He interrupted his own thoughts before they went too far south and off the company radar screen. "No golf today. Maybe tomorrow...after we get this misunderstanding straightened out with your assignment."

"Thanks, but I don't golf." She angled her head, peering at him through narrowed eyes. "Hmm, I bet you're referring to the Mitch Wulfrum assignment."

He could almost hear her purr of satisfaction at landing the celebrity-related mission.

We'll see about that.

"Yeah." He shoved his hands into the pockets of his khakis to prevent the automatic thrust for a handshake. It was what he'd normally have done had it been anyone else but Punk-rock Polly he'd unknowingly initiated business with. His perusal took in a quick glance of the long, purple nails—make that claws—adorning the tips of the hand currently curled around the edge of the door. "Uh, mind if I come in? We really need to discuss a few crucial things."

"Do we?" Her voice was raspy, like some cigarette-smoking, whiskey-drinking madam in a bordello. He ignored it even as it seemed to reach out and caress his ears. And grab him by the cock and stroke up, down, around.

Gulp.

"We do." He nodded. "There's an issue or two I wasn't aware of. This is important. And obviously, time is of the essence here."

"Mmm, obviously." She pursed her lips and concurred, stepping back to wave him inside. If he didn't know better, he'd say she knew exactly what he referred to. "Sure. Come on in, Mr. Manning."

"Jager'll be fine," he murmured, taking a few long strides into the luxurious room complete with separate bedroom, sitting room, and stocked wet bar. He knew every detail about her accommodations. He'd blindly booked them at Heloki's insistence.

Before doing his homework on the woman, goddamn it. Not his customary way of operating, by far, but he'd been unusually wrapped up in another client's Hollywood drama and had stupidly taken his contact's raving recommendation of Ms. Montrose as gospel. *One of these days, after this all blows over, I'm gonna deck the bastard for lying and risking my career.*

He shuddered to think what Heloki would do if Jager didn't rectify this problem now. Jager couldn't risk losing KPCS as a client, and Heloki paid him well, very well. He'd been the first to take a chance on Jager ten years ago, an eager, twenty-four-year-old just out of college, and nothing to show for it but a master's degree with a focus on marketing and public relations. Jager had built his publicity management company on that first lucrative account with Heloki. The man's business and the 'Alohi family didn't deserve the potential headaches this woman could bring to the table. Jager had been unaware of her recent connection to the gossipy Hollywood tabloid *Superstars* when he'd first contacted her. The mere possibility she could out Mitch's bisexuality—something Jager was almost certain Heloki didn't know about—would bring some bad publicity to KPCS that Heloki hadn't bargained for.

In addition, if it did come out worldwide, and Heloki ever discovered the part Jager had played in Mitch and Kiona's marriage—not even factoring in the addendum he'd just drawn up two nights ago to include Kol in the marriage—he'd be looking at pure ruin.

Career right in the fucking shitter.

Sure, he now had a lot of celebrities on his client list, but Heloki had power all over the world, in far-reaching places and ways even Jager hadn't been made privy to.

Therefore, Jager wasn't leaving here without firing her.

She closed the door and crossed to the bar. His attention was drawn to the colorful edges of a tattoo peeking out from the strap of her shirt near her right shoulder blade. What was it a picture of? Did she have anymore? he suddenly wondered, his gaze exploring the salon-made tan glowing over smooth skin, toned arms, the small bare ankles and feet. She spun around to face him. And father of angels, he couldn't help but notice the flat belly just now revealed below her shirt when she reached up and drew tumblers out of the overhead cabinet.

Fuck me. Another piercing caught his attention. And how could it not, all sparkling and dangly hanging from the top rim of her cute little navel? He rubbed his fingertips together, wondering what it might feel like to—

"Suit yourself. Jager it is," she said in a sing-song tone, peeping at him beneath the cabinet as she clinked ice into glasses. She stilled her movements. Her perfectly shaped eyebrows arched. "Care for a drink...Jager?"

Not on your life. You've got to focus, you idiot.

"Uh, no." He tried to fling the sexy sound of his name from his mind. It had tumbled a bit too sensually off her tongue. "Thanks, though."

She busied herself pouring rum and cola. "Mind if I do?"

"No, be my guest." He located a plush chair near the bar and sank into it. He sure could use one of those drinks, but he needed a clear head. "Look, about the wedding..."

"Yes?" None too ladylike, she spit her gum into a nearby trashcan. Stirring the drink with a finger, she then slid the digit into her mouth and sucked the wetness off with a slurp and pop. Her eyes never left his during the entire motion.

Mother fucker.

Jager shifted in his seat and propped one ankle over the other knee, subtly repositioning his rising hard-on. From the first moment he'd laid eyes on her, his cock had traitorously stirred in his pants. All he needed was a damn boner to turn this meeting into a farce.

Wasn't gonna happen.

"Well, you see, it seems in my rush to secure a photographer for Mr. 'Alohi, I took another client's recommendation as gold and neglected to study your credentials."

"My credentials?" She set the glass aside, rounded the bar, and her small breasts jiggled when she hitched her little bottom up onto the opposite side of the counter. Her eyes, wide and mockingly innocent, never left his as she reached for the glass again, raising it and sipping slow and deliberate. "Are they in question?"

"Well, no, not really. But you see..." He leaned forward, clasping his fingers together, and propped his elbows on his knees to further conceal his crotch from her probing stare. "I, uh, wasn't aware of your prior credits with *Superstars*."

She threw her head back, tossing those long blonde and pink locks over her shoulders, and laughed so melodiously, he wondered if she had a talent for singing. In the process, he caught a glimpse of metal flashing on her tongue.

Goddamn it, what's next, a strap-on dildo in her pants?

His body went rigid at that depraved thought. He couldn't afford to think about that, or the images flashing in his head of that silver little ball sliding over and around his cock while he—

"And that's a problem?" she asked innocently enough, her smile quickly fading. Or was she mocking him?

"Well…"

"Usually, given that particular tabloid's fame, this would be the thing to get a journalist's foot in the door, not prevent it. Is that really why you've come here, Jager, or—" she halted her words and trailed a finger from her plump lips, down her silky neck, to just short of burying it in her small but distracting cleavage. "Or did you have something else in mind?"

Do I ever.

He ground his teeth together. Yep, she was mocking him all right. Somehow—and he wasn't quite sure why—she seemed to think she had a very strong chain to yank where he was concerned.

Like hell you do.

"No, what I had in mind, Ms. Montrose, was—"

"Please. Call me by my first name," she purred, winking at him. "You do remember my first name, don't you, Jager?"

"Yes, of course. It's Anjelee. So Anjelee it'll be, then," he said on a sigh, doing his best to keep his eyes from rolling heavenward. "But getting back to why I'm here. You see, Mitch Wulfrum would really like his privacy in this personal, intimate union. He, the 'Alohi family, and KPCS, all can't afford any potential...negative publicity."

She sipped, regarding him over the rim of the glass. "So it's your feeling that I might compromise the reputations of all these people. And most especially, for the celebrity in question who you worry—at your own expense, as well—might end up between the pages of *Superstars*."

They were statements, not questions. "Yes. Well, possibly."

She slid off the bar, her small breasts bouncing within the confines of the snug little shirt, and sashayed toward him, ice jingling in the tumbler as she went. Very primly, she kept her back straight and held the glass between both hands, lowering herself onto the plush sofa opposite him. The corners of her mouth curved up in a smile so faint, he wondered if he imagined it.

"How, might I ask, could the news of Mitch Wulfrum's nuptials to the gorgeous KPCS heiress ruin anyone's reputation, or be a bad thing to announce in a magazine?"

He started to speak, snapped his jaw shut.

"Well?"

He wiggled in his seat, leaned back, crossed and uncrossed his legs. "It's rather...complicated."

Batting her eyelids, she asked, "You wouldn't be referring to the gay rumors, now would you, Jager? Are you worrying I might photograph evidence that this whole hasty relationship and ensuing wedding are nothing more than a farce to cover up his fondness for men? And that I might secretly sell my story and photos to *Superstars*?"

Shit.

"The gay rumors are just that. Rumors."

"Right. How could they be anything else if he's getting married to a woman?"

Goddamn it, Punk-rock Polly was a sly one.

"Look, I apologize. But the truth of the matter is, it was a big mistake for me to hire you on such short notice. You'll still be compensated very well, if not better than if you'd completed the job."

She gasped theatrically, pressing a hand to her chest. "Are you firing me?"

"No, it's just that I've got someone else already lined up. You'll still be paid for your time and trouble. But in this business where celebrities are involved, it's very—"

"Mr. 'Alohi already paid me."

For one long moment, her words ricocheted between his ears.

Fuck me.

Jager tried like hell to keep his jaw from dropping open. He clamored to his feet. "Excuse me?"

She stood up slowly, shoulders held back, eyes daring him to look away. But he couldn't help it. His gaze lowered against his will, drawn to the peaks now tipping those two just-a-handful mounds. Crap, exactly as he'd suspected, she wasn't wearing a damn bra. Her pink little nipples perked up and strained against the thin white fabric. He could well imagine the flavor of them in his mouth, and whoa, the feel of them against his chest as he slipped his cock into her—

"You heard me. I just came from KPCS and a meeting with Mr. 'Alohi. He paid me a very tidy deposit equivalent to half my fee, and he thanked me for coming all the way here on such short notice. He instructed me on when and where to report, and directed me to get tons of pictures...all to be viewed and approved by him the day following the ceremony. Even before the bride and groom get to see them."

"He did? B-but he told me to pay you after the—"

"You must be mistaken, about that and one other thing..."

Her many telling words amassed in his head like a pile of shit. The stench, the horror of what this could mean for Jager, made him want to vomit. Then there was the *before the bride and groom saw them* thing. What the hell was Heloki up to? Sonofabitch, this could only mean one of two things. Either there'd been a misunderstanding between Jager and Heloki, or Heloki was beginning to suspect something wasn't right with this wedding, and had therefore taken the bull by the balls, himself.

Did he think—or rather, had he discovered—that the marriage was all a sham, and that Jager had orchestrated the hasty love match behind Heloki's back? Heloki rarely kept up with the news or media, so Jager was almost certain he was oblivious to the gay buzz. But maybe he'd somehow found out, and then had learned of Anjelee's connection to the tabloid?

He paid me a very tidy sum. Her words echoed in his head, making him dizzy with apprehension. Was Heloki buying her silence about the rumors, or paying her to find evidence to keep his daughter and KPCS from associating with its bad publicity? Or could he be devising some sort of bribery plan to get Kol out of the picture for good?

Goddamn it, Jager hated being put in the position of sleuth in order to cover his own ass.

"One other thing? What one other thing?" Jager asked hesitantly, swallowing a lump of bitter dread.

Her kissable pink mouth curved into a chilly smile, complete with dimples and sparkling gems in her eyes. "Eh, never mind. That other thing is confidential between me and my...employer."

He thrust a hand through his short hair. "But I'm the one

who contacted you and—"

"Jager?"

"What?"

She crossed her arms over her midriff. "I believe, if I have my facts straight, that you were just the messenger. Correct?"

"Well, yes, but—"

"I need this job very badly. You have no idea just how much. So I believe I'll be taking my orders from the top, which is where the money's coming from. Got it?"

Mother fucker.

He could almost feel the heat of ire steaming out of his ears and nostrils like a pissed-off dragon. It appeared this little slip of a woman was going to try to single-handedly ruin his career and the long-standing, father/son-like relationship he'd built with Heloki.

Like son of a bitching fucking hell!

He folded his arms, mimicking her insolence, and rounded the coffee table. There was now only two inches of space between them. He could feel the warmth of her body, smell her alluring scent, and this close, he looked down into eyes that burned with something more than greed, more than ambition. If he didn't know better, he'd call it fear and vulnerability.

Jager snorted at his own foolish thought. The last thing this woman should be called was vulnerable. "Oh, I get it all right. I get that you're a ruthless, ladder-climbing golddigger who'll apparently do anything for money."

She sucked in a breath of distain. Her upper lip curled. "Why, you son of a—"

"And I get that you have an agenda that has nothing whatsoever to do with being loyal to your employer. Yeah," he nodded, "I get it all right."

She was so small, she had to tip her head back to snare him with her hissing cat's glare, and he could feel her warm breath against his arms and neck even as she spoke through clenched teeth. "You son of a bitch. You know nothing about me. Nothing."

"And I'd like to keep it that way."

"What the hell did I ever do to you?"

"Nothing, really, but I know what you can do to patch things up..."

"Not on your life, you bastard. I've already cashed the check, and it's mostly already spent. I'm not backing out on this job."

"Figures." He turned and stalked to the door. It was useless. He was wasting his damn time. He should be using it trying to talk Heloki into his other recommendation instead.

"What figures?" Anjelee stomped along just one step behind him. "What?" she demanded, her small, cool hand curling around his biceps and yanking barely hard enough to swat a fly aside.

He swung around to face her, obliging out of nothing but morbid curiosity at what she would do when he answered her question. "That you would already have the money spent. Supports my theory."

"Fuck you and your theory." Her voice was like acid, burning his ears.

He spun and reached for the knob. *Fuck this. I'm out of here.* Rather than beat his head against her barricade of stubbornness, there were other ways of solving this problem. He needed to get to Heloki, like yesterday.

"Oh, Jager?" Her tone suddenly turned sweet again, albeit dripping with sarcasm, all traces of the ire gone.

“What?” He couldn’t help growling the word out. The woman was just so exasperating.

She lifted one hand and wiggled her fingers in a girlish wave. If he didn’t know better, he’d say the fake smile on her face had been painted on. “See you at the wedding.”

He yanked on the knob, stepped out into the hallway, and slammed the door shut behind him.

Mother fucker. I’m done for.

Chapter Nine

"Thank you, Father, for hiring the wonderfully adept florist." Kiona rose on bare feet in her floral *luau* wedding dress and kissed Heloki's cheek. The camera flashed. She ignored it and brushed his perspiring brow, inhaling the familiar scent of antacids mixed with martini on his breath. The camera flashed again. "And for finding us such a...thorough photographer."

"Where'd you get her, anyway? She looks kind of familiar." Mitch slid an arm around Kiona's waist and drew her curves against his hard body. The evening ocean breeze blew in through the tent openings where the florist had tied back the flaps with colorful strings of *leis*. It stirred his scent, and she smelled some sort of expensive, faint aftershave she couldn't quite place. It was entwined with brine and the sharp aroma of hibiscus. Now and then, she also caught the essence of the white blooms on the *naupaka* bushes edging the beach. In the background, beyond all the soft ukulele music and tinkling laughter of the lingering guests, she could hear the crash of waves upon the shore as the tide moved in.

Their vows suddenly swam through her head, altered as, "'til *bliss* do we part." All Kiona could think of was all that muscle and man taking her to the gates of that particular bliss...while Kol watched...and then joined them.

Her pulse skittered at that wicked thought. Soon it would

be time for them to retire. Hoping to cool her ardor until then, she looked away, yet her eyes seemed to have a mind of their own. She gave up and studied her husband—God, had she truly married Mitch Wulfrum?—but that only made her horniness worse, her pussy wetter.

He held a glass of champagne in one hand, and to her quiet surprise and delight, he hadn't let go of her with the other hand since the ceremony had ended hours ago. Maybe it was just for show, but nonetheless, something about it made her heart and her loins stir with lust and pride.

She glanced around in search of Kol. Where was he anyway? She hadn't seen him since she and Mitch had been pronounced man and wife. He'd held her gaze from the last row of guests, watching with an indiscernible glitter in his dark eyes as Mitch had kissed her senseless in front of all their guests. Kol had risen then, crossed to the outdoor bar, downed two shots of tequila in a row, and to Heloki's seeming glow of satisfaction, strode into the house. Had he changed his mind and left? Was he angry and jealous again?

God, she hoped not. With smoldering heat igniting in her belly, Kiona took one more sweeping glance of the tent area. There were only perhaps a dozen people remaining out of the original seventy-five guests, mostly employees of KPCS and a few local friends. Unable to locate Kol, she bit her lip and prayed he awaited them in their wedding bed as the three of them had planned.

She swung her thoughts back to Mitch in hopes of easing her worries. He wore a *lei* strung around his neck. It lay on his wide chest over a red, yellow, orange, and green Hawaiian shirt, and he'd paired it with crisp white trousers. Kiona's system had been in overdrive since she'd laid eyes on his striking handsomeness while walking up the aisle. She'd felt as if she were the heroine in one of his movies, but this was far from fiction.

It was reality in all its bizarreness.

The florist and caterers had done a fabulous job forming their tent-covered, seaside wedding atmosphere on the rear deck of Jager's house, complete with a spread of various *luau* hors d'oeuvres, fire-lit torches, a tinkling, soft-lit champagne fountain, a Hawaiian-decorated, dark-chocolate cake, and all the Polynesian decor and flora needed to give it just the right romantic touch.

If Kiona didn't know better, she would think she'd just gone through a traditional wedding. With a traditional husband. With a traditional life ahead of her.

But oh no, there would be nothing traditional about her marriage to movie star Mitch Wulfrum.

And the thought of that sent a renewed tremor of sexual electricity racing through her system and swimming in her groin.

"Of course, Jager found her for me," Heloki replied curtly. His voice sounded distant, almost cross, but Kiona knew her father couldn't be happier that she'd finally gotten married. And to a famous man, at that, one whose association would boost KPCS's sales and world visibility.

"You know her?" Mitch asked, directing his question at Jager.

Jager shuffled his stance. He was used to dressing in suits, and other than *lei*-print swim trunks, he'd always despised wearing Hawaiian garb. Being a tall, well-built man with short-cropped, chestnut hair and penetrating hazel eyes, he didn't look Polynesian in the least, but he was a good-looking man in that sexy, businesslike, *GQ* sort of way. He'd donned the floral shirt and white pants with just one quick grumble of protest, and had stood at Mitch's side as his best man.

He took a long draw on his beer now, and narrowed his gaze on the photographer. "No, not really. When Heloki phoned me to ask if I knew of anyone who could take on the job with such short notice, I contacted a client of mine on the mainland. One I figured could give me a good recommendation."

The slim blonde photographer, Anjelee Montrose, sent Jager a chilly smile. She lifted the 35mm camera, peered through the lens, and it seemed she defiantly aimed it at Jager. *Flash*!

Jager blinked and rubbed his eyes. With a sigh, he added, "Sorry, the fact is, I didn't know who, or *what*, I was recommending. Until it was too late."

Heloki sipped his martini. "*Ahahana.* She's working out just fine."

"Right, shame on me," Jager mumbled. Kiona knew he fully understood the translation of Heloki's chastising words. Demonstrating some insolence of his own, Jager guzzled his beer, his narrowed stare never leaving the woman.

Hmm, what's this all about? Kiona wondered. For someone who claimed not to know the photographer, there sure appeared to be *some*thing going on between them.

"Don't know a damn thing these days," Jager added with a bored drawl to his tone.

"That's enough," Heloki snarled. "We already went through this. You did fine, just fine in finding her for me. She's doing just what I hired her to do."

"Is there a problem?" Mitch demanded to know, his eyebrows arching in suspicion.

Jager blinked. "No, of course not. Not at all." He tipped the bottle and drained the last few ounces of his beer.

"Well," Heloki said on a sigh, "I believe it's time for the

newlyweds to retire and for me and all the guests to go."

Thank goodness. Kiona didn't think her small G-string could hold anymore wetness. "It was a lovely wedding, Father. Thank you for everything."

"Yes," Mitch added. Kiona shivered when his palm grazed up and down her arm. "I know it was all on such short notice, so it's very much appreciated. Handpicking the guests and using discretion with all the wedding coordinators made it much more memorable for us all. It was very refreshing not to have a media circus at every turn."

Jager cleared his throat.

Heloki's lips thinned. "It was my pleasure. No one could be prouder than me to have a renowned person such as you as a son-in-law. Now I really must be going." He raised a hand and snapped his fingers at the head staff member.

The plump woman nodded at Heloki and rushed over to the DJ, whispering in his ear. The DJ glanced up from his CDs and took his cue, halting the music immediately.

"I've just been informed," the man announced over the microphone, "that it's time for us to depart and offer our farewells and final congratulations to the bride and groom. Thanks to everyone for coming. It was an honor to MC the wedding of Mitch Wulfrum and the outrageously gorgeous Hawaiian princess, Kiona 'Alohi."

Unintelligible chatter and laughter followed, and the lingering guests walked over one by one to offer their best wishes for a long and happy union. As Kiona hugged each friend or relative, bidding them good-night, excitement swirled in her belly. Soon she would be in bed with two intense men, one her lover, the man she loved beyond life, and the other her husband, a man she'd already become extremely fond of.

That is, she'd be with them both *if* Kol hadn't changed his mind and left.

Heloki held out his arms to her. "Come here. Give your daddy a big hug."

She let go of Mitch and walked into the circle of her father's thick arms. He was soft, warm, and as big as a bear. She inhaled the faint scent of his cologne and the alcohol on his breath. He squeezed her tight and whispered in her ear, "My little Kabana girl, all grown up now. I love you, Kiona—my valuable company CEO."

"Love you, too, Papa." She ignored his mention of her job and the odd tone to his voice. Instead, she kissed his rotund cheek, surprised to taste the salt of tears.

He framed her face in his thick hands and said, "I will bring by the paperwork tomorrow before you leave on your honeymoon."

"Paperwork?"

"The documents showing transfer of the trust fund over to you."

Thank God! "Oh yes, thank you." She pursed her lips and gave him a quick kiss on the mouth. The camera flashed.

Heloki turned, waving as he went. "Good night, all."

"Night," Jager murmured, closely watching Heloki as he waddled into the house. "Well." He blew out a long breath. "Guess it's time for me to split too. What do you want me to do about the photographer? Looks like she's still at it."

Flash. As if to taunt him again, Anjelee took a shot of Jager and Mitch.

"Get rid of her," Mitch growled good-naturedly as he yanked Kiona into his arms and kissed her long and hard. His mouth was wet, demanding, and tasted of champagne. He pressed her body against the hard length of his own, and she caught the unmistakable feel of his half-hard erection against her lower abdomen.

Flash.

"Yes," she added, winding her arms around his neck. "Get rid of the annoying woman and that damn camera of hers. In fact, get rid of everyone."

"Um...sure." Jager didn't move.

Mitch's hands went south, cupping Kiona's ass. The flash of the camera winked again. "Something wrong?"

"Uh, no, no." Jager tossed the empty beer bottle into a nearby trashcan. "I do need to speak with you about something, but I guess it can wait until tomorrow. Have a good night...all of you." He sauntered off.

Kiona watched as he stopped to talk to Anjelee. They appeared to have a brief, heated discussion, then Jager stormed into the house.

"What do you suppose is going on between Jager and that photographer chick?" She tucked herself up tighter, clinging to him. All the while, her pussy engorged, hoping, just knowing Kol waited for them.

"Hmm, knowing him, he's probably trying to get in her pants. Looks like he's not getting anywhere, though. Don't think she's his type—or maybe he's not her type. But you know what?" He kissed her mouth, nipped at her bottom lip, and made a wet trail of sucks and licks down her throat.

She quivered, her response erupting on a moan. "What?"

"You're my type, all right, and I don't really give a damn one way or the other about Jager." He nuzzled his way up to her ear and whispered, "All I care about is making love to you and Kol on our wedding night."

"I thought you'd never suggest it." She pulled away and slid her hand into his. Warm, long fingers closed around hers and squeezed with a tenderness she was convinced had to be genuine. “Let’s go.”

“’Bout damn time.”

Five minutes after the DJ, the photographer, and the wedding planner had packed up and gone, and Mitch and Kiona had bid their last guests farewell, they strolled into the master suite hand-in-hand.

Kol lounged naked on Mitch’s huge bed, his cock stretched flaccidly along that sexy crease where thigh joined hip. She studied his buff body with the colorful array of tattoos, her fingers curling into her palms with a sudden need to explore those familiar adornments on his flesh. Proudly native, he had one tattoo depicting each of the four gods.

Kane, the procreator, was represented on Kol’s left outer biceps by an owl in flight, its eyes two glowing yellow suns. Kanaloa, lord of the seas and winds, was opposite on the right arm, formed by an interwoven octopus and squid amid crashing ocean waves. Though by his position she couldn’t view the tattoo of Ku, she knew its details well. Its colorful beauty adorned his left shoulder blade, and was a masterpiece of scarlet *i’iwi* feathers gilded with serrated dog’s teeth and mother-of-pearl eyes. Finally, he’d had Lono, the god of thunder, etched onto his hip just above the spot where his cock currently lounged. The half-man, half-wolf image howled at storm clouds wrought by jagged lightning and crashing seas.

Kiona had always thought its position near his manhood to be extremely sexy. But now, at this pivotal moment in her life, she welcomed the irony of its shape-shifter form. It not only paralleled his dark and tempestuous moods, but his newly admitted bisexuality, as well.

Warm cream gushed into her panties at the thought of it, of that and everything that was to be consummated tonight between the three of them.

Kol punched the remote control buttons, his gaze never leaving the TV screen. “I’ve gone from soft to hard to soft again like ten times already, just waiting for you two. What took you so damn long?”

“Looks like the wait was well worth it,” Kiona purred, leaving Mitch at the door and padding barefoot across the plush carpeting until she reached the bed. She gazed down at Kol and stripped off her *lei*. Cool air gusted in through the open bay window and caressed her perspiring flesh. She unbuttoned her dress, slid it down her arms and over her hips, and let her breasts bounce free. They were heavy and engorged, the nipples so tight and achy, it felt as if they might burst. Kiona cupped one mound, skimmed the other hand down her belly and into her G-string. She filled her palm with her drenched cunt, rubbing, soothing herself.

“Guess what? It’s happening, Kol. Finally. He said he’d bring by the paperwork and sign the trust fund over to me.”

“When?”

“Tomorrow before we leave on our honeymoon. Isn’t it exciting?” Exhilaration bubbled up inside her as she dove onto the bed and crawled atop Kol’s thick, warm chest.

His arms went around her, squeezing her on a sigh. He clamped his eyes shut and kissed her temple. “You sure?”

Ducking her head, she smacked her lips against his and let the glee of triumph soar through her veins. “Positive. It worked. The marriage to Mitch, the wedding, everything. Even your addendum to our contract is going to work for us.”

“Mmm.” He dragged a thumbnail up and down her bare

back making her tremble with gooseflesh. She glanced around and saw that he'd lit lots of candles in preparation for their wedding night. The flames danced, both emphasizing and shadowing the planes and angles of his sculpted body and darkly handsome face. Kol's warm breath fanned her cheek, his anxious panting the result of months of pent-up emotion inflicted by her father, finally released. She caught the lingering scent of tequila on his breath entwined with the salty sea breeze wafting in through the window. His arms held her tenderly, his gaze alight with hope.

The curtains billowed inward and the rush of the sea played musically in the background. The bedroom was positioned on the opposite end of the house from the rear deck. It shared a cliff-like, uncovered *lanai* with the den, both overlooking a rocky tumble to the beach and the Pacific below. Perfect. So romantic. She couldn't have asked for a sexier ambiance than this on her wedding night.

I'm so happy!

Kol's gaze shifted to look over her shoulder. Her belly quickened and moisture flooded her panties when she saw the gleam of lust there the moment his eyes met Mitch's.

Kiona slid a look at Mitch. He stood near the closed door right where she'd left him. In his Hawaiian wedding attire, he exuded male elegance and raw sexuality. His tanned complexion shone light-bronze against the white background and colorful flowered fabric of his button-up shirt. He had his hands shoved into the pockets of his white trousers, but still she could discern the outline of his rising, enormous erection.

Heated lust quickened in her belly; her nipples tingled. Wow, this man was her husband. And here she lay atop another man, also her husband in spirit and in her heart. Leave it to Kiona to fall into such an unconventional sort of arrangement.

But heaven above, she loved it!

"How about we try out that contract now and see how we all like it?" Kol suggested, reaching down to hook a finger in her panties. The silky, soaked fabric briefly stuck to her sex-lips when he dragged the G-string down and over her hips. She obliged, wiggling and rising up to allow him to peel them off. He tossed the undergarment onto the floor and continued to stare expectantly at Mitch.

Kol's hard body and warmth permeated her flesh from breasts to toes. His sparse chest and leg hairs tickled her bare skin, and his quickly hardening cock had been sandwiched between their bodies. She rubbed her abdomen against him, doing a dance over him while kissing his salty neck. She rode the wicked thrill of it with reckless abandon, knowing Mitch studied her nude ass and, from his view near the door, she was well aware he caught glimpses of her drenched mons between her spread legs.

A sidelong glance proved Mitch had just shed his clothes, his wedding *lei* now piled atop his garments. What a glorious sight, she thought, to study the famous movie star, not on the big screen, but within reach, right here on their wedding night while Kol willingly shared the awesomeness of it with her. Acutely aware of Kol's warmth running the length of her front side, Kiona's gaze scanned Mitch's lean limbs as he sauntered nearer, the sleek jaguar circling his prey. His penis stood at a rigid angle from his flat belly, its swollen head crowning the veiny length of steel. She scanned higher, longing to scrape her nails down his wide, sinewy torso and sculpted, smooth chest with its dark, erect nipples. Her mouth watered, fully ready to taste and suckle the manly nubs.

The bed shifted slightly when he climbed onto the mattress

and crawled across the slick emerald comforter, his eyes seeming to drink in the sight before him. “I don’t think there’s going to be any question whether any of us likes it or not,” Mitch murmured, his voice deep and laced with arousal.

Kiona glanced down at Mitch’s hands. On the left, he wore the single, wide gold wedding band she’d placed on his finger during the ceremony tonight. On his other hand, he wore a platinum band, one that Kol had slid onto Mitch’s right ring finger during their private three-way wedding ceremony a few nights ago following their meeting with Jager. Kiona wore an identical one on her right hand, as well—the one Kol had placed on her finger that same night. Finally, Kol wore one from Mitch and one from Kiona.

They were all now connected in their hearts and under God’s eyes by a three-sided commitment.

The arrangement Mitch had come up with had been mutual without any disagreements. A contract had been drawn up to coincide with their clandestine wedding. It had outlined the fact that Kol and Kiona were a couple first and foremost, that they loved one another, but had mutually approved of Mitch as part of their partnership. It stated that at no time could Mitch and Kiona as a legally married couple exclude or divorce Kol unless all three agreed, and that to do so would be the only factor that would allow Kol the option of writing a tell-all book about the famous icon and his true predilection for both women and men. True, it had been a chancy thing for Mitch to agree to, but then again, all three of them had their own specific risks, and of them all, Kol had the most emotionally to lose, and the least amount of legal leverage in the arrangement.

The basis of their contract was, of course, illegal in that the essence of it implied polygamy. But it wasn’t as if it had been filed in the higher courts. It simply was private insurance between them all—known and held only by the three of them,

God, and Jager—that gave them each peace of mind and allowed them to enjoy their newfound triad.

Mitch had netted a Hollywood trophy wife to parade around on the red carpet, as well as the added bonus of being able to live out his true private fantasies without ruining his career in the process. Though he'd have to remove the platinum ring in public so as not to get tongues wagging and speculating, he vowed always to wear it in private.

Kiona would be able to keep the man she loved, while finally getting access to her trust fund. A perk she hadn't planned for, but couldn't help being thrilled about, was she would not only be the publicized wife of Mitch Wulfrum, but also his private one with all the amenities! Though she'd continue to have to hide evidence of her ongoing relationship with Kol from her father and from the public, she would walk that rocky path when and if she ever came to it. For now, she'd achieved all of her dreams. And then some.

Finally, Kol would possess the woman he loved once and for all. He'd have to continue to dodge Heloki, but he now had the security of their marriage, and the added benefit of being able to further exercise that bisexual side of himself that, as it had turned out, had been far darker and sexier than Kiona could ever have imagined.

Life couldn't get any better, she decided as Mitch stretched out beside Kol, both men hard and manly, one blond, one dark. Happiness welled up inside her. It was her wedding night, and she couldn't wait to make love to them both, to consummate their threesome marriage and to further explore this naughty little pact they'd formed.

Chapter Ten

Kol dragged his knuckles down Mitch's chest, skimming them over one taut nipple. Mitch groaned when Kol went lower over his quivering abdomen and closed his hand around Mitch's cock. He clamped his eyes shut, surrendering to the moment.

"I think you're right," Kol replied, his voice thick with lust. "We're all going to enjoy this immensely."

Kiona squelched a vague sense of shyness by reaching out and wrapping her hand around the back of Kol's. She urged him to stroke up, down. "No one is going to have a better time than me." She gyrated her pelvis, rubbing her pussy up and down Kol's cock, while her hand assisted him in bringing Mitch to a full hard-on. "I mean, look at you two. I'm so lucky. Do you know how many women in this world would envy me if they could see me now?"

"Uh-uh, no one's going to see you but me and Mitch." Kol whacked her rump, leaving behind a sting and the warm ease of desire flooding her quim. "Now, how about we take this into the bathroom?"

One eyelid popped open and Mitch croaked, "The bathroom?"

"Mmm, yeah." Kol eased Kiona aside and leapt to his feet. She would never forget the rare but genuine grin on his face. It was boyish, mischievous, and she hoped to God it foreshadowed a life of love and satisfaction for them all. "While you two were out there playing bride and groom, I was in here setting the ambiance like a good third wheel. Got the Jacuzzi tub bubbling, candles lit, champagne chilling, and enough hors d'oeuvres for an army. Even got a bisexual porno flick set to play on the flat-screen TV above the big-ass tub."

"A bi porno?" Mitch rolled over and got to his feet. He threw a smoldering smile over his shoulder and clutched his left chest. "Ah, a man after my own heart."

Watching sexy videos with Kol was nothing new to Kiona. But they'd never watched one with another person present, especially not another man.

Kiona pressed a hand to her forehead. She felt giddy, totally dizzy with ribald lust. Crawling from the bed, she fixed her gaze on the doorway she knew led into the master bath. She could see the flicker of candlelight on the open *koa* wood door, and now that she honed in on it, she could hear the faint bubbling of the jets in the tub, and could detect the aroma of coconut-scented wax. Anticipation spun around in her gut, tumbled over nerves, and shot up to close around her windpipe. She couldn't catch her breath. Though she felt as if she'd just run a marathon, she took a few wobbly steps toward the bathroom, her heart knocking against her ribs.

"Wait." Mitch took her hand and yanked her into his arms. He positioned his warm body flush against hers, and planted a wet kiss on her mouth. His tongue dragged in a dizzying path around her open lips. She tasted champagne and sweet fruit, longing for more.

She stretched, rising up on tiptoe, her arms sliding up to hook behind his neck. The kiss deepened. He moaned into the cavern of her mouth, she moaned back. His tongue worked her lips open wider, testing the strength of her tongue against his, tracing her teeth, and nibbling at her lips. Mitch splayed a hand over her ass and pressed her pussy firmly against his stone-hard penis. Knowing Kol watched, a flame erupted in her swollen clitoris—embers to fire, inferno to billowing smoke. Before she could bask further in Mitch's heat, he tore free of the kiss. She gasped when he bent and lifted her into his arms.

Kiona hesitantly glanced at Kol. Her lips were bruised to tenderness, her breathing ragged, and her pussy soaked with intense want. Was Kol okay with seeing her in her legal husband's arms? Apparently, Kol didn't seem to mind that Mitch had dominated the moment, and there didn't appear to be any reason at all to worry that Kol had felt neglected. His inky-black, lust-filled eyes never left Mitch and Kiona. Kol stood there several feet from the bathroom door, a Polynesian god, tattooed muscles flexing by candlelight, jacking himself off to the sight of Mitch kissing Kiona, then lifting her into his arms. Kol stared, clearly mesmerized, as Mitch held Kiona possessively against him, both nude and fully aroused.

Mitch's own eyes were glazed with need when he directed his comments to Kol. "Being the bride and all, she should be carried over the threshold. Do you mind? Or would you like to do it? I mean, she's your bride too."

Even though, in reality, she was Kol's bride only by their private ceremony and not by law, just the fact that Mitch offered, said it all. It meant he honored their arrangement, whether a court would or not.

Kol shook his head. "Go right ahead. Kiona and I have had our moments alone." She knew Kol referred to their recent romantic tryst on the beach. He'd carried her into the house in the midst of a storm, and no one could refute that, at that moment, they were married heart and soul.

"Besides, I've discovered I like to watch," Kol added with a wink.

"Are you sure?" She asked it even as Mitch started toward the bathroom.

"Never surer of anything in my life." Following on Mitch's trail, Kol massaged his own balls and then slid his hand back up to caress himself as he walked.

She kept her gaze on Kol, watching him over Mitch's shoulder. She could almost feel his intent look caressing her, firing up her loins. He held her stare and she caught the unmistakable gleam of confidence there. Yes, that stormy night on the beach had been time well invested.

They passed through the doorway, but even from the short distance with Kol just outside in the bedroom, something else formed in his eyes, and it made her shiver. It was intense, one man completely sharing and surrendering his woman to another man he had grown to trust in less than a week's time. It made her breathless and sent hormones rushing through her system.

Kiona suppressed an eruption of lightheadedness. She had one cock pressed against the underside of her thigh, and yet another only five feet away from her, erect and ready to please her...and Mitch. How had she gotten here in this surreal place in her life?

Her mind raced from one thought and question, to another. Was this really happening to her? Tonight, mere minutes away, would she truly experience her first taste of being made love to by two husbands at once? Would she get to watch as Mitch and Kol made love with each other?

She let out a lungful of air and pressed a hand to her shuddering chest. "I-I... Whew. I'm so keyed up, I feel dizzy."

"You and me both, babe. I've been wound up ever since you fell into my arms that first day we met." Mitch kissed her cheek, lowering her into the hot, bubbling water until she stood in the center of the emerald tub. It was the size of an outdoor spa, big enough to hold six people, and the jetting water's depth swirled at hip level. Beneath the surface, she could see the indentations of a bench seat on either side. One long lounge seat jutted out into the middle between them, and it had a grooved and padded headrest.

She glanced up and saw that two TV screens opposite one another above the ends of the tub indeed played a porn movie, the volume low enough to hear just the faint grunts and groans of ecstasy. A well-built man kissed another hot man—whew, how much stimulation could she take?—while a beautiful buxom brunette woman held their cocks together and tried to take them both into her mouth for a double blowjob.

For now, Kiona shifted her gaze away from the television screens for fear she might embarrass herself by coming just from visual stimulation. Instead, she perused the wide marble tub ledge. It held thick, rolled-up terry towels in scarlet, butterscotch, and bright green. It also was laden with a large tray of *pupu* hors d'oeuvres, champagne on ice in an elegant sterling-silver bucket, and a woven *lauhala* basket full of various body oils, lubricants, condoms, and...adult toys?

Oh wow.

Her pulse thumped out of control, her legs went weak. She pressed a trembling hand to her chest and tried to still her erratically beating heart. Her mouth watered at the chocolate-dipped tropical fruits and whipped cream, but that didn't even come close to the moisture that gushed out of her pussy at the sight of all those naughty dildos and odd-shaped toys.

She swallowed audibly, forcing down a lump of exhilaration. "You, um, thought of everything, didn't you?"

Kol sauntered forward, stopping next to Mitch. To look from

one naked man to the other, made her feel all winded, almost apprehensive. Holy shit, they were hers—both of them. What would she do with two men the rest of her life?

"Damn right," Kol drawled. "My wedding gift to you both. And I intend for the three of us to have the hottest marriage ever, starting with our wedding night."

"You know something?" Mitch canted his head. He took in the two televisions screens, the candlelit room, and Kiona's nakedness. Her clit tingled, instantly engorging at the visual caress. Her ears drank in the soothing, deep tone of his voice. "I don't know where the hell you two've been all my life, but I don't think I can wait another second to get this night started. You know how hard it was to socialize and keep my mind from straying during the reception—not to mention making sure I didn't walk around with a boner? I mean, look at you both." He swept Kol with a lusty perusal, then Kiona. She felt the steam of it right down to the tip of her womb. "Jesus, you're both so hot."

"Thanks, man, you're not too bad yourself. And hell, her? I think I could just ogle her all night long," Kol drawled conversationally to Mitch, though he never took his glittering gaze off Kiona. "What about you?"

They studied her nudity, one pair of warm, dark-chocolate eyes, the other as blue-green and cool as the waters of the Pacific. Kiona waited like a virginal bride, her flesh zinging with anticipation at their hungry scrutiny while her nipples perked into aching arrows. She inhaled the tropical-scented wax entwined with the faint aroma of the sea wafting in through the overhead skylight.

Angling her head, she heard the rush of the surf beyond the audio of the movie. She imagined it to be the rumble of her world tipping on its axis instead. Here she was at an unexpected yet exhilarating crossroad, offering herself up for a liftetime to two men at once. Nostalgia gripped her, and she welcomed the sting of tears behind her eyes.

I will remember this moment forever.

"Uh, no. Looking isn't nearly enough for me. I definitely need more." Mitch stepped over the tub's side, splashing as he went. He reached out, his long fingers curling around the nape of her neck. She caught the essence of his musky cologne when he pulled her close, melding her body against his warm, long length. "You've sampled her plenty of times before, so if you want to ogle, you go right ahead and ogle all you want. But me? I'll be touching, tasting, smelling, and making love to her all night long."

"Mmm..." She didn't know if the purring sound of concurrence came from her own throat, from the movie, or from Kol, but clearly there was no disagreement as to Mitch's privileges.

Looking up into his handsome face, Kiona gazed beyond him to the beautiful picture the skylight made on the vaulted ceiling. Kol had drawn the shutters on the massive picture window above the tub, no doubt to ensure no prying eyes from the paparazzi. During the wedding and throughout the night, Jager had seen that bodyguards had been posted down by the shore, as well as along the road and at various posts on either side of the property. But in Mitch's world of fame, there could still be the possibility that one persistent reporter—or perhaps even a disgruntled employee—could get lucky enough to have been tipped off about the wedding and permeate the defenses. Apparently, in the extraordinary world of Hollywood, one could never be too discreet.

As a result, to provide them a hint of the outdoors while still maintaining their privacy, Kol had instead opened the large window built into the slanted ceiling. The faint candlelight in the master bath drove away any lunar glow that might have angled in from the screened opening, but it didn't diminish the beauty above them. The skylight was enormous, and it framed a scatter of white stars over the black velvet of night. Every now and then, she could see the swaying shadow of palms against the backdrop. Wispy gray clouds highlighted by the moon's silver rays, streaked across the picture, making her wonder if another storm brewed.

"Hell with that, I'm not going to watch the whole time." Kol climbed into the tub behind Mitch and reached for a tube of massage oil. Kiona caught the fruity scent of honeydew seconds after she heard the flip of the cap.

Mitch held her gaze captive with his. "Then get to work," he replied with a grin just before he ducked his head and captured her mouth in a voracious kiss.

Mitch's moan of pleasure vibrated on her lips and tongue. She heard the woman in the video whimper, and cracked one eye open to see a well-built man now licking her pussy while the other man forced his cock into her mouth. Kiona's cunt ached, dampening as she imagined her own clit being devoured in the same way, her mouth invaded by a swollen shaft.

With her eyes still open, she set her hands on Mitch's hard biceps and swept her tongue deeper into his mouth, exploring his delicious dampness, inviting him to spar with her. Kiona's fingers dug and caressed as she shifted her gaze and watched Kol over Mitch's brawny shoulder. He worked the oil between his palms and started rubbing down Mitch's back. With Kol's increasing pressure and movements upon Mitch's back, Mitch leaned closer to Kiona, escalating the intensity and speed of the kiss. His mouth moved hard and wet over hers as he let out a muffled groan of pleasure. He still tasted of the faint traces of effervescent champagne. It made her drunk on his kisses, and she opened wider, offering herself up to him completely.

Kol's attentive massage forced Mitch's body to move and sway in the water, which in turn had her nipples brushing and bumping Mitch's smooth chest. Her areolas puckered, aching for more stimulation. She pressed closer, rubbing harder, her nipples dragging over Mitch's. Her nubs tightened almost painfully, causing a flood of desire to spread down from the tight tips and spill into her loins.

Mitch moaned his approval, his nipples as hard as hers. His tongue retreated, traced her lips, then pushed back in even as his hands skated down her back and cupped her buttocks. His body shifted and rocked in the water, moving with Kol's ministrations on his back. It caused his hard-on to grate over her moist-hot cleft, which in turn, ignited her libido into a full-fledged inferno.

She groaned into the kiss, finally closing her eyes and wrapping her arms around Mitch's neck. There could be nothing more erotic in this world than being devoured by an attractive celebrity, while the man she loved worshipped that same person with the talented hands she knew so well.

She surrendered to the madness of it, leaning into Mitch. He kneaded her ass cheeks, sending repeated frissons of heat to her loins. He wedged his manhood closer, and her come oozed out onto the head of his cock before being washed into the water. She wanted to be filled just like the woman in the movie, one man's huge cock now pummeling her glistening pussy while the other one sucked on her pink areolas. Kiona's clit engorged, throbbing with the desperation of that sudden craving. Her nipples stung with need when he reached between them and closed one hand over her breast, grazing the tight pebble with the palm of his hand.

"Mitch...Mitch," she purred against his mouth. "I—oh, God, I want..."

She hadn't finished her plea, but he sensed her urgency. He responded by leaning down and lowering her onto the reclining seat just beneath the water's surface. His mouth remained sealed to hers, his hands and arms cradling her with gentle care. Whirls of steam wafted up to engulf her face as her bottom settled back onto the hard surface, and hot water embraced her from her toes to her shoulders. She let her head fall back onto the headrest when Mitch finally tore his mouth from hers and stared down at her.

"You're so damn beautiful," Mitch rasped, kneeling on the seat to her right. His eyes glowed with lust, yet there was also something else intense and oddly emotional that Kiona couldn't name. He trailed his hand down one of her legs, lifting it out of the water. "So stunning, lying there naked in the water. So fucking sexy, I can't catch my breath."

Mitch's finger whorled around the tattoo on her ankle. His brow furrowed as he studied it. "Ah, so that's what it is. Kol's name surrounded by a pretty little red heart. Well, you know what that means don't you?"

She shook her head, his hot touch making her breath catch in her chest.

"You're going to have to put my name on your other ankle."

"I-I...okay, I'll be sure and do that first chance I get."

Mitch chuckled. "Come here," he said to Kol. Apparently loath to shun Kol, Mitch reached behind him and tugged Kol's arm until Kol's chest and narrow hips were pressed against Mitch's backside. The move, both sexual and endearing, beset Kiona with another rush of giddiness and desire that snaked into her womb.

Looking over his shoulder, Mitch's gaze locked onto Kol's with a level of heat Kiona had never seen in a man before. "And you. Goddamn if you're not the hottest guy I've ever laid eyes on." Keeping his head turned, Mitch captured Kol's mouth in a quick, tongue-delving kiss. As he devoured and growled his pleasure, Mitch guided Kol's oily hand down to his cock and closed Kol's palm around the steely hardness.

God help her, it made her heart stop and her mouth water.

Kol sighed, broke free of the kiss, and voraciously attacked Mitch's neck with sucks and nips. All the while, he jacked Mitch off with his lubricated palm, eliciting such a salacious response from Mitch, Kiona gasped in speechless awe.

At that one earth-shattering, carnal moment, Kiona saw an unleashed, hungry side of Kol that she hadn't fully realized existed, even with his recent confession of bisexuality. It was as if there had been one piece of the puzzle missing in their relationship, but not loud or large enough to make her take full notice before now. Had she known sooner, it certainly would have spiced things up in their already kinky love affair. Now this...this was mind-boggling. She was nearly delirious with thrilling, pussy-soaked confusion at what she should do next. Just let them go at it, or reach out and insist on being a part of it?

But there was no need to stress over it for long, she concluded when Mitch leaned down and caged her in, planting his hands on the rim of the tub on either side of her. He nudged her thighs apart, settling his knees on the bench between her calves. "There ya go, spread those gorgeous legs for me. Let me in."

Lowering himself into a half-floating position over the top of her, he bent and took her mouth with his again, pillaging and plundering every last inch and crevice of her orifice. She arched upward, winding her arms around his neck, bringing him further down into the water so his body stretched atop hers beneath the foamy surface, skin-to-skin, heat-to-heat.

Kol shifted with Mitch, settled onto the seat at her left, and continued to jack Mitch off between her body and Mitch's.

"I need it now," she whispered against Mitch's mouth. Kiona raised her hips, and what maddening glory it was to feel the head of Mitch's penis periodically brushing her labia while Kol jerked him off harder, faster. "Watching you two like that is so—God, I need your cock inside me before I explode."

He smiled at her with a tenderness that made her breath catch. Reaching one hand between them, he closed his palm over Kol's knuckles and let out a hiss. But Kol didn't let up on his hand movements. Instead, he relaxed into the underwater seat and groaned, gripping his own rod with one hand while he continued to pleasure Mitch with the other.

Mitch squeezed his eyes shut, bracing himself on the tub's rim and tipping his head back. He tightened his grip around Kol's wrist. "If you keep that up, I'll come before I even get inside her. Let's slow it down."

Mitch's gaze scanned the tray of appetizers as if he searched for a miracle to help achieve some patience of his own. He floated over, settled onto the other underwater bench, and reached for a huge, chocolate-covered strawberry. Dipping it in the whipped cream, he winked and said in a husky voice, "I have a feeling the three of us are going to be up all night. We'll need all the energy we can get."

When he held it to her lips, she opened her mouth and closed her teeth over the pointed tip of the berry. The sweet-cocoa, creamy flavor burst in her mouth all at once. She chewed, sighing, her eyes rolling back in her head.

"I still can't believe this. It feels like I'm in a dream, in some Eden somewhere off on a distant planet or something."

"I have a feeling this is only the beginning of the dream." Mitch dipped the remainder of the berry into the fondue bowl and leaned across Kiona's breasts to offer it to Kol. "We'll start our Eden with fruit, then move on to more...interesting things to dip."

Kol bit off all but the stem. He grinned, speaking around a mouthful of food. "Like bananas and melons."

"Damn right." To prove his agreement, Mitch chose a banana piece, dunked it in chocolate, and popped it in his mouth. "Every last one."

"Wow, we're really married," Kiona said, a breathy tone escaping from deep in her throat. Steam wafted up from the surface, and she stretched, basking in the heat of the water. Her muscles gradually relaxed as the jets pounded against her back and rear end. "We actually pulled it off."

Kol poured a half-glass of champagne into each of three fluted crystal wineglasses. He handed one to Kiona and one to Mitch.

"To us and a long, happy, three-way marriage." Kol raised his glass in a toast.

Kiona and Mitch beamed their agreement. "To us," they murmured in unison, then lifted their stemware to clank them against the rim of Kol's. The ping of crystal echoed in the room. Together, they drained their first glass of champagne as a married trio.

"Now for some fun..." Kol set his glass aside and plucked a long, penis-shaped vibrator out of the basket. "But not to worry," he grinned boyishly, twisting the end so that it leapt into a whirring song. "They're all waterproof."

"That's handy." Mitch laid his arms along the edge of the tub. His gaze drifted to the movie when one man started sucking the other's cock. Still holding his empty wineglass, he nodded his approval, twirling the stem between his thumb and forefinger.

Watching Mitch study the porn flick with an approving eye stirred Kiona's libido with wicked heat. She let out an exaggerated sigh, but cut the sound off abruptly when Kol dipped the toy into the chocolate and held it to her mouth. "Go ahead, babe, eat my cock."

She giggled. "Your cock?"

"Make that our cock." Waiting expectantly, he arched one dark eyebrow. "Go ahead, lick it off. Don't want to get anything sticky in the water, now do we?"

"Mmm," was all Mitch could contribute to that as his lust-filled gaze shifted from the TV to Kiona and Kol. Obviously enjoying the show, he poured himself another glassful of bubbly, then sipped leisurely as he splashed some into their glasses, as well.

The image Kol's words conjured up caused something warm and gooey to settle in her womb. She opened her mouth, locking her eyes on Kol's, and let him slide the chocolate-dipped, quivering faux-cock into her mouth. The flavor of sweet cocoa melted on her tongue, oozing along her now chattering teeth and inside her cheeks. She sucked and swirled her tongue around the vibrating bulk, and knowing they watched her, as if she gave yet another man a blowjob, induced her to plunge her hand under the water and ease the ache between her legs. Her sex-lips were swollen, her clit as hard as a nugget. And her cunt—she slipped a finger slowly inside herself—was hot and moist, ready for a man. She moaned around the bulk of the toy, deep-throating it faster, excited when the two of them groaned at her uninhibited interplay.

"Goddamn, that's so fucking sexy," Mitch muttered, palming himself beneath the water.

"No shit." Kol dragged a finger along her jaw, down over her collarbone to one light-brown peak. He pinched and twisted it, making her breasts ache and lust ignite in her bloodstream.

Kiona whimpered around the bulk in her mouth while running the tip of her finger along her clitoral nub in a circular motion. Applying more pressure, lifting her hips in a dance beneath the water, she played with herself while sucking the toy, loving the sensation of flames burning hotter in her pussy and the water thrashing warm and bubbly over one sensitive nipple while Kol tortured the other.

They might as well shut off the porn movie. It was apparent she'd turned them both on and drawn their attention away from the screen. What a sense of extreme power this was, to tease them and know that soon, one of them—or maybe both—would be inside her, bringing her immense pleasure.

"Oh yeah, gotta agree with you there," Kol added, twisting the vibrator as he pushed it in and out of her mouth. He, too, couldn't stand the foreplay much longer. Kiona knew that by the familiar, stormy glaze in his dark eyes. He released her nipple, resumed stroking his shaft, and she watched enthralled as his eyelids fluttered shut on a grunt.

She couldn't take it anymore, and drew back so the vibrator fell from her mouth. Kol caught it, but didn't turn it off. "Mitch..." She desperately needed to be filled by a real cock. Leaning close to Mitch so that her mouth touched his, she murmured, "Make love to me. As man and wife."

His gaze shifted over her shoulder, as if to get Kol's permission. That look did something odd to her. She felt her heart swell with the first fluttering of deep affection for another man besides Kol. The thought stunned her.

He's your husband. You can let yourself love him if you want, while still loving Kol.

Did she want to? But she didn't have time to ponder her own question. It was as if uttering "man and wife" had sparked something in them both.

Kol shut off the vibrator, rose, and leaned over to pluck a small sample tube of flavored lubrication oil from the basket. "You heard the woman. Make love to her." Kol's command was thick with arousal. He watched with heavy-lidded eyes as Mitch obeyed, positioning his big body so that he returned to that kneeling position between Kiona's legs.

"No arguments here," Mitch murmured, stabbing his wet hand into her hair, angling her face up so he could kiss her again. "I want nothing more than to make love to my wife." The kiss didn't last long. He tore free of her mouth and moved across to her cheek in a tender path, up to her temple, then down to her ear.

She shivered at the sensation of his hot, wet tongue tracing the rim of her ear, and his teeth biting just short of painful on her earlobe. He pressed closer, his cock probing at her entrance beneath the water, his hips forcing her legs further apart. As if that weren't enough stimulation, she watched over Mitch's shoulder as Kol chose a purple toy. It was much thinner and shorter than the one she'd just sucked on, and reminded her of a mini space shuttle, its base thick in circumference, while its length tapered to no bigger around than his finger. No longer than about five inches, it was covered in tiny bubbled ridges. The last inch of the very tip was bent at a right angle, and Kiona almost fainted with excitement when she realized what Kol intended to do with it.

No doubt, it was a vibrator meant for deep anal stimulation. And in this case, she was certain Kol planned to use it on Mitch while Mitch made love to Kiona. The mental images that depraved thought conjured up in her head caused her breath to hitch in her windpipe. A warm flood of desire settled in her groin making her pussy throb and dampen.

Wicked, this was all so wicked. But she wouldn't give it up for anything in the world.

Mitch took a detour down to her breasts. He slid an arm around her waist and lifted her up so that her breasts broke the water's surface. She plopped her head back on the rim of the tub and screamed out her pleasure when his cock skimmed over her clitoris at the same moment he sucked one nipple into his mouth.

She heard the splash of water, but she didn't have the strength to open her eyes. Mitch's tongue played havoc on her areolas, first one, then the other, and back again. It was like a blazing rod branding her with its fiery heat, pulling and flickering so that those very flames back-lashed into her pussy and left her bucking her hips in search of his cock.

Mitch's head popped up on a groan. She finally opened her eyes and stared into his glazed, aqua pools. The man was stunning, a sex god in his own right, a man every woman in the world—and no doubt a lot of gay and bisexual men—lusted after, and yet here she was about to accept him into her core.

It was only when she dragged her gaze from his and peered over his shoulder, down his long tanned back, that she realized what had caused him to abruptly halt his adoring ministrations on her breasts.

Kol stood tall in the center of the tub behind Mitch. His muscles were well-defined and glistening, his body taut with excitement. He tossed aside the lubricant package, obviously having drained its greasy contents onto his hand, and had just reached down to caress Mitch's ass. She caught the faint essence of it. Strawberry.

Was Kol going to…?

"Ah, yeah, there you go. Relax," Kol rasped, and his arm made a small circular movement that told her he must be slickening up Mitch's anus.

She tried to catch her breath. Kiona hadn't seen anything quite as sexy and wanton as that in her entire life. If Mitch didn't get inside her soon, she feared she'd have a spontaneous orgasm without so much as a brush of a finger upon her clit.

Mitch shuddered. His eyes clamped shut, and he grasped the sides of the tub on either side of her. "Oh, Jesus. Oh fucking God, that feels so damn good. Mmm, yes, do it. Stick it in."

A wicked gleam entered Kol's eyes, the kind she recognized as the side of him that enjoyed it rough. She watched as his arm shifted again. If Mitch's sudden, strangled reaction was any indication, no doubt Kol had just slipped his finger inside Mitch's rectum to ready him for the toy. But he didn't stop there. He raised his other hand and whacked Mitch on the buttocks.

Water splattered all three of them, raining out across the tiled floor. Mitch's howl was definitely one of shocked pleasure. It was clear by the wide-eyed look that no one had ever spanked him before.

"That does it," Kiona panted. She wrapped her arms around Mitch's neck and her legs around his waist. "You two don't know how much you're turning me on. Make love to me. Now, before I faint from an overdose of horniness."

Kiona was totally delirious. She couldn't wait for a response from either one of them. Aligning herself, she let out a long, drawn-out sigh. Her eyes crossed and her eyelids closed as she clung to Mitch and slowly impaled herself with his enormous, granite-hard cock.

The incredible sensation of finally being filled and being able to clamp her muscles around girth was accompanied by the faint whir of the toy. She didn't need to look to know that

Kol teased Mitch's asshole with it. Mitch twitched, shoving himself deeper inside her. He groaned, his voice nothing but an animal's growl. Gradually, she felt the vibrations moving through him, into her, and she knew that meant Kol had penetrated Mitch to the hilt with the little vibrator.

"*'Û!* I'm so *pili lani*, and I haven't even fucked anyone yet," Kol groaned. Just then, a beam of moonlight filtered in from above and, combined with the flicker of candlelight, cast him in a dancing glow of silver and gold that made him appear godlike. She saw the torture on his face, so at odds with the proud erection jutting up from the nest of dark curls in his groin.

It was apparent Kol needed relief. But she didn't have to say a thing to Mitch. He was sympathetic, or rather, in need of Kol as much as Kol was in need of stimulation.

"Do it," Mitch growled through clenched teeth as he gripped the edge of the tub and drove into her again. Water splashed out of the tub. A gust of cool, salty air blew in from above making the candle flames dance and flicker, casting romantic shadows upon the tiled walls. "I'm ready."

Kiona blinked. He meant for Kol to... Heaven above, despite the breeze, could it get any hotter in here?

"Are you sure?" Kol asked, tossing aside the toy and leaning over Mitch's back, licking and nipping his shoulder.

"So damn sure," he replied, kissing Kiona's neck. "I know I'm going to blow as soon as you get inside me."

Kol's eyes rolled back in his head in mock ecstasy. He reached for a condom, tore open the package with his teeth. She smelled the faintest scent of latex, scrutinizing him as he rolled it down over his cock. She didn't think her pussy had ever been this wet. It was going to happen. Her fantasy was about to come true here in this huge Jacuzzi on her wedding night with two of the hottest men on Earth. She marveled at her patience, but she knew she was on the edge just as Mitch was.

Kol leaned over Mitch's back. Kiona made room for him by unhooking her legs from behind Mitch and planting her hands and feet on the underwater recliner instead. Mitch still held her up, but the movement caused his cock to jolt inside her, and little bursts of pleasure shot off in her belly, spreading out to bathe her entire body in sexual heat.

Kol reached around, massaging Kiona's breast. The nipple tightened, making her long to buck her body against Mitch's, but she knew she should hold still for what was to come.

"If you're sure…" Kol bit and sucked along Mitch's neck as he supported himself by propping one hand on the tub's rim next to Kiona's head.

"I'm sure, goddamn it. Do it. Now." Mitch's voice came out strained in a tone of impatience wrapped firmly by lust. He turned his head and softened his voice. "Sorry, but I'm so turned on, it's not going to take much." Their eyes met over Mitch's shoulder. Kol captured Mitch's mouth in a voracious, open-mouthed, tongue-dueling kiss that made Kiona's toes curl.

She felt the skim of Kol's hand as he wrapped his other arm around Mitch's narrow waist, preparing to hold him steady for entry.

Mitch broke free of the kiss and directed his attention on Kiona. "Ready, beautiful?"

"You have no idea," she said breathily.

His response was a nonverbal one that shook her world and had her gasping. He thrust forward, pulled out, then drove back in one last time before holding himself deep inside her canal.

Kol must have taken that as a cue to make his move. She stared into Kol's eyes and saw happiness and love like never before. Then the pressure built in her pussy when he aligned his cock and pushed forward, slowly, gently, inch by maddening inch. Mitch opened his eyes and held his breath, his body rigid. She saw ecstasy there, pure lust-filled need and a glow of pleasure that made her heart melt. Kol's gaze met hers over Mitch's shoulder, and she knew the very instant complete satisfaction seized them both.

Mitch panted, fighting to keep his eyes open. "Yes, oh God, yes..."

Kol's body twitched as he pushed slowly forward, every muscle taut with restraint. She watched the emotions flicker across his face and settle in his dark eyes. There was something beyond satisfaction there, almost a coming-home glow that completed the puzzle of Kol. He stood in the bubbling water, legs apart, hands gripping Mitch's hips, and his gaze never leaving hers. Fire built inside her loins as she started to move, stroking Mitch's cock with her slickness, forcing Kol deeper inside Mitch's ass.

With each of Kol's thrusts, she could feel a glorious pressure against her G-spot. The stimulation and timing of it all couldn't have been more perfect. As she and Kol gained a rhythm, gradually fucking Mitch hard and fast, they sang a trio of moans, hers high-pitched, theirs deep and all male. Beyond the rhythmic splash of the tub water and the orgasmic cries of the two men and the woman fucking on the video, she could hear the distant thrash of the ocean. Candlelight flickered across their handsome faces emphasizing the need that smoldered there. She could still smell the faint traces of the strawberry lubricant, but it was now overpowered by the potent aroma of sweat and arousal.

Her mouth watered for the flavor of her new husband. She wanted to taste Mitch when the rising orgasm washed over her. "Kiss me," she whispered, and he groaned his agreement, finding her mouth in a frantic search. His tongue dipped deep, parting her lips and teeth. He moaned into her mouth, following each of Kol's gentle penetrations with a swirl of his tongue around hers and a thrust of his cock into her soaked passage.

Her body hummed and bucked. She closed her eyes tight, the image of Kol entering Mitch emblazoned on the back of her eyelids. Mitch held her close, giving her limited freedom to explore. Her hands skimmed frantically over hard chests, strong shoulders, handsome, stubbled jaws.

She clamped her pussy around Mitch's cock and stroked him faster, grinding her clitoris across his pubic bone as she sucked his tongue deeper into her hungry mouth. Kiona's pussy had never been so wet, so totally filled. Elated, she sensed the outer edges of ecstasy reaching for her, starting first in her loins then spreading out to ripple through her legs and arms. There was no escaping it—no wish to. She surfed on the unbearable wave of climax, reaching for the final crest, amazed that it rose higher, hotter, faster than ever before. Kiona felt the surprising sting of tears in her closed eyes, the ceasing of her heartbeat, when the orgasm finally crashed over her in shattering disarray.

She was just about to tear her mouth free and scream her pleasure at the final wave of release when Mitch beat her to it. His head came up and he stared with glazed eyes at the wall behind her. "Oh, fuck, oh my fucking God..." His body shuddered on a deep groan at the very same moment Kol let out a rabid growl. His head was thrown back, his eyes tightly closed. Long, damp strands of his blue-black hair trailed down over his sculpted chest. Between the two gorgeous men, she had never seen anything so hot and sexy in all her life.

And they're both mine.

"Wow," she panted, plopping her head back onto the rim of the Jacuzzi. They held still, linked together as one. Amid Kol and Mitch's gasping agreements, she heard a thump and scrape above the tub. “What the...?”

“What’s wrong?”

She caught something out of the corner of her eye. Her gaze flicked to the window directly above them. “Shit!” Kiona shrieked, scrambling out of Mitch’s arms and yanking herself from his cock.

“What—?”

“On the roof. There’s someone there. I just saw a head peeping over the edge of the skylight window. A blonde head with pink streaks!”

Chapter Eleven

Anjelee held on for her dear freaking life. Her fingers ached like a mother fucker where she had them curled around the blunt edge of the gutter. Her heart beat so fast, she could hear it thumping in her head, as if someone held a drum to her ear and pounded like mad. She was nearly sick with the smell of their tropical-scented candles still lingering on the salty night breeze, and she wished like hell she could puke her guts out first before having to make a decision on how to get herself out of this perilous mess she'd suddenly found herself in.

With her body dangling from the rooftop, she prayed to any god who would listen that, if she decided to let go—*if* being the operative word—she would land safely on the veranda rather than on its precarious edge just below and to her right.

Holy crapsake alive, would a tumble down that rocky slope ever hurt like a bitch. All she needed was a broken leg or two. That would definitely make her flight back to L.A. tomorrow afternoon a drag and a half—or maybe delay it by several days. Not to mention it would probably put her out of commission long enough to keep her from earning the money she desperately required.

A muffled shriek sounded from deep in her throat when the gutter suddenly creaked and shifted, dropping a fraction of an inch lower. She peered through her upstretched arms and looked down the length of her body. There was a wash of cloud-covered moonlight casting a silvery glow over the damp stone floor of the terrace about eight feet or so below her shoes. The walls on the main level were slightly higher than most normal people's homes—damn all the rich sons of bitches in the world and their unnecessary extravagances. As if that wasn't enough, the roof was steeply vaulted to boot, so this particular section where she hung was up in a gabled peak, which left her a good distance yet to drop before landing smack-dab onto that hard, slippery stone patio... Or plummeting down over all those goddamn boulders that led to the angry sea below.

God help her, she didn't want to crack her noggin and drown. She'd been on the swim team in high school, so she could get around in water pretty well. But falling all that way would certainly injure her, which would make staying afloat—and remaining conscious—that much harder.

The Pacific breeze seemed to be picking up in velocity, and she tried not to think of something as disastrous as a sudden hurricane ripping her from the house and tossing her down the precipice and into the razor-sharp teeth of sharks. She could hear the taunting rush of the waves, the slap of the incoming tide against the narrow stretch of beach and its adjoining rocky drop-off. Her body swayed treacherously in the wind, and she tried her damnedest to keep from smacking her shoes against the wall and alerting them to her location. If she'd made as much noise as she thought she had, and they even knew someone was out here in the first place, that is.

Think, you dummy, before someone comes and finds you dangling here like a damn puppet on a string.

She drew in a shaky breath and tightened her grip, determined to figure this dilemma out. If she let go of her right hand, it might swing her body toward the left so she could avoid landing near the dangerous cliff edge. But did she have time to ponder the geometry of things?

Fuck no.

From inside, she could hear the faintest of voices and the subsequent slosh of bathwater. Was that alarm in their tones? Alarm, maybe, at the loud thunk she'd just made when she'd slipped off the fucking thatched roof?

Jesus Christ, what had she done to deserve this life-or-death situation?

The fact of the matter was there wasn't time to contemplate her pitfalls or her bad luck. All it would take was a quick heads-up phone call from Mitch Wulfrum to one of his guard dogs positioned around the perimeter of the property, and she'd be toast.

Burnt-to-a-crisp toast.

Luckily, she'd had the camera on its strap and anchored around her neck when she'd slipped. The weight of it currently bumped against her chest, and she realized she wasn't so unlucky after all. Every last one of those incriminating, extremely intimate pictures she'd just taken through the skylight window was worth a bank full of gold.

Oh yeah, the precious camera around her neck was her lifeline...as long as she survived.

As it turned out, she hadn't needed to use the key Heloki had provided her. Something about just letting herself into someone's house without knowing how many people were really in there, and where, had given her the paranoid willies. It wasn't like she was a professional criminal. Until now, she'd never done anything illegal in her life, and didn't have so much as a parking ticket listed in the motor vehicle database. Well, on second thought, she did have several speeding tickets on her driving record, but who the hell didn't?

So instead of waltzing in the front door—that had been an

idiotic plan anyway—she'd counted the remaining people before leaving the reception, hid in a copse of *loulu* palms near the road, and waited for the last person to leave. During the party, she'd spied the trellis she'd climbed up to get to the rooftop. It was positioned on the back of the house near the deck where the ceremony and reception had been held. But that was on the opposite end from the current gallery she swung above, so no help there. Unless she could somehow pull herself back up, scale across the roof, and then descend safely back down from there? It had been the original plan, of course—not the falling, but the going back the way she'd come—yet it seemed an awfully far distance now that she no longer had her footing.

Well, she worked out five times a week. She could do a chin-up, no problem, and if the damn gutter would just hold still, she could probably swing herself back up onto the roof if she really tried. So Anjelee inhaled, closed her eyes, and curled her fingers tighter around the rim of the gutter. Flexing every muscle in her arms and hands, she raised her knees and pulled herself up with all her strength.

Creak.

Anjelee gasped when the gutter shifted slightly in response to her upward movement. She paused, lowered herself carefully back down, and swallowed a dry lump in her throat. "Goddamn, what a cheap-assed piece of crap for such a rich man," she muttered under her breath.

She hung there immobile for a moment, holding her breath, only letting it out when she was certain the gutter wouldn't have some sort of delayed reaction and finish separating from the eaves.

"So much for that plan."

There were no choices left. Even though her stomach churned with terror, she forced herself to look down again. Not down along that scary, rocky plunge, but at the terrace surface to her left. Well, she decided, back to the letting-go-of-the-right-hand-in-order-to-swing-left strategy.

Which petrified the fucking piss out of her.

"Pull yourself together and concentrate, hun," she whispered to herself. Anjelee narrowed her eyes, forcing her brain into overdrive. She could imagine—no, almost feel—the synapsing and electrical activity firing off hot and all zappy inside her skull.

"Okay, so here's the deal, self" she muttered, knowing the overdrive had resulted in something just short of panic rather than the composed problem-solving she so needed. "No one seems to be about yet, and the noises inside have died down, therefore, you most likely have time."

But not all fucking night. That any idiot could figure out. She had to either let go now and risk breaking a few bones, or try Plan B. Or was it Plan C?

She'd begun to lose track, but who really gave a shit which one it was? All she wanted was to get the hell out of there before they caught her, hauled her off to jail for trespassing, and confiscated her precious camera. With all the shocking, rumor-confirming shots she'd just taken of the movie star in his little rub-a-dub-dub bathtub threesome, and all that homosexual activity she'd just captured on film—whew, and had that ever made her heart race—holy shit on a damn stick, was she ever going to be worth a fortune!

Anjelee didn't even want to think about the fact that just watching them do all that touching and kissing and naughty foreign sex moves had made her breathless and her pulse hammer just a bit too quickly.

No, she had much more important matters to attend to than to analyze her body's peculiar reaction to that amazing aerial view she'd had of such depravity. Later. Maybe she'd lie on Freud's little couch and analyze herself later, but Jesus, not now. Before she took the time to do or think about anything else, she first and foremost had to get the hell down from here. She had a lot more to live for now than she'd had just an hour ago, which meant in order to reap her rewards, she'd have to take a chance and just fucking jump.

Her entire body trembled with fear and exhaustion. What she wouldn't give for a damn Valium right about now. She didn't know how much longer she could hold on. Her arms and fingers were beginning to go numb. And crap, she was starting to get dizzy from all the nervous tension jumbling her brain up in knots and her stomach into chaotic rumbles.

Time to go, you pussy.

"One...two..." She made herself look down, held her breath. "Three." Finally, she opened the grip on her right hand and let it slip. "Mmmm," she groaned as her body swung sharply left. And then she released her left-hand hold.

It seemed she fell for hours before she hit with an umph. Her right foot hit first, but slipped backwards out from under her. The force promptly brought her down onto that knee, and the abrupt pain that shot through her leg had her suppressing a howl. The camera knocked hard against her chest—*shit, please don't let it be broken*—but in the next flash, she managed all at once to bite her tongue, reach down, and break the rest of her fall with both hands.

Ignoring the throbbing in her knee, Anjelee remained crouched. She dragged in a lungful of moist air and glanced around the huge terrace. She saw no one, so she rose and started to limp toward the low wall that prefaced the rocky decline below.

Up the shore to the right, she caught sight of a giant of a

man—most likely one of the hired bodyguards—running like a marathon sprinter toward the house, his footsteps pounding on the packed sand. She stopped in mid-step, perking her ears, her pulse pounding painfully, her breath ragged. Inside the house, shouts rang out, lights flipped on, drowning her in a sudden white glow. She heard the click of a lock on a sliding door nearby and hobbled back to the house. Flattening her body against the wall, she waited, planning, knowing she wouldn't be there for long. Her time was nearly up.

It's now or never, you idiot. Run! Get the hell out of here!

Gripping the camera securely against her chest, Anjelee dashed for the stone wall. She climbed over its low height and scaled the boulders like a wounded mountain lioness being tracked by hunters. Grimacing as throbbing pain shot through her knee, Anjelee pressed on, climbing downward toward the beach in the direction away from the approaching guard. And as she went, she prayed like a bitch that any others stationed on the premises hadn't been alerted in time to cross paths with her.

Her vehicle was parked a half-mile up the road. But what a victorious journey it would be if she reached it without discovery. Then it would be time to implement her next plan, one that most likely would not include Heloki 'Alohi as he'd hoped.

Oh no. Now that she'd hit the jackpot with all those unexpected, juicy shots, she had a cleverer strategy than to just earn a few measly bucks by turning the photos over to the sugar-cane tycoon.

If she kept the pictures herself and offered them to the movie star for a price, Anjelee would be filthy rich. And all her horrible troubles would finally be over.

With a groan of regret, Jager dragged himself out of an erotic dream at the buzz of his cell phone. He clawed his way through the lingering fog, popped one eye open, and snatched the offending object from the hotel bedside table. How could one small piece of electronic equipment be so damned loud and bright all at the same time?

Focusing on the little window, he saw that the call was coming from his own beachside house. Shit, it must be Mitch or Kiona. What now? He added a grumble, swung his legs over the side of the bed, and flipped open the phone.

"Jager here," he barked. "And at—" he flicked a gaze toward the digital alarm clock, "—two a.m.?"

"One forty-five," came Mitch's snarl, which made Jager's irritation level rise all the more.

"It's your damn wedding night, for Christ's sake, not to mention I was sleeping like a baby. This better be good."

"Goddamn it, it's not good at all, believe me," Mitch growled, instantly churning Jager's stomach with dread. "What the fuck kind of photographer did you hire, anyway?"

And churning some more.

"What..." *God, please don't tell me that little bitch caused some trouble.* He shot to his feet, readjusting the hard-on tenting his boxers. "What're you talking about? What'd she do? You mean she's still there?"

"No, she's long gone. But she was here. Apparently, she stayed long after everyone else left."

No...

"And I'll tell you what the hell happened, all right. The three of us, we were...enjoying our wedding night, like anybody just married would be doing. Kiona just happened to look up, and she swore she saw someone's head peeping over the edge of the skylight above the tub. Then, guess what, pal?"

"I, uh, don't—"

"Uh-huh, we heard a loud scrape and thump noise. Had to haul my naked ass soaking-wet from the Jacuzzi tub, locate my phone, and alert Larson. Seems after my call, Larson ran up the beach and spotted a woman with long blonde hair running up the road."

Jager gulped down a knot of dismay. "Blonde?"

"Yeah, blonde…with goddamn pink stripes."

Aw, fuck.

"Pink stripes?" Jager didn't know what else to say but to echo Mitch's angry words. Already Jager could picture his hands closed around Anjelee's scrawny little neck, never mind the fact she was the one he'd just been screwing in his dream. Fuck that. It was just a damn dream. In reality, he'd kill the conniving little twit before he'd ever slide his cock between her legs.

"Yep, just like that photographer chick you hired for Heloki. Remember? Anjelee whoever." Mitch forced out an exaggerated breath. The phone shifted. "And guess what else?" he added with a jaw-clamped growl.

"What?"

"I suddenly remembered where I'd seen her."

Jager's head fell back. *Fuck.* He closed his eyes, fantasizing about squeezing Anjelee's little neck until her gorgeous green cat-eyes popped from their sockets. "You did? Where?"

"Her picture was in *Superstars* a few months back. As a reporter. One of those little side boxes crediting the writer. Perched right next to the ball-busting feature article she did on Randy McConnell and the torrid affair he'd had behind his wife's back. It published the day before his new movie hit theatres. The movie tanked, by the way."

"Oh, her." What else could he say? That he'd already known who she was? That he was responsible for this whole mess? *Hell no.*

"So help me, Jager, if that woman isn't apprehended, my whole career's going to tank just like Randy's movie."

"Why? What makes you think so? Did she do or say something?" As if he didn't already know.

"Did she do something?" he repeated incredulously. "You're damn right she did. She climbed on your fucking roof, and I'm pretty sure—no, make that damn sure—she saw us. All three of us. Naked. Going at it, for Christ's sake. Even if she didn't have her damn camera with her, she has eyes, a mouth, a memory, and a journalism connection that could completely ruin me. The fact she went to all that trouble to climb on the damn roof and spy tells me you can bet your precious Mercedes this'll be in next week's tabloids. Christ, what the fuck am I going to do?"

"Uh..." Jager whistled for lack of a better response. "I take it you didn't call the police?"

"Hell no! Why would I do such a stupid-assed thing? The media'd be all over it in minutes."

"Yeah, yeah. Right. Good thing you didn't." He inhaled, held the hot air in his lungs until they ached, then slowly let out a shaky breath. "Okay, let me think..."

"Well, you better think fast, because she's got a huge head start. Larson lost her."

Shit, shit, shit.

"Okay, all right—"

"It's not all right, goddamn it!"

Jager winced, hearing Mitch's pissiness loud and clear. "I

know, I know, that's not what I meant." He wedged the phone between his jaw and shoulder, and jammed his legs into a pair of jeans. "Look, calm down, I'll see what I can do. I know where Heloki put her up. I'll head over there and confront her, and confiscate her camera. Don't worry, I'll— Hold on, someone's pounding on the damn door."

"Fuck that. Tell them to get lost. You need to get your ass over there right this minute and get that camera from her before she skips the islands and heads back to the mainland. Tell her I'll pay her five grand, ten, hell, I don't care how much. Just get the fucking camera from her and make her sign some sort of gag agreement." He groaned. "Holy shit, I can't believe this. Jesus, she was on the damn roof watching us. Didn't you do some sort of background check on her?"

"I...well..." *Yes, I did. But only after it was too late.* He crossed to the door and yanked it open. And there she stood. "Um, you're not going to believe this, but it looks like she's here."

"What? Who?"

"Anjelee. She just showed up at my hotel suite."

Anjelee tilted her head and winked at him. Soft light from the hallway spilled in around her, outlining her curves and putting her face in bedroom-like shadows.

"You're kidding me. Put that fucking bitch on the phone right now," Mitch said through gritted teeth.

"No. No, let me handle this." Jager flipped a switch by the door, and a small desk lamp illuminated one corner of the suite near the sitting area.

Anjelee leaned against the doorjamb, her long hair spilling down over her small breasts, and stretched lazily, adding a fake yawn for effect, no doubt. She sent him a smirk of satisfaction, lifting a slim shoulder as if to say, "Do you blame me?" It reminded him of a purring cat who'd just caught the fattest rat in the alley.

Without taking his wary gaze from her, Jager's pulse hammered with ire as he continued to speak to Mitch. "Believe me, I'll take care of it. Call you back, okay?"

"You better call me right back. And with good news, goddamn it, or you're fired," Mitch snarled before the line went dead.

Jager punched the disconnect button even as he watched her eyelids flutter with mock innocence. "Something wrong, Jager?"

"Don't you have more important things to do," he asked, tossing the phone onto a nearby table, "than to spy on unsuspecting, harmless people?"

A brief flash of something almost sorrowful lit up her eyes. But it was gone so quickly, he was certain he'd imagined it.

"Yeah, actually, I do." She breezed past him, leaving behind the fresh scent of the ocean entwined with her sporty yet feminine perfume. "Which is why I'm here."

Jager closed the door and turned to face her, arms crossed. "All right, where is it?"

"Where is what?" Anjelee asked in a mocking, sing-song voice. She strolled her way around the room, trailing a finger across furniture.

"You know damn well what. Your camera."

She plopped down into a plush chair near the patio door and propped her feet up on the round table meant for dining-in with room service. "In a very safe place." Her gaze raked him from his bare feet to his dull-throbbing head. But her eyes suddenly dropped. And zoned daringly in on his hard-on.

She may as well have closed her palm around him. He

hadn't thought to zip up his pants before answering the door, and knowing she boldly perused the head of his cock—which barely peeped over the elastic of his boxers—was like sex itself.

Jesus Christ and Mary, get back to the current crisis.

He thrust a hand through his short-cropped hair. "What's on it? What sorts of shots did you get?"

The corners of her plump little mouth tipped up. He wondered what it would feel like to plant the tip of his finger into one of the deep dimples that just then emerged on her cheeks.

"All kinds of kinky stuff. For instance, that rumor about him being gay?" She let out an unladylike snort. "Um, believe me, it's nooo rumor. As if you didn't already have knowledge of that particular little tidbit."

"Look, I don't know what you're trying to prove, or what it is that you really want, but I gotta say you are one deceitful, malicious little cunt if you think you can come here and—"

Her feet hit the floor. "Fuck you." The cunning smile vanished, and he fielded a brief sense of regret when the dimples went with it.

"Ah, so is that what you're after? To fuck me? Because if it is..." He made a show of gripping the waistband of his jeans as if he fully intended to whip them off.

"No."

"No?" He held out his hands, shrugged. "Could have fooled me."

She leaned forward, slapped her hands onto her thighs, and fisted them in the white pants she'd worn to the wedding. He noted a tear in her right knee with a splotch of red soaking the edges of the ragged hole. Maybe earned during her little trespassing act? Well, at the moment, he didn't give a damn how it had gotten there. Still, his gaze moved up and over her thin build, took in the fragile, feminine shoulders. The curves of her small breasts were outlined in the shimmery-blue, low-cut camisole shirt she wore, and even though he tried to look away, he couldn't help but notice the pebbles of her taut nipples straining against the thin fabric.

"Look, you asshole, it seems besides harboring some arrogant, idiotic notion that I've got the hots for you—which I don't—you're also forgetting one minor detail. I'm the one in the driver's seat," she hissed through clenched teeth, her eyes narrowed to slits. "So you just shut the hell up, you hear me? And all your immature name-calling crap, by the way, isn't scoring you any points with me, you goddamn prick."

That did it. His rage had officially reached a level he'd never experienced before. His face burned like Hades, and his hammering heart seemed to have taken up residence in his tight throat. He could almost taste the bitter flavor of his fury, could nearly smell its acrid odor fuming up to suffocate him.

Hands quaking like a son of a bitch, he just couldn't help himself. Jager did what he supposed any man in this particular she-devil's life did when she pissed him off. He stalked over and jerked her up out of the chair. Her forearm felt so small and fragile in his grip, he instantly readjusted his hold, loosening his fingers. But he didn't let her go. Oh, no, he wasn't going to let the little shrew out of his sight until he had his hands on her camera, and her written promise she'd keep her spewing, plump mouth shut. Yes, it would be easy to snap her bone, but he wouldn't. Jager wasn't an abuser by nature. At the moment, he might be a bully for the first time in his life, but he'd never lay a hand on anyone, especially not a woman.

Oh, but you can bet your ass I feel like laying a hand or two on this one.

With his nose mere centimeters from hers, he drilled his gaze into her defiant, glittering one. He could smell her fiery scent, and goddamn if she didn't make his cock twitch and start to ache with the need to sink into her depths and—fuck that. This was madness.

It was career suicide.

"Let go of me, you sonofabitch." She tried to wrench her arm free, but he tightened his hold enough to prevent it. He had to admit, even while being overpowered by a man, the woman had more balls than most men he knew.

"Do you know just how much I'd love to close my hands around that skinny little neck of yours and squeeze the life out of you for this? Huh? Do you?" He shook her, and her head bobbled around before she got control of it. "Watch your big, beautiful eyes bulging from their sockets?"

"I'm starting to understand just how much." Anjelee swallowed and her gaze wavered. It was all a vague gesture of uncertainty he hadn't expected to see so soon. But it didn't last long. She abruptly changed tactics.

Her knee came up and plowed him between the legs.

Jager let out an umph of surprise and doubled over in mind-blowing pain. He let go of her arm in the process, and cupped his crotch with both hands. Nausea assailed him. His sac was on fire, scorching so intensely, his eyes went cross and the room spun in circles around him. He stumbled to the bed and collapsed, curling into a fetal position, sweat beading on his brow.

"You...bitch," he managed to roar between pants and groans. "Not only will you...have trespassing and extortion on your prison record...but assault too."

Though he had a hard time keeping his eyes open, he noted that she crossed her arms, a sign of bravery that, if he weren't all balled up in agony at the moment, he might have admired.

"Uh-uh, I don't think so. I've got all my bases covered, pal."

He groaned as his stomach threatened to let loose of all that beer he'd drunk at the wedding. "What the fuck's that...supposed to mean?"

"Emailed myself copies of the photos." As an afterthought, she added a shrug.

Goddamn mother fuckin' son of a bitch.

"You expect me to believe that?" he moaned, attempting to sit up. *Oh, my poor balls, my poor balls, my poor balls.* He breathed in, out. "I just hung up with Mitch. You couldn't have left there fifteen minutes ago. No time to go Internet surfing. No cafes open this time of night, either."

She giggled. "Laptop's in my rental car. Got a satellite Internet subscription with one of those thingies you slide into your computer to connect. After I easily got away from Mitch's incompetent bodyguard thugs, I fired up my hard drive, slipped the camera's chip in, and *voila*, downloaded them all—every last naughty one of them—to My Pictures. A few more little clicks and I had them all zipped into a tidy little file and sent them off through cyberspace to myself. They're sitting in my inbox as we speak."

No, no, no, no, no!

Jager finally dragged himself up to a full sitting position and dropped his head into his shaking hands. He did his best not to reach down and cradle his poor throbbing sac. He was going to throw up, he just knew it. "So? You emailed pictures to yourself." Time to use a bit of reverse psychology. "I hardly think that's going to save you from any legal action. Or from disappearing off the face of the earth."

She sat down next to him and leaned her head on his shoulder. The spiteful, sarcastic move made him cringe, but he tried to play the game her way for now. And he forced himself to breathe lightly so as not to inhale too much of her provocative scent.

"Ah, Jager, Jager, Jager." She sighed and clucked her tongue, rubbing a hand in a circle over his back. He attempted to overlook the fact that it caused goose bumps to shimmy up his spine and made him partially forget the painful swelling of his scrotum. But attempted, he was beginning to realize, didn't always work where this woman was concerned.

"You see, I have this safe-deposit box at a certain bank in California." Anjelee patted his back, rubbed again. She tossed her head in a show of arrogance, and he got a whiff of her apple shampoo.

"One of my siblings has a copy of the key," she went on in a baby tone one might use to relate a nursery tale to a child. "She doesn't know what it goes to or where the bank is located, but—" she thrust up a finger, "—she has instructions that, in the event of my death or disappearance, or even incarceration or attempted prosecution, she's to go to my lawyer and obtain written instructions on where to go to use the key. See, there's a certain...document I've left there in that little safety deposit box. My lawyer has his own instructions as well. Those include to never turn the document over to dear old sis...unless any or all of the aforementioned circumstances have come, shall we say, to light? So...wanna guess what's in that important document?"

Mother fucker.

This was a son-of-a-bitching career nightmare for both Mitch and Jager. He'd never been so pissed off in all his life, and he briefly wondered if Hawaii carried the death penalty, or life sentencing for murderers. But he had to get a grip. He couldn't let this happen. He shoved her away and got to his feet, ignoring the excruciating throbbing in his balls. His legs were shaky, and his stomach continued to hurl, but he forced himself to focus on the pretty painted face staring mockingly up at him.

"Let me guess. Email logins and passwords, maybe?"

She leapt to her feet and clapped like an elated child. Her voice bubbled with glee, and when she smiled, he caught a flicker of the little silver ball on her tongue. "Yes, excellent guess! And permission to sell any of my existing photographs, including the new ones now in my email box or already on my hard drive, to any publication in the entire world! Isn't that just so clever?"

His cock had gone completely flaccid, more so from her words than from her assault. He disregarded it—had his dick really responded to her in his dream?—and planted his hands on his hips, snaring her with what he hoped was an intimidating, nasty look. "You bitch. Why are you doing this? Do you realize I could lose Mitch Wulfrum as a client over this?"

And holy shit, he didn't even want to think about what it could do to Mitch and Kiona's careers.

Anjelee merely arched a brow, as if she hadn't thought of that—which he didn't believe for one second—but still didn't give a shit one way or the other.

"Are you doing it for money? Is that it?"

She shrugged. "Among other things."

"You know something?"

"Hmm?"

"You're pathetic."

"Thank you," she replied sweetly, and those damned dimples emerged again.

"How much, goddamn it. How much do want?"

"Enough to keep the boogeyman away."

Jager rolled his eyes. "What, are you like five years old?"

"No, thirty-one, as a matter of fact."

Damn, he'd never have guessed that. The little hellcat didn't look a day over twenty-one. He sighed and spoke through clenched teeth. "I'm going to ask you one more time before I resort to choking the life out of you. How much money to get the camera and now your laptop, see that you delete the email in your inbox, and keep that fat little mouth of yours shut forever?"

"Hmm, excellent question. Now let me see..." She fixed her twinkling gaze somewhere over his shoulder while tapping her claw-tipped finger against her chin. "About...oh, say, fifty thousand?"

"What?"

"I said fifty thousand. Not one penny less." Her voice went hard. No more joking sarcasm. It was apparently time to get down to business.

"You're crazy. There's no way in hell—"

She spun and marched to the door, her small little ass jiggling as she went. "Fine. Your choice. I can probably get even more for them somewhere else, anyway."

"Wait. Where are you going?"

"To call *Superstars* and let them know I have a story and supporting pictures that'll make their subscriptions and sales on the stands skyrocket."

He raced to the door and whirled her around. "I said wait, goddamn it."

She canted her head and blinked with disparaging innocence. "What for? It seems you've made your choice."

"No, no, you win. Fifty thousand it is." He scrubbed his

face, narrowed his gaze on her. Mitch was a millionaire, but holy crap, was he ever gonna freak. “But you have to hand over the laptop and camera, let me witness you deleting the email account, and then sign a legal agreement to keep your mouth shut—no future articles, no selling your story on the side, nothing. Agreed?”

Anjelee wrinkled her nose and made a play of thinking hard for a few seconds. She finally nodded. “Sure. Agreed. What an excellent idea.”

Chapter Twelve

"I still can't believe I paid that bitch *fifty* thousand," Mitch muttered.

At an exhausting four a.m., after resisting one final urge to choke Anjelee, Jager had uttered an eager farewell and driven to his house to meet Mitch. He pushed past him now, made his way into the living room, and popped open his briefcase on the coffee table. "You said whatever it took. And that was her bottom dollar. It's done."

Mitch collapsed next to Jager onto the leather sofa. "Jesus Christ. It's still making me nauseous."

"Yeah, I know." Jager sat down carefully, wincing at the tenderness between his legs, and briefly thought how Mitch didn't know the meaning of the word nausea. He drew out his laptop, fired it up, and shuffled through a stack of papers inside the briefcase. He had Anjelee's PC in his car and would deal with it later—including combing every inch of her hard drive for any photos she'd missed pointing out to him, or any incriminating files. She'd also turned over the login information to her email box, which had allowed Jager to get in and delete the account right after she'd left his hotel with dollar signs in her eyes and the money already electronically transferred into her account. Oh, he was on to her, all right, the vixen. He could just see her racing over to the business center in her hotel, logging onto her email account, and restoring the deleted file. But nope. Wasn't going to happen, not if Jager could help it. Deleting the account had solved that mess before she could even think to implement another catastrophe.

There was no need to mention to Mitch she'd gone two steps further in her devious plan by downloading photos and emailing them to herself. Mitch needed to get on with his wedding celebration and take time to relax and enjoy himself while he could with his new partners. His next movie was scheduled to start filming soon. No, no need to add to his worries. Jager had it covered for now.

But still, what a fucking mess it had all been.

"What about the camera?" Mitch propped his elbows on his knees and shot Jager a sidelong, wary look. Maybe he didn't completely trust Jager to handle his affairs anymore, but from here on out, Jager would prove to him he was capable of continuing the job.

"Got it right here, along with a signed agreement to keep her mouth shut." Jager dug the camera out of an inside briefcase pocket, held it up along with the adapter cord for uploading photos, the CD, and the battery charger. "All the wedding pictures are there, too. It's digital, so just load this software onto your desktop when you get back to California. Or feel free to load them here on my desktop too if you want to take a look, then just delete them off the hard drive before you go. At least the incriminating ones."

"Nah. We'll just look at them this way for now." Mitch had the camera on, and was scrolling through the shots on the little screen. He arrived at one that depicted him in a hot and naked clench with Kol. His face went hot-pink. "Shit, these would have caused some damage, all right." He switched the equipment off and let out a long, breathy sigh. "Thank God you got her to agree to everything."

You have no idea how much I'm *thanking God.*

"No kidding. Anyway," Jager said, in a rush to get this all over with, "then you connect this cord from camera to computer. Snapshots'll upload in an instant."

"Mmm, handy," Mitch mumbled, going back to fiddling with dials and buttons.

"Yeah. So everything's taken care of, even the funds transfer." He saw that his laptop had almost finished connecting to the wireless Internet. While he waited, he handed Mitch a manila envelope containing the gag document Anjelee has signed. "Your copy of the agreement."

Jager's own copies also contained yet another paper stating she'd voluntarily turned over the laptop and the camera to him. He'd thought that to be the best way to prevent her from coming back later and trying to have him arrested for theft. Oh yeah, he could easily see Anjelee Montrose turning the tables on him and seeing him put behind bars for something he hadn't done. The blackmailing bitch.

Jager went on as he put fingers to keyboard and logged onto Mitch's personal bank account. "I think this electronic transfer was the wisest way to conduct the transaction. No check or signature by you for her future forgery use, which I wouldn't put past the little sneak. I figured sending it from your personal account to hers, and labeling it as payment for wedding photography services, or something to that effect, in the comments section would be best. That way, there'd also be no tax questions in the future like there would be if the money was to come from PR or marketing funds."

The bank page popped up on the screen. Jager turned the laptop toward Mitch to show him where he'd already transferred the fifty grand from Mitch's account to Anjelee's.

Jager rifled through more papers and located one of their usual authorization-of-funds-transfers forms used between them when Jager conducted Mitch's PR business. He slid the paper with a pen onto the coffee table. "Just sign your approval of the transfer and I'll be on my way."

"I can't believe this." Mitch snatched up the pen, scanned the document, and scrawled his signature on the line.

"I know." Jager tore off Mitch's copy, slipped it into the manila envelope, and stuffed the duplicate into his briefcase. "I'm sorry the three of you had to go through all that. But it looks like it's handled now, so you can head out on your honeymoon without any worries. Everyone doing okay?"

Mitch got to his feet. He wore a navy blue silk robe knotted at the waist, looking every bit the handsome, masculine movie star. He jabbed a thumb over his shoulder. "They're sleeping. It's been a long night."

You have no idea.

Jager shut down the computer and gathered his things. He had to admit he'd secretly looked through all the pictures. He'd known Mitch's hush-hush sexual preferences since day one, but seeing it happening in the flesh, so to speak, had been a stunning experience. Before this week, Jager never would have guessed Kol to go along with homosexual activities. But apparently, after their little private trio marriage ceremony Jager had witnessed, and now the obvious proof of it in pictures, there was no denying Kol definitely had a thing for the male gender too. Obviously, Jager hadn't known Kol well enough, but now that he'd seen it all in action, it made sense, and they all seemed to fit so well together.

Kiona's obvious acceptance and enjoyment in the photos hadn't surprised him one bit, either. She was a sexual creature by nature, and though he'd had to avert his scrutiny from her nakedness—she was like a sister to him, for Christ's sake—Jager had thought how happy and fulfilled she'd looked in the shots.

He rose, shook Mitch's hand. "Well, I'm glad it all worked out in the end."

Mitch blew out a breath and pumped Jager's hand. "You can say that again."

"Yeah, I was worried for a bit there, I admit, but we're all good now." He retrieved his briefcase and laptop and turned, making his way to the front door.

Mitch followed. "Uh, you don't think she let anything out to Heloki, do you?"

Jager turned to face Mitch. He shook his head, silently praying to all the gods in the universe that Anjelee wouldn't breach their contract. "If you read the agreement she signed, you'll see I specifically named Heloki as off limits too. She swore not to reveal any of it to him, or anyone for that matter."

"Kiona'll be relieved to hear that. He's supposed to come by sometime today to sign her trust fund over to her."

Jager pulled open the door, grinned. "Yeah, I know. Remember? Besides your need to cover up those rumors, that trust fund's partially responsible for starting this whole huge ball rolling."

Mitch snickered. "Yeah, I suppose in that respect, I should be thankful to Heloki." His smile faded. He searched Jager's eyes. "I'm happy with them, really happy. Thanks, Jager."

"No problem. Have a great honeymoon." He stepped out onto the front porch, drew in the sultry night air scented by ginger and hibiscus, and spun to face Mitch again. "And like I mentioned last week, remember the cabin and the whole island I reserved for you is extensively private. Everyone who's rented it is close-mouthed about its location and existence. It's got acres and acres of lush rain forest, a long stretch of concealed beach and lagoon, and a fully equipped and stocked house. Not to mention the island is never booked by more than one guest at a time."

"I know, sounds great. We can't wait to get there."

"Lots of my clients reserve it when they need to get away without worry of the media prying—even stars as famous as you. So you won't have to worry about being photographed or spied on while you're swimming or walking the beach or whatever. Enjoy your freedom while you can."

"Will do. Thanks, man." Mitch smiled, and Jager thought for the first time since he'd known him, it was a genuine, relaxed expression.

"You're welcome. Now go back to bed." Jager heard the door close behind him as he made his way down the front steps to his car.

The sun wasn't up yet, and the sky was still a black expanse speckled by white diamonds. The moon had been brighter earlier that night, but now it hung low and dull near the craggy, palm-lined horizon. He caught that scent of ginger again, this time sharp and heady...

Like her.

No. He wasn't going to go there, not ever. He climbed into his expensive rental sedan and started the engine.

Okay, he would admit there was something fascinating about her. She could even be classified as beautiful...in her own impish way. She smelled like the kinkiest of sex, and he imagined she probably tasted like sin. But she'd schemed and extorted and even hit him below the belt in more ways than one. The woman was trouble with a capital T. She'd nearly cost him one of his biggest clients, perhaps two if he included Heloki, and she'd been ballsy enough to steal fifty thousand dollars without even blinking an eye.

No, not the woman for him. Not at all. Never, ever.

Good fucking riddance.

Jager was just getting ready to slide the gearshift into reverse when he glanced up and saw a star shoot across the pre-dawn sky. Its white fire blazed in a diagonal path across his vision, and he could swear he saw faint streaks of pink in the long tail. He blinked, but the pink disappeared. In a split second, the whole damn star was gone leaving only the expanse of dark ocean below it, and darker space above. Mysterious and intriguing.

Like Anjelee.

"Yeah, good riddance," he said aloud this time. Jager raced the engine and shot out of the driveway. He followed the ribbon of the coast road, thanking that lucky shooting star she was out of his life for good.

Anjelee crisscrossed the strap of the overnight bag across her chest. Limping down the hotel hallway—her knee still hurt like hell, but it had been worth it—she rolled her suitcase behind her. It was almost six a.m. and she'd been successful in rebooking an earlier flight.

It was time to go home.

She punched the elevator button, soaring on elation. Finally, things would calm down! She now had the money to fix all her problems in her sorry life back in California. Stepping into the elevator, she let her mind wander, thinking of the family she'd left behind, of all their bad luck and how she would now be able to come to their rescue. No more piled up bills, no more collection agencies, no more scrimping for crumbs.

Maybe life *would* go on after all.

"God, I'm so glad I came here!" The bell sounded, indicating she'd arrived on the ground level. She shot out of the elevator, grumbling when her cell phone buzzed on her hip. Stopping in the main corridor, she snatched it off her belt and glanced at the caller ID.

"Shit, it's Heloki."

Maybe she should ignore it? She didn't owe him a thing. She'd taken and delivered wedding pictures as instructed—minus the incriminating ones—already having attached and emailed them to Heloki well before visiting Jager and scoring that hefty supplement from Wulfrum. True, the first check Heloki had given her was more than enough to cover her fee for the regular, innocent wedding shots. But hadn't it been an unusual wedding in that it was celebrity in nature? Hadn't she dropped all her obligations back home and come running as soon as Jager had called and offered her the job for Heloki? Besides, what was wrong with getting money from both Heloki and Mitch? God knew she needed every penny, and they sure could spare it. And Heloki would never know about the hush-money she'd accepted from Mitch...

Probably. Hopefully.

The phone continued to ring. Anjelee pondered answering it, still unable to believe her good fortune. She knew she wouldn't be receiving any more money from Heloki simply because, due to the agreement she'd signed with Jager, she'd withheld the juicy photos Heloki had been after. They would have netted her the other half and a possible bonus from him, but fifty thousand clearly outnumbered Heloki's smaller payment. Little did Heloki know she now could do without his filthy money because the star had outbid him. Yep, his payment had been raised fivefold by Wulfrum.

And Anjelee may not be a genius, but she knew the difference between the two amounts of money would be life-altering for her. It hadn't taken a mastermind to decide which offer to go with.

Besides, there had been no signed agreement between Anjelee and Heloki like there'd been between her and Mitch Wulfrum. All there had been was a private conversation where she'd verbally agreed to turn over the wedding pictures to him. Oh, he was probably disappointed that she'd gotten him no dirt to dish, there was no doubt about that. For some reason, he'd been banking on having something to hold over his son-in-law and daughter's heads. Why, Anjelee didn't know. But he was a controlling bastard who apparently had his reasons, reasons she'd love to be privy to.

But no one understood such motivational factors when a person was desperate, more than Anjelee did.

Well, she was out of the picture now. She'd earned her pay, and her aching knee could attest to that.

She grinned, poising her thumb over the connect button. No sweat. She had plenty of pay now.

Anjelee pressed the button. "Hello?"

"Montrose?" His voice was a gruff bark that told her he wasn't in the best of moods this early in the morning.

"Yeah."

"I just opened your email. Why aren't there any pictures of Mr. Nakolo Huaka?"

"There are, but—" Shit, Heloki had caught her off guard. She didn't mean to let that slip, not now that she'd signed Jager's agreement to keep things to herself. For now.

"Ah-ha. Then where are they? The file you sent me contains

none of him, or them all together."

"I...I didn't mean there were shots of him available. I just meant I'd taken some, but several of the photos didn't turn out." Damn she was such a good liar. "I guess it was the wonky terrace lighting under that tent or something."

"'Û!" He made a growling sound before replying, "You're supposed to be a professional photographer. Lighting and camera adjustments should be elementary to you by now."

"Right. So sue me."

"Do you think I'm *lôlô*? I can tell when some gold-digging *malihini*'s trying to pull one over on me." There was a rustling noise accompanied by heavy breathing. She could just picture His Rotundness sweating like a pig, his coal-black eyes glittering with fury as he dug for an antacid tablet. Well, too bad. "Now give me the rest of the pictures, damn you. You either get over here now, or email them to me this instant."

Crap, here we go. "First of all, *lôlô* and *malihini* whatever you said, those words don't mean a thing to me, so you might as well just talk English. Second of all, you're flat-out wrong. Nakolo just wasn't around that much. He sat in the back row during most of the ceremony and reception, then he suddenly up and left. I never saw him again." *Except in the tub, ass-shagging Wulfrum.* "And like I already told you, the few snapshots of him I did get didn't turn out."

She really was a fantastic actress. Maybe *she* should try out for a part in one of Mitch Wulfrum's movies.

"You're lying to me, you little bitch."

She sighed, playing the role well. "No, sir, I'm not."

"There has to be more pictures than just those of the bride and groom cutting the damn cake," he replied with incensed sarcasm, "or dancing together, or hugging on the terrace like two lovebirds who've known each other for years. But we all know that's bullshit, especially after what I saw."

Hmm, interesting. I wonder what he saw. Maybe a man-on-man liplock?

Her pussy flooded with sudden desire. *What the fuck, Anj?*

Heloki's tone brought her out of her horny mental flash. His voice changed abruptly from terse to deadly. "Send me the damn pictures, Ms. Montrose. Or you will pay dearly."

The prick is threatening me? "I'm sorry, but I don't know how to make it any clearer. How can I send you something I don't have? I sent them all to you, I swear it."

She pulled the phone away from her ear when he growled, "*Ahahana*! You're a liar!"

"For the last time, no, I'm not."

"I'll put a stop-payment on your check."

She snorted. "Too late, I already cashed it." Thank God.

"I can still put a stop-payment on it."

"It already cleared both our banks. Believe me, I checked."

He barked his frustration. "What about the key, then? If you don't turn it over to me, I'll have you arrested."

She headed toward the lobby. "Arrested? For what? I already dropped it in the mail to you."

"Did you use it?"

"I-I..." she stammered, but quickly got her tongue under control. "Yes, and all I saw was the bride and groom, then I got the hell out of there. Would you like details of what I saw them doing?"

"No!"

"Well, then, that's all I have to say on the matter." She paced in the tiled atrium of the soaring, fancy lobby. "You got what I got."

"There had to be more, you *lôlô* little bitch. The three of them weren't hanging out at the pool together half-naked just to discuss the weather."

Ah-ha. Interesting. Now that would have been some great shots.

"Something's going on between them all, and you were supposed to get pictures of whatever it is."

Oh-ho-ho, you have no idea just how much is going on.

She approached the front desk. "I can't photograph what's not there, sir. If you're saying you want me to manufacture something, maybe do a little...hmm, like cropping and doctoring, now that's a different job-for-hire entirely." With her free hand, she gestured her room number to the clerk. The woman nodded and began closing out the bill on Heloki's credit card account.

"You know damn well I want real photos and real evidence."

"Well then, I'm sorry, but—"

"All right. You don't get the other half of your fee, then."

She shrugged, reached for her receipt and stuffed it into her bag. She'd already expected he'd withhold the second payment from her. But fifty-thousand sure helped ease the sting.

"Look, I'm *pau*. Done." She had picked up on that one little Hawaiian word during her stay. Kind of easy to remember, and it felt good rolling off her tongue. "I did what you hired me for. I got some nice pictures of your daughter's marriage to a celebrity. And lots of them, but that's all there was to be had. Take it or leave it, Mr. 'Alohi. Be glad you got some memorable snapshots of your daughter's first marriage, and to such a famous idol, at that. Not every father in America can claim that."

"He was there, wasn't he? More so than you claim."

She dragged her roller-suitcase across the lobby and made her way to the bellhop's station. "Who?"

"You know who! Nakolo Huaka. She was with him last night, not her husband. Am I not right? This whole wedding was a scam just so she can get her hands on my trust fund. It allows Mitch to cover up the gay rumors you mentioned, while she gets to keep her damned lowlife lover. *'Ea?* Isn't that what you saw?"

If you only knew the half of it.

Anjelee climbed into the shuttle van and let the bellhop load her luggage. Heloki's words intrigued her. She hadn't known about a trust fund, but now the whole hasty engagement and subsequent wedding was starting to come together and make sense. Clever, very clever. God, she wished she'd have known all the gory details before signing the agreement. It would have been worth ten times what she'd gotten.

"Speak to me, you conniving little *malihini.* I will pay you your other half if you just tell me the truth and turn over the evidence."

Don't tempt me.

"Look, God knows I could use the money, but I've told you all I know, and I gave you all I got. I tried, I snooped, but nothing came of it. What more do you want from me?"

Heloki let out a deep, exaggerated sigh. "Why are you being so *pa'akiki*?"

She mouthed the words "the docks" to the driver and said to Heloki, "Um, I don't know what that means."

"Hard-headed, stubborn."

"Okay, I'm done with this conversation, Mr. 'Alohi." She

watched as the orange arc of the sun started to peep over the horizon. Sugar cane swayed in the early morning breeze, and tiny white glitters of dew shone on their stalks. It was no doubt a beautiful place, but Anjelee was ready to go home.

"While I appreciate the assignment opportunity you gave me," she went on, "I can't tell you what I don't know. I can't conjure up pictures that just don't exist. I can't go put them in bed together and shout 'cheese!' while I take their picture, just so you have proof you plan to use for who knows what. And I can't confirm your bizarre suspicions if I saw nothing to substantiate them. Now I really need to be going."

"You better remember...all I did was pay you to photograph a wedding, nothing more. You will keep your mouth shut about any further issues." It was an order, not a question.

"Of course I will." They swung onto the coast road toward the docks. A charter boat would take her to Oahu where she would catch her flight. She watched the magenta and purple streaks glaze across the sky and reflect on the choppy sea. She had the window down a crack and could smell the sharp scent of sea salt, as well as that of coconut and something floral she couldn't quite place. "And in exchange for my loyalty, I'd hope you might consider keeping me in mind for your future needs."

"Ha. You didn't deliver this time. Why would I hire you again?"

She rolled her eyes, but her breath caught when she saw three dolphins break the ocean's rippled surf in a choreographed display. "Whatever."

"Goodbye, Ms. Montrose. And remember, silence is your friend in regard to our original agreement. I happen to know people in high places—right there in your own hometown, in fact—who could make your pathetic life hell."

"Really? Well you can just—" She started to tell him just

what he could do with those people, but he hung up on her before she could tear into him. "Asshole."

She flipped her phone shut and shifted her eyes to the curve of the road ahead. He might know people in high places, but it was Anjelee who had some really naughty pictures she'd copied to her inbox...a second email box that Jager didn't know about.

Pictures of Heloki's precious daughter and her two bisexual lovers. Yes, no doubt Heloki was worried their possible torrid affair just might destroy his beloved sugar cane empire if it were to be revealed. And she assumed he also wanted some sort of blackmailing leverage to hold over their heads just so he could continue to run his daughter's life.

Fuck that. Anjelee was the one with the control now. She held the proof, and she'd let it out of the bag without a second thought if Heloki chose to sic his *people in high places* on her. Damn right. The lovers' shocking ménage a trois would be front-page news in a second if he so much as looked at her wrong. And to hell with contracts.

You threaten Anjelee Montrose, you pay dearly.

Anjelee cackled. She might be without the financial resources Mitch Wulfrum and Heloki 'Alohi had, but she was no fool. It was always a good idea to have a back-up plan. Insurance, just in case those moles of Heloki's started coming out of the woodwork in the future. Or just in case she ran out of money again.

Chapter Thirteen

"Papa, what are you doing here at this time of...?" Kiona's words trailed off as her father pushed his way through the front door into the foyer. He wore crisp white pants and his usual floral, button-down shirt, but clearly he was anything but calm and cool. He was so agitated she could practically cut the tension with a knife. Sweat dribbled down his chubby cheeks and soaked the fabric of his shirt. His dark eyes gleamed with unmistakable fury, and his silver-streaked, midnight hair was tousled as if he'd raced over here without bothering to roll up the windows in his car.

She clamped her eyes shut and drew in a cleansing breath. Her forehead briefly touched the closed door before she gathered her bravery and spun back around to face him. But she didn't even have time to speak again before Kol entered the foyer shirtless and in boxers.

"Hey, babe, who was that at the—" his bare feet skidded to an abrupt halt on the marble floor, and his eyes widened at the sight of Heloki, "—door," he finished softly.

Heloki's big body trembled with his booming voice. "I knew it!" He jabbed a finger in Kol's direction, then at Kiona. "You're still seeing him. Your marriage was a farce after all, just like I suspected."

"Now, Father, let me explain the—"

"Don't you 'Father' me," he roared, jamming his fists onto his round hips. "I see what's going on here. I knew it. You're all going to ruin me." He snarled at Kol. "What a *lapuwale* you are, you pathetic, worthless scoundrel."

"Papa!"

"*Hâmau*!" He rounded on Kiona and leaned down, thrusting his face into hers. He must have been stewing over this for some time, because she got a strong whiff of antacids on his breath. "I don't want to hear your scolding or your excuses. What you're doing is *kapu*. Forbidden and shameful! You are nothing but a *milimili* whore for these two men."

Kiona gasped at the insult. Never had her father called her such horrible things. If he only knew she was not a plaything, she was not a whore for them. If he only understood how happy she was—how happy they all were—and that it's possible to love and be loved by two men at once without being a slut.

"Goddamn it, that's the last time you're going to talk to her that way," Kol growled, and with his hands balled up and white-knuckled, he stalked across the hallway and whirled Heloki around by the arm.

"Kol, no!" Kiona reached out to halt Kol's flying fist, but Mitch was already there. He stopped Kol just short of plowing a blow into Heloki's fat face.

"Get a hold of yourself, man. Do you want to be in jail instead of sunning on that private island with us?" Mitch muttered under his breath. From behind, he slid a free arm around Kol's waist and dragged him backward.

Kol writhed against Mitch's hold. "I'll kill the bastard. I'll fucking kill him."

"You *lôlô hûpô*," Heloki spat, his beady eyes boring into Kol. "You sicken me." His glittering gaze moved from one to the other. "All of you do. And you, Kiona? It shames me to call you daughter. You are no *kamali'i* of mine."

His words seemed to reach right into her chest, squeeze her heart, and twist. With the sting of tears in her eyes, she replied, "That's nothing new. You've simply spoken it for the first time."

"The bastard," Kol mumbled, still struggling to break free of Mitch's hold.

"Kiona," Mitch barked. "Come here, sweetheart. Get away from him."

She never took her eyes off her father, but she stepped backward until she stood between her husbands. The move suddenly hit her as symbolic. Even though she'd married last night, even though Heloki had given her away in the ceremony, it was as if she hadn't fully broken that tie with her father until now. She'd battled all her life to please Heloki, to win his love and approval. But it was only at this very moment—perhaps since it had come *after* the amazing wedding night she'd had with Kol and Mitch—that she realized she would never win no matter how hard she tried. He'd always hold things over her head like her trust fund. He'd always manipulate her and try to rule her life. There was nothing she could ever do that would ever please him completely and finally get him off her back.

She supposed she had one thing to thank him for. If he hadn't pushed her to marry in order to get the trust fund turned over to her, she never would have met Mitch, and the three of them wouldn't be so deliriously happy with their arrangement.

Still, she knew what this meant. Heloki would not be handing over her inheritance to her.

Almost as if he'd read her mind, Heloki said, "I was fully prepared to come over here today and sign over your trust fund to you. But if you choose to go with them and live such a deplorable lifestyle, then I choose to deny you."

"You can't do that. You promised. I got married just like you forced me to do."

He narrowed his eyes and folded his arms. "Watch me."

Kiona swallowed a lump that tasted more like bitter rejection than poverty. "Fine. And my position at KPCS? Are you yanking that out from underneath me too?"

"I'm seriously thinking about it. Unless you agree to a divorce from this sorry excuse for a celebrity, and then sever your ties completely with Kol."

Mitch shoved Kol behind him and sauntered forward. "You mother fucker."

Heloki snorted. "I rest my case."

Mitch growled and pounced. He was just about to close his hands around Heloki's stout neck when Kol seized him, lugging him back. "Do *you* want to be in jail instead of sunning on that private island?" Kol hissed in Mitch's ear. "Frankly, I'm looking forward to our honeymoon, so get a grip, man."

Heloki's body tensed, but he didn't move. "You sicken me. All of you! A honeymoon for three? That's disgusting and shameful. That does it." He turned and waddled to the door. With his hand on the knob, he peered over his round shoulder and sneered, "You're officially disowned, Kiona. The trust fund will be turned over to charity."

The tears wouldn't come. They'd since dried up behind her eyes. If she had to, she'd go get a job waitressing at the pub where Kol bartended. Or at the mall. Or maybe she'd start her own sugar-cane company and compete with her father? She didn't really know what she'd be doing now, but she was certain she no longer cared about the trust fund, or pleasing Heloki.

For a long moment, she stared at the man who'd once called himself her father. Finally, she murmured, "You're disowned, too, then. If you can't accept that I'm happy, that I love them, and that I'm no longer putty in your hands, then fine. I resign from KPCS, and I *officially* denounce you as my father. By the way, you can forget ever seeing any grandkids."

Mitch jerked out of Kol's hold and growled, "Fuck the trust fund. What a cold bastard you are to hold that over her head all her life, and then pay her practically minimum wage when she's working her ass off as head of your company." He hooked his thumbs in his jeans pockets. "Well, how about this? You go right ahead and give her inheritance away. I already donate millions to charity every year. But since you'll be, in a sense, donating it for me, I'll turn right around and give those millions to Kiona instead."

A strangled noise escaped from Kiona's throat. "What?"

Mitch shot her a look that briefly softened before lighting back on Heloki with the fires of hell. He shrugged. "It's no secret that I'm rich. Probably ten times what your father is. Handing you over a few million isn't going to break me in the least. Besides, you're my wife."

"Whoa." That from Kol. He was beaming, his handsome face all aglow, no doubt with a combination of fulfilled revenge for Heloki, and happiness for Kiona.

"B-but I can't," Kiona rasped. "I-I mean, thank you, but I can't take money from you when I should have my own to bring to the marriage."

Mitch had recently emerged from the shower, and his golden hair was slicked back from his gorgeous face. She caught the clean scent of soap and shampoo when he pulled her into his arms. The hardness of his well-muscled chest and arms was like a solid, protective wall to lean on. Heloki's words and attitude had chilled Kiona to the bone, but suddenly, heat poured into her core, and she was assailed by a deep affection for her new husband.

Mitch smiled, and a twinkle of some unknown but breathtaking emotion shown from his aqua eyes. “Darling, you’ve brought something to this marriage that can’t be quantified or paid for with money.” He ducked his head and planted a firm, wet kiss on her mouth. She tasted the delicious remnants of orange juice and buttered toast.

“Besides,” Mitch conintued, “I’ve already set you up accounts, stocks, the whole thing. Even a shopping-spree allowance so you can pamper yourself until your heart’s content. And if you decide you want to start your own business, fine, go for it. But I suspect with all your experience, you’ll be sought after by every company here and on the mainland once they hear you’re available. Either way, whatever you decide to do with your future, what’s mine is yours.” He paused, winked. “Babe, believe me, you don’t need his money.”

She was still trying to process Mitch’s words and close her gaping mouth when Heloki screeched, “Kiona, are you really going to fall for this? Can’t you see what he’s doing? He’s making you dependent on him, buying your love and your silence just so he can have his butt-buddy on the side.”

“She’s perfectly capable of supporting herself without my money,” Mitch replied.

“You son of a bitch,” Kol grumbled. He shifted his stance, his body straining to keep from leaping across the distance and attacking Heloki. “You are the biggest prick I’ve ever known. Why don’t you just get the fuck out of here?”

“No, wait,” Mitch interjected. He hooked an arm over Kol’s shoulder. “I have one more thing to say to him before he leaves.”

Heloki yanked open the door. “I don’t want to hear anymore of this nastiness.”

“Kol here, you’ve got all wrong, Mr. ’Alohi,” Mitch drawled, gesturing with a tilt of the head.

Heloki halted his movements. His curious eyes slid back to Mitch.

"He's not my butt-buddy at all. He's my new personal assistant—you know how celebrities always have a shadow following them around?" To that, he added a mocking wink. "Just hired him a few days ago. It's why he was at the wedding, why he's here right now helping me prepare for our trip. And he's handling some business for me for my upcoming trip to my next movie set. See, since you foolishly fired him, I got smart and hired him myself. Kiona and I might be spending a week honeymooning, but in Hollywood, business has to go on as usual. Which is why Kol's going too. I need him probably more than he needs a job."

Kol blinked, doing his best not to appear surprised. She thought she heard Kol's breathing stop for a beat, but he didn't say a word so as not to blow Mitch's best-ever acting scene.

All of Mitch's declarations were starting to sink in. Kiona tamped down a rush of giddiness. How had she gotten so lucky? She certainly owed Jager a big hug and kiss for bringing them together.

"Unbelievable," Heloki huffed, throwing up his hands. "A famous movie star paying off his wife and hiring his male lover just so he can cover up his dirty little gay secret."

"Think what you want, Heloki, but I can *guarantee* he's not gay," Kiona said nonchalantly, sliding an arm around Mitch's narrow waist. It was the first time she'd ever called her father by his first name, and his flinch didn't go unnoticed. "But that's really none of your business either way, is it?"

He didn't answer, just stood there, his body quaking.

Kiona took the opportunity to further have her say. "And since you've just disowned *and* technically fired me, it looks like even though it saddens me, I have no ties to you or KPCS anymore. But there is that possibility of those grandkids in the future, so perhaps you better keep your suspicions to yourself..."

Heloki stood there for what seemed like several minutes jerking his wild-eyed gaze from Kol to Mitch to Kiona. He opened his mouth four different times, then snapped it shut. Sweat trickled down his temples and neck, and his hand shook where it continued to remain clamped around the doorknob.

The door was ajar, and just through the open space, she caught a glimpse of a brilliant red flock of tropical *i'iwi* birds flitting from the many palms to the *koa* and *hala* trees clustered in the front yard. An early-morning breeze rushed in, sweet-scented by the blooms of the many *naupaka* bushes lining the forest and the beach. Entwined with it, she detected the familiar aroma of Heloki's aftershave. It conjured up memories of idolizing him while sitting on his lap as a child, having him hunched over her in the KPCS office mentoring her to run the business, or giving him a hug and a kiss every morning even though he often resisted her affections. It saddened her to know it had all come to this, but at the same time, she experienced a sense of freedom she'd never felt before.

It was a shame she couldn't have both her freedom and his love—KPCS had been her life. She'd practically grown up there, and she would sorely miss it and working with him. But now she'd found an unexpected love and freedom elsewhere, and she wasn't giving it up just to please her father. Hopefully one day, he'd come around. Maybe, based on the look of regret on his face, it would be grandkids that would be the deciding factor for him.

"You would do that, wouldn't you? Keep my grandchildren from me?" Heloki asked, his voice cracking. Was that a tear she saw in one eye?

"I wouldn't wish to, but..." Her throat ached as she held back the emotion that threatened to spill. She leaned on Mitch who in turn kept his arm around Kol. Kiona felt whole, complete, loved. Why couldn't her father just be happy for her? Why did he have to be so difficult, and so opposed to Kol?

"I see. Well, *pau*. I guess I'm done here. Have a good honeymoon. You have my word I won't say a thing." And he was gone, leaving the door wide open.

She swallowed back the tears. Kol swung around and gathered her in his arms. His body was warm, hard, and scented by the remnants of their early-morning lovemaking. "He'll be back groveling for forgiveness in no time, because there's no way he'll be able to pass up his own grandkids."

"He passed up his own daughter," she whispered.

"And he's a fool for doing so," Mitch pointed out, wrapping his arms around them both.

She gulped in air, fighting off the tears that threatened to spill.

"*Kulikuli*, my love," Kol murmured, stroking her hair and her spine, sending shivers along every cell of her body.

Kiona let out a slow breath, basking in the strength of the two men she'd promised to share the rest of her life with. She suddenly realized there was a knot in her stomach that had been there since she was a small child left motherless with a father who bordered on being a tyrant.

But it was time to let it go.

And she did in that one loving moment standing there cradled by both men. It was as if the knot in her stomach slowly unraveled, caught on the tropical breeze, and floated away, right out the door.

Then something glorious happened. Unrehearsed, both

Mitch and Kol simultaneously kissed her cheeks and uttered, "I love you, Kiona."

Epilogue

Kiona didn't know why she'd allowed years to pass since her last trip to the small getaway island miles off Kabana's sunny western coast. Heaven didn't even begin to describe the atmosphere of the private chartered slice of paradise that few knew of, and fewer still could afford to frequent. It didn't have a name she was aware of, but she liked to call it *Kupaianaha*, which meant amazing. And it was just that. They were away from the lush, windward side, so the rain would stay to the island's eastern coast. Their honeymoon on the leeward side of the land mass was bathed by glowing, hot sun and arid breezes.

Blessed by Kane, the god of gods, wielder of sunlight, fresh water, and lush forests.

Kiona so loved her Hawaiian heritage.

Reaching for her mai tai, she sipped and thought how her life had changed so much in the two weeks since meeting Mitch. The years of obsessing over her trust fund and yearning for an honest life with Kol seemed like a lifetime ago. And in hindsight, a waste of energy.

She no longer felt anger toward Heloki. For reasons only he understood, he'd needed to control her. He'd figured out that using the promise of money, and thus her independence, while keeping her practically destitute, would be the best way to go about it. It was sad that a father could treat his own flesh and blood that way, but Kiona didn't care anymore. She pitied him, but she still loved him in spite of it all.

She'd earned that trust fund over the years working at KPCS for pennies. But she supposed in a roundabout way, she was still receiving it just as Mitch had rationalized. Spitefully, Heloki had held true to his word. He'd donated it to charity.

With a snort, she stared out at the thrashing sea beyond the calmer bay and thought how ironic it was that she no longer cared about the money. She'd instead ended up with something far more valuable—two men who loved her, and an exciting, private lifestyle she would never have dreamed of in her wildest fantasies.

Heat coiled in her belly at the memory of their lovemaking. "Mmm, wild doesn't even begin to describe it."

Drawing in a lungful of fragrant air, she sipped some more, letting the tension of the past years finally melt away. The sweetness of the chilled cocktail slid down her throat like wet silk, its potent spirits going straight to her head and making it swim pleasantly.

With a purr of contentment, she relaxed back into the chair and thought of their temporary vacation home. At the area behind the lagoon's wide pier where she lounged, sand met foliage, which in turn embraced the bamboo-styled cabin built into the small cliff that had once been an active mini-volcano. Yellow and white *plumeria* blooms, and *hibiscus* flowers of pink, orange, and lavender, swayed in the gentle winds carrying fragrant puffs of air out to tease her nostrils. Still, she could smell the sex and sweat on her skin from their morning romp, and she marveled that the scent could stir her libido once again.

This morning had been amazing, but thoughts of last night's lovemaking assailed her. It had been an unusually chilly night, so Kol had started a fire in the hearth of the great room. They'd fed each other tropical fruits and cheeses, and had gone through three bottles of wine as they laughed and related stories of their childhood. Naturally, they'd moved on to discussing their past sexual conquests, which had gotten them all horny. Before she knew it, they were having vigorous sex right there on the rug, Mitch entering her from behind and Kol kneeling before her as she sucked him off like a starved harlot. A Michael Bublé CD had been playing in the background, and the fire had warmed their nude, glistening flesh while the empty bottles and half-eaten food strewn around them, went forgotten.

She now stretched naked in the padded lounge chair, basking in the warmth of the high-noon rays, just like she'd done last night by the fire. Her muscles had that faint, delicious soreness to them. Kiona smiled wickedly. It was the kind that meant her body had been well used and treated to riotous, kinky sex.

Lots of riotous, kinky sex.

Kiona tossed aside the straw, and gulped down the rest of her drink. She contemplated all the naughtiness she'd experienced since arriving here for their honeymoon three days ago. Wow, how many times had they made love, anyway? She furrowed her brow. And how many different combinations of positions could there possibly be with three people involved?

Well, there was one she hadn't yet experienced, that Kiona knew. She giggled, her head spinning pleasantly. "Oh, but I'll be trying it today," she decided as she set the glass aside. "Very soon."

Behind the dark sunglasses, her gaze drifted out to the center of the inlet where Mitch and Kol playfully wrestled unclothed in the turquoise water. Kiona sighed and slid her hand down her belly. Fielding a jolt of bliss, she pushed a finger through her damp folds, swiped come onto her finger, and circled her clit with the wetted tip.

"I can't believe I want them *again*," she murmured huskily.

But instead of acting on it, laziness won out. Settling back, she devoured Kol's tattooed, tanned body and the corded muscles along his biceps and backside. He wrapped an arm around Mitch from behind, holding him captive in a throat lock, flexing those hard muscles.

"Think you're clever, do you?" Mitch chuckled, his lean, bronzed form breaking free and whipping around to face Kol. Mitch didn't gloat long. "Look out." He tackled Kol so that they both plunged beneath the surface of the waist-high water.

She held her breath, stroking herself, waiting to see what her two good-looking, virile husbands would do next. Her clit throbbed, swelling to the size of a pea. Pinching a nipple, she sucked in a breath at the hot pull that snaked down from her breast into her groin. Warm juices trickled out of her pussy and soaked the lounge chair.

But instead of rising to join them, she forced herself to keep watching—she suddenly understood how Kol could enjoy being such a voyeur. He loved to watch her and Mitch making love almost as much as he relished participating with them.

Drawing up a knee, she listened to their sparring words when they broke the surface. They faced each other, their arms wrapped around one another's waists, eyes locked. Kiona could well imagine they were both hard and their cocks were probably touching, grinding, aching to slide into slick heat, or to be sucked off to orgasm.

Keeping that mental vision intact, she slid a finger inside her tight, tender cunt. She could hear their murmurs, moans, and the deep tone of male laughter. There was the lulling backdrop of the rush and ebb of the Pacific just beyond the mouth of the bay. Entwined with it, the gentle tumble of the small waterfall across the lagoon sang a mesmerizing song that nearly put her to sleep even as she masturbated.

She was just about to close her eyes and bring herself to a quick climax when they both stopped talking and pivoted their heads to stare at her. One pair of eyes as aqua and lively as the water they stood in, the other as dark and promising as sin.

Their faces, both so handsome, yet in such different ways, spread simultaneously into blinding-white grins.

Kol's blue-black hair was slicked back from his Polynesian features. He lifted a hand out of the water and crooked a finger at her. "Come here, babe. Come join us."

"Yeah," Mitch agreed, waving her in, his shorter golden locks tumbling down to frame his striking, strong-boned face. "We're both as hard as petrified lava. Get in here with us so we can ease your discomfort." His smile widened into a mischievous grin. "And ours."

Her pulse quickened, sending hormones racing through her blood. She rose and plucked up the waterproof coconut oil she'd been using to tan. Without taking her eyes off them, she poured a puddle in her palm, tossed the bottle on the lounge chair, and slowly, deliberately worked the slickness between her hands.

When she reached behind her and massaged the cheeks of her ass, Kol groaned and rolled his eyes in a show of bliss.

Mitch's jaw fell open, and when she angled around so they could get a better view, lingering to grease up the crease between her buttocks—an area she intended one of them to explore—he let out a breathy, "Jesus Christ."

Once she had her rear prepped, she slathered the excess onto her breasts and then dug a condom out of her tote bag. She was on birth control pills, so it wasn't like she needed them for that kind of protection. No, Kol and Mitch had already used them with each other, but there'd been no need to with her... Yet.

She crossed the pier, the condom nestled in her hand. Her bare feet soaked in the warmth of the slats of wood as she went. Seagulls cawed overhead, and a fluffy white cloud briefly dimmed the sunrays, casting a shadow across her men as it drifted across the azure sky.

Arriving at the end of the dock, she curled her toes over the edge. Dropping her sunglasses at her feet, she slid her gaze from one husband to the other. "I'm ready for you to ease my...discomfort," she purred.

She kept her eyes on Kol and Mitch while massaging one of her slick breasts. The nipple tingled, and the weighty mound felt engorged, the skin satiny and smooth. She tweaked the areola, pinching and rolling it between her fingers while never taking her eyes off the two gawking hunks.

Kol and Mitch licked their lips. It was a lot like being ogled by hungry wolves. Unmoving, predatory-like, they kept their prey in sight, incensing her further. They held the air in their lungs, their corded muscles tense as they waited for her to come to them, to do something besides standing there, continuing to tease them. Their unmasked, fevered perusals—double the fire, twice that of Kabana's scalding heat—made her heart knock against her ribs and her breath clog in her lungs.

A gust of wind blew into the lagoon and fluttered her long hair. Mixed with the coconut essence of the oil, she smelled salt on the air, and caught the distant chatter of dolphins out to sea. Palms swayed along the shore, aiding her in imagining she was a native Hawaiian woman on a sacrificial platform, offering herself up to two virile gods.

Kol arched a single inky brow. "You're ready? Again?"

Mitch shook his head as if to clear away the sexual stupor

he'd been in. He blinked, switching roles. "What *exactly* are you ready for, babe?"

He really was quite the actor, Kiona decided with a smug smile. She knew damn well he understood what she intended, despite the fact she'd made it clear their first day on the island that she wanted to delay any...*complete* attention bestowed upon her in that...area. Even though the concept had intrigued and aroused her, and she knew what to expect since Kol had made anal love to her before, she'd feared trying *two* men at once for some odd reason. She'd allowed some touching and foreplay there, but it had intimidated her to think of including anal sex with normal sex in their three-way lovemaking.

Double penetration, as it were.

Would it hurt? Would it be too much stimulation too soon in their relationship? Would she disappoint them?

Maybe. Maybe not. But there was only one way to find out...

For some reason, today the thought of it made her shiver with anticipation rather than tense up with uncertainty. Yeah, so she guessed now that she'd become more familiar with Mitch, she was finally over that little hang-up and ready to embark on yet another journey in their marriage.

Continuing his act of feigned bewilderment, Mitch turned away from Kol and faced her, the water lapping around his narrow waist. "Well? What is it that you're ready for?"

"As if you didn't already know." Her tone was husky, playfully scolding. "But just in case you don't, I'd be glad to demonstrate..."

She dove in and swam beneath the water. Her head spun, though she wasn't sure if it was the alcohol she'd consumed, what she was about to do, or the combination of lust and love that assailed her senses. Ahead, she could see them, their strong thighs side-by-side, their erections standing tall, and their balls swollen with arousal.

Kol's cock was slightly smaller than Mitch's, she mused, swimming lazily through the cool water, gliding closer. Kiona had grown used to Kol's size and gentle anal play. He knew just the right way to prepare her and make her want it rather than resist it as she had in the beginning. He'd seduced her, and eventually, with a thrilling sort of capitulation, she'd willingly allowed him to experiment on her with vibrators, dildos, and butt plugs. But while he'd trained her to crave attention in that area, she was worried she wasn't quite ready for Mitch's larger size invading her derriere.

Baby steps, she thought, now arriving a mere foot away from Mitch and Kol. Yes, they had a lifetime ahead of them to experiment and take all those naughty little steps. The men had certainly engaged in their own anal wickedness and experimentation, and she'd been content and highly aroused just watching it. She'd been fine with merely being a link to it in their lovemaking, taking one man into her pussy while he accepted the other into him. The thought of what they'd already done, and what awaited her in mere minutes, made her entire body zing with sexual need.

So it must be time.

Kiona broke the surface face-first so that her hair slicked back away from her face. She wanted to see everything, bare it all, feel everything. Placing one hand on Mitch's shoulder, she leaned away from him and captured Kol's mouth with hers. He tasted of sharp whiskey and the macadamia nuts he'd been snacking on before diving into the cove's crescent pool. She groped for Kol's hand during the kiss and slid the condom into it. He pulled back, a lusty gleam of understanding in his eyes.

Kol twined his fingers in her hair and yanked her head

back—ah, yes, a little rough around the edges just the way she liked it—dipping his tongue between her lips. “Mmm, pineapple and rum. Addictive,” he added, tracing the tip of his tongue around her lips.

Mitch floated closer and ducked, wrapping one arm around her lower hips. He straightened, lifting her until she became buoyant in the water. Pressing himself firmly against her belly, he stepped toward Kol and turned her so that her left side became trapped against him. Now sandwiched between two hard abdomens, she slid her arms around their necks and reveled in the tingling, throbbing sensation in her loins. Cool droplets dribbled over her shoulders and down over her bare breasts. Each nipple became a pert, aching arrow brushing against the faint hairs on their chests. She inhaled, catching their sea-salted scents, one cool and sophisticated, the other raw and untamed.

“Let me have a taste,” Mitch insisted, claiming her mouth with his.

Keeping one arm hooked around Kol, Kiona leaned into Mitch’s kiss, so moist, so sweet. Mitch tilted his head, opening his mouth wider. His tongue vibrated against hers when he moaned deep in his throat. Water splashed as he lifted his dripping-wet hands, stabbed his fingers into her sodden strands, and framed her face, forcing her lips to seal to his. His eyes were still open, and there was the adoring sparkle of forever in them. Simultaneously, their eyes fluttered shut, though the brilliance of the Hawaiian sun continued to light up her vision.

It was at that vibrant, profound moment following that look in Mitch’s eyes that she heard the slosh of water. She popped one eye open and peered over Mitch’s shoulder. Kol swam around and levered himself up so he lay on his back atop the water and behind Mitch. His erection rested thick and hard against his taut, water-slicked abdomen. Kicking his feet to stay afloat, he tore the condom package with his teeth and quickly rolled the rubber down and over his cock.

Mitch opened his eyes and tightened his hold on her, raining kisses over her jaw line, down along the side of her neck and her shoulder. Kol floated around toward her back while Mitch's arms went around her. He held her up so that Kol could explore her shoulders and upper spine. Kol licked and sucked the water off her skin, his tongue and lips warm and satiny-soft everywhere he explored. His warm hands followed, reaching around to gently cup her breasts and tease her nipples as he went.

She'd been floating on arousal, but Kiona needed more. She shivered and returned to Mitch's mouth, wrapping her legs around his hips so that he was forced to face her. Kol kneaded the flesh along her spine and ribs, moving lower to her buttocks. At every simultaneous touch, every kiss and moan, goose bumps shimmered from her scalp all the way down to her ankles. The delicious sensations fired up nerves so intensely, she had to break free of the kiss, let her head drop back, and drag in a breath. Mitch tasted her neck, slurped down along her collarbone, and lifted one breast to his mouth. His tongue and teeth did sinful things to her nipple while Kol's fingers started to play with her anus, preparing it in the way he always had, first with fluttering touches to begin arousing her, then with a flickering penetration of just the very tip of one finger.

Maybe she'd imbibed in one too many mai tais, but it seemed as if her universe spun out of control, causing colorful bursts of gold to rain down behind her closed eyelids. Kiona sighed, smiling wickedly to herself. Was this what she had to look forward to the rest of her life? Total heaven? Complete and brazen indulgence?

Though she didn't have time to gloat at her own gluttonous

question, she already knew the answer.

Kol delved deeper beneath the water until his warm palms cupped her fleshy, greased rear. He growled, nipping the side of her neck with his teeth, stretching her cheeks apart with his hands. He moved closer, pressing his cock to one slick butt mound. Using the tanning oil to his advantage in both areas, he circled her anus with his finger while sliding his condom-covered shaft against her slippery flesh.

"Are you sure, babe?" Kol murmured in her ear. "You sure you want us both at the same time?"

Mitch reached up, curled one hand around Kol's neck, and drew him closer. Three wet, panting mouths hovered together in a near-kiss. "Yes," he growled, answering for Kiona. "She wants us both in more ways than one. In fact, she's stuck with us. No name-only crap anymore. The contract says so."

He forced their lips together, and Kiona let out a guttural sigh as two male tongues searched her mouth simultaneously, their soft lips exploring and skating over hers, then each other's, in the most erotic kiss she'd ever experienced.

But Mitch's words slowly permeated the sexual fog in her brain. "What?" she asked, pulling away. "The contract says what?"

Mitch nuzzled at one side of her neck while Kol devoured the other. She tried to stave off the delicious feeling of being worshipped by two lovers at once. Her mind rewound to that first day she'd met Mitch at Jager's house and they'd signed their name-only contract.

"Before you arrived that day, I'd spoken on the phone with Jager about concerns that'd occurred to me. I wondered if our living apart might be uncovered by the media, or cause strain in the relationship that could begin to show to the public." He shrugged, burying his nose in her damp hair. "I didn't see any reason why we couldn't give a real marriage a shot for the paparazzi's sake at least. Wow, and meeting you in the flesh really sealed that decision for me. So with Jager's help, I rewrote it to reflect that we were to at least try a true trial marriage first before the separate-lives, separate-beds shit was put into force. Then I printed up a new copy for you to sign—which being in such a hurry, you thankfully overlooked—and I left it up to Jager to advise you of the changes."

"You left it up to Jager? You coward," Kiona squealed, shoving against him. "You know, I could get that contract voided very easily. It's called misrepresentation, breach, cooersion, whatever I want to claim, would probably do."

He grinned. "But you won't."

"You're one cocky bastard, aren't you?" Instead of allowing him to respond, she gave him a long, tongue-delving kiss.

"Mmm, see. You wouldn't do it."

"Okay, okay, I admit it. I won't." She narrowed her gaze on him. "You know, to this day, that asshole Jager has never once mentioned the changes in the contract to me."

"That's because he was too damn busy trying to keep our secrets from your father. Then there was that photographer bitch. I'm sure she was a handful and a half who kept him from tying up all his loose ends."

"I'll be damned," Kol finally muttered with a conspiratorial grin. "Clever. You let her sign it without knowing if she knew of the changes or not."

Mitch pulled back and grinned boyishly. His eyes glowed with mischief. "Well, I did suggest she read it—which she did, but apparently she missed it since she was in such a hurry to get back to you."

"You're such a deceitful jerk." She giggled and slapped Mitch's shoulder.

"Pot and kettle here. Besides, you did say you loved Kol, so I assumed it would be a lost cause in the end, anyway. But remember..." Mitch winked, then his smile slowly vanished. His gaze locked with hers. He leaned in and kissed her softly, tenderly. She tasted saltwater and soaked up the heat of his body. The security of commitment and something warm and glowing seemed to wrap itself around her heart. "When we first made the agreement through Jager, neither he nor you told me about Kol here." He gave Kol a quick, apologetic kiss over her shoulder. "A man so hot, I can't really blame you for keeping him to yourself."

Kol snuggled up behind her, wedging his cock in the crevice of her buttocks. Her ass was still slick from the waterproof oil, and the frictionless feel of it made her pussy engorge with the hot, heavy sensation of arousal. He skimmed his hands along her ribs, reaching farther still until he had both her and Mitch in a tight hug. He moaned, rocking his hips and sliding his shaft up and down, making her anus tingle.

"Speaking of hot..." Kol murmured in her ear. "If we, um, don't get past this contract shit very soon and get on with things, I'm going to combust." Kol lifted her up and slid one hand down between her belly and Mitch's. He closed his palm around Mitch's cock eliciting a hiss and groan out of him, and aligned the tip with her pussy. Her limbs and torso shuddered in response to his tender ministrations, causing her bare labia to close around the head of Mitch's manhood.

Then Kol gripped her hips and gave a firm downward pull, impaling her with Mitch's shaft. "Got it?" Kol asked on a growl.

Water sloshed around her waist. She got a brief whiff of the coconut oil she'd slathered on her body. Her eyes crossed at the sudden carnal wakefulness permeating her loins. "Yes," she whispered. "I definitely got it. How about you?"

"Mmm," Mitch moaned, the deep timbre of it mingling with the caw of seagulls overhead. She felt him twitch inside her. He held his breath and let it out in small hitching gasps.

"Yeah, I've got *you*." Kol pressed his chest to her back, one hand sliding up her spine to tangle in her hair. He pulled her head back and sucked along the pulse point below her ear sending shivers through every limb and cell of her body. Beneath the water, he gripped his cock with his free hand and circled it around her rectum.

"Feel good, baby?" Kol asked, pushing the head a mere inch inside her slick ass.

Unable to speak, she bit her lip and nodded instead. Flames sparked in little frissons around the sensitive nerves. At first, her involuntary reaction was to tighten her cunt and sphincter muscles. As a result, she gloved Mitch's full girth tighter with her moist canal. It caused him to groan again, and apparently at insanity's door, he started to move inside her, pulling out, pushing back in. He released a sound of impatience and alternated kissing her with reaching out to drag Kol's mouth to his over her shoulder.

Mitch's tempo picked up. Kol held on, allowing himself to bob in the water with them, little by little sliding further inside her. She forced out a guttural cry as the flames teetered back and forth between her pussy and anus. Her entire pelvis felt heavy and deliciously achy, and she knew it wouldn't take much more to raise the level of heat and bring her to paradise.

Gradually, she forced herself to relax, even as her clitoris ground over Mitch's pubic bone. She had a rabid urge to feel Kol completely sheathed inside her ass. But this time, what filled her pussy wouldn't be a small toy.

Her sex surrounded Mitch's hardness. She threw her head back with an animal cry of ecstasy when Kol slowly, completely filled her. His erection nearly touched Mitch's somewhere deep inside her. Their strong thighs were tangled together, their balls almost as one beneath her. She had four arms surrounding her, two mouths devouring her flesh wherever they could. She reached behind her, pulled Kol close over her shoulder, and kissed him on a growl.

When she switched to kissing Mitch, Kol breathed heavily, "Wow. I can feel him. I can feel Mitch inside you. It's like we're almost cock-to-cock in the same hole. Jesus, this is so fucking sexy..."

It was the tone of a man out of control, one experiencing a level of bliss he'd never attained before. That in itself propelled her own desire forward. She hung on the precipice of the orgasm, amazed by the thrill of it, the fullness and fulfillment that racked her core with barely any movement at all. Finally being filled by two cocks at once rather than a toy substitution, it was as if her life at last made sense and had direction. However her father, or the world, or Mitch's fans might look at it, this was who she was—who all three of them were—and it was where she always wanted to be. Though she never even suspected before Mitch had strolled into her life, she understood now that she needed to receive the love of two men at once. And she needed to offer her love to more than one, as well.

"Mmm, you have no idea," Mitch countered.

The sun warmed their skin as they bobbed, but the cool water splashed around them, soothing their hot flesh. Mitch slid in and out, his shaft aligned with Kol's inside her as Mitch expertly stimulated her G-spot. His eyes were glazed over as they locked with Kol's then shifted back to hers. She nearly drowned in his aqua gaze, the pupils constricted, his expression one of deep emotion.

"Both of you..." Mitch shook his head, perspiration beading his forehead. "I think I'm falling. This—the two of you—it's exactly what I needed in my life."

Kol rocked with him, treating her to a gentle but devastatingly arousing rhythm. "I agree...didn't think I had room for anyone but Ki in my life..." His voice was strained, choppy, as if he used every bit of his strength to talk. "But oh, God, I'm going to..."

When Kol groaned, twitching behind her, and reached out to clutch her and Mitch together, it pushed her over the edge. Kiona laid her head back on Kol's shoulder and clamped her eyes shut, waiting for the tide to wash fully over her. Mitch tightened his embrace pulling them both closer, the move causing her clitoris to rub harder against him. Her orgasm rose higher, hotter, exploding violently. All at once she felt a flood of Mitch's heat in her womb, and Kol's deep inside her ass within the confines of the condom. Her inner muscles spasmed, contracting around the thicknesses of both cocks at once. In between the two hard bodies, she jerked her hips up one last time, jammed herself back down, and reached for the final barrage of rapture.

Pleasure. Ecstasy. Utter bliss. She'd never experienced it quite so intensely before. Gasping for air, she slowly opened her eyes. Kol pulled out of her replacing his heat with the coolness of the water upon her tender flesh. She was left with Mitch inside her. He had his face buried in the hollow of her neck, kissing her, murmuring unintelligibly.

Kol floated around to their sides and wrapped them in a tight embrace. "Do you two have any idea how happy I am? Didn't know I could love so much."

She noted his voice had cracked with emotion as he spoke, and it made her heart ache with joy. "We have a very special, wonderful thing here. I hope to God no one ever ruins it for us."

At Kiona and Kol's words, she could swear she saw tears in the corners of Mitch's eyes, but they held the unmistakable glitter of happiness. Overwhelmed with love, she dragged both mouths to hers and sparred with tongues and hungry lips.

Kol chuckled. "Nah, it'll be fine. We might be a secret scandal right beneath the world's nose, but no one'll ever know for sure." He made a face, lifting one inky-black eyebrow. "Hmm, kind of hot to have such a wicked secret, huh? Makes me want to do it again."

Mitch sighed with an air of exaggerated drama. After all, he knew his theatrics well. "You are one horny bastard, you know that?"

"You haven't seen the worst of it yet," Kiona advised.

Kol grinned his agreement, kicking his feet in front of him and his arms to the side so that he floated backwards away from them. "I might be a bastard, and I might be horny," he said to Mitch, "but at least I'm not thick-headed and careless enough to allow my...sexual preferences to get hung out on the line for the whole damn world to see." He roared good-naturedly at his own wit.

Mitch's body tensed. He lifted her away from him and set her aside until she got her footing on the sandy bed of the lagoon. He raked a hand through his damp hair, leaving it standing on end, and shot a look of pure male competitiveness at Kol. "Thick-headed, huh?" He gave her a sidelong glance. "Honey, you didn't happen to bring an extra condom out here with you, did you?"

She giggled, already feeling the heat firing up in her loins again. "No...but I'd be delighted to swim over to the dock and get one for you."

"Ki, don't you dare," Kol warned, starting to swim away

from them with quick strokes. "Don't you fucking dare."

Mitch pushed his way through the water. "Go get one, Ki. I think it's time I show him just how thick my head really is..."

Kiona's laughter carried out across the bay. She watched as Mitch dove atop Kol and dragged him under the water. They came up locked in a passionate kiss, their hands racing haphazardly over each other, as if to channel their male aggressiveness into foreplay.

She reached down and touched herself. God, they'd done it so many times in the last few days, she was tender as hell. Maybe this time she'd just watch, and masturbate if worst came to worst. As she swam, she watched Mitch work his way down Kol's torso, trailing kisses along Kol's rippled abdomen. Then Mitch went under the water and Kol's head fell back with a growl.

Hmm, screw that. Maybe she'd watch the time *after* this?

Her clitoris engorged, and that heavy warmth of arousal spilled into her pussy. With euphoric love soaring in her heart and warming up her loins, she swam toward the pier to fetch that condom. Oh yeah, the temperature in Kabana was only just starting to rise.

Hawaiian Glossary

ahahana—shame on you; you're gonna get it
aloha—greeting for hello or good-bye
aloha wau iâ 'oe—I love you
auê!—oh! [used to express wonder, fear, scorn, affection, pitty]
'ea?—isn't that so? that's it, right? [often added to the end of sentences, ie., "It's that way, is it?"]
hâmau—silence
hemolele—perfection; flawless
hiwahiwa—precious, beloved, darling
ho—wow
hoaloha—friend
hûpô—fool; stupid
i'iwi—a colorful red Hawaiian bird with a long hooked beak whose feathers were often used to make capes, helmets, and other symbols for use by royalty
kamali'i—child
Kanaloa—Hawaiian god of the ocean and ocean winds
Kane—Hawaiian god of procreation, sunlight, fresh water, and forests
kapu—taboo, forbidden, out of bounds
koa—native Hawaiian tree used to make furniture, and other items
koa congo—large drum with a warm beat, made with koa wood
kulikuli—hush; be quiet; be still

kupaianaha—amazing; fantastic; wonderful; phenomenal
ku'u—my
ku'u aloha—my love
lanai—porch, veranda, balcony, sometimes enclosed
lapuwale—fool; worthless; wretch; scoundrel
lauhala—leaves from the hala tree used to weave baskets; also used to make roofing, flooring, mats, bedding mats, clothing, boat sails, jewelry, etc.
lei—garland, necklace
lôlô—stupid; dumb
Lono—Hawaiian god of thunder, clouds, winds, fertility, agriculture, and sea
loulu—low and bushy palmetto-type palm plant
mahalo—thank you
makakoa—bold, fierce, unafraid
makuakane—father
malihini—visitor, newcomer to the islands
milimili—toy, plaything, pet, beloved
Mikeke—Mitch
Mikela—Mitchell
nohea—loveliness; handsome
naupaka—thick green beachside bushes with white blooms, native to Hawaii
pa'akiki—hardhead; stubborn; difficult
pau—done; completed; the end
puka—hole, opening
pupu—Hawaiian hors d'oeuvres, snacks
pupule—crazy
'û!—a grunting, groaning, moaning, sighing, or humming exclamation

About the Author

To learn more about erotic romance author Titania Ladley, please visit www.TitaniaLadley.com, or drop her a note by email at TitaniaLadley@yahoo.com.

For monthly contests with prizes, and to keep abreast of her latest releases and exciting news, subscribe to her announcement-only monthly newsletter *Titania's Hot Sheets* at:

http://groups.yahoo.com/group/Titanias_Secret_Seductions/

For some chatty fun with Titania and other award-winning erotic romance authors and readers, check out the following links:

http://groups.yahoo.com/group/Fantasy_Club/

www.sizzlingscribes.com

www.sensualromances.com

Titania also invites you to explore her other hot titles written under the penname Roxana Blaze: www.RoxanaBlaze.com

Printed in the United States
146571LV00004B/69/P

9 781605 04305C